Books by April Wilson

McIntyre Security, Inc. Bodyguard Series:

Vulnerable　.

Fearless

Shane (a novella)

Broken

Shattered

Imperfect

Ruined

Hostage

Redeemed

Marry Me (a novella)

Snowbound (a novella)

Regret

With This Ring (a novella)

Collateral Damage

A Tyler Jamison Novel:

Somebody to Love

Somebody to Hold

A British Billionaire Romance:

Charmed (co-written with Laura Riley)

Audiobooks by April Wilson

For links to my audiobooks, please visit my website:
www.aprilwilsonauthor.com/audiobooks

Somebody to Hold

A TYLER JAMISON Novel
Book 2

by

April Wilson

Copyright © 2021 April E. Barnswell/
Wilson Publishing LLC
All rights reserved.
Cover by Steamy Designs
Photography by Jean Woodfin Photography
Model: Daniel Rengering

Published by
April E. Barnswell
Wilson Publishing LLC
P.O. Box 292913
Dayton, OH 45429
www.aprilwilsonauthor.com

ISBN: 9798707170140

No part of this publication may be reproduced, stored in a retrieval system, copied, shared, or transmitted in any form or by any means without the prior written permission of the author. The only exception is brief quotations to be used in book reviews. Please don't steal e-books.

This novel is entirely a work of fiction. All places and locations are used fictitiously. The names of characters and places are figments of the author's imagination, and any resemblance to real people or real places is purely coincidental and unintended.

1

Tyler Jamison

At six o'clock, I shut off my PC and lock up my office. It's time to head home. This sense of anticipation I feel is relatively new for me. I've never been so eager to go home because I never had anyone to go home to—just a dark, empty condo awaited me. Now that I'm sharing my boyfriend's townhouse, I feel like I have a real home. It's not just the place I hang my holster and gun every evening after a long day of hunting murder suspects.

Tonight's special because it's *date night*—Ian's exact words.

"Don't be late, Tyler," he told me this morning. "Dinner is at six-thirty."

I'm not sure how eating dinner together *at home* constitutes a date, but apparently it does. And I'm not about to argue the point. Ian's been texting me reminders all day, and just thinking about his eagerness puts a smile on my face. Whatever makes him happy, makes me happy.

They say opposites attract. Well, it's definitely true in our case. Ian and I couldn't be more different—and yet it works for us. I'm the stoic, brooding, controlling type, while Ian is life and energy and emotion bubbling over. Whereas I'm a glass-half-empty kind of guy, his cup runneth over. My favorite color is any shade of black—hence the lack of variety in my wardrobe—while Ian wears the colors of the rainbow.

We're like yin and yang, two contrary forces that complement each other perfectly.

As I'm nearing the exit to our Gold Coast neighborhood in Chicago, my phone rings. I glance at the screen and see that my station captain is calling. *Damn it.* There's only one reason Jud Walker would call me after regular work hours—to assign me a new case.

I accept the call. "Hello, boss."

"Tyler. You're needed in Rogers Park. We just received report of a body discovered in the alley between Murphy and Irwin. Victim is a Caucasian female, early twenties. Cause of death appears to be blunt force trauma to the back of the head."

And just like that, this evening's dinner plans evaporate. "I'm on my way," I say with a resigned sigh.

I call Ian to tell him the bad news.

"Hey, babe," he says. "Are you on your way home?"

"I was."

"Oh." I can hear the disappointment in his voice, but he doesn't give voice to it. He knows my job has erratic hours, and he's not one to complain.

"Yeah. Walker just assigned me a new case, and I have to head to the scene. I'm afraid it'll be a while before I can make it home. I'm sorry, baby."

"It's okay. Duty calls, right?"

"I'll be home as soon as I can, I promise."

"Be safe, and I'll see you tonight."

After we say our goodbyes, I turn on my flashing lights, make a U-turn, and head back toward Rogers Park.

Even though my evening plans haven't worked out the way I thought they would, it still feels pretty damn good that I have someone in my life who cares whether or not I make it home.

* * *

I arrive at the scene and park next to the two units already on site. When I get out of my car, I nod at the familiar face of the officer standing at the mouth of the alley. "Hi, Phil."

"Hey, Tyler." Phil Ingrams nods down the alley. "The victim's down there, just past the dumpster. Clements is with the body."

As I walk down the narrow alley, stepping over puddles of

questionable origin, I mentally block out the cloying odors of human excrement and rancid trash. As I approach Officer Clements, my pulse picks up and I automatically switch into homicide detective mode. I've been doing this job—investigating murders—for well over a decade now, and it still rattles me to come upon a murder victim. A life cut short is always a tragedy, but in this case, it's a life ended far too soon.

Ray Clements, looking as gray and grizzly as usual, nods curtly as I approach. "Tyler."

"Hello, Ray."

He shines a flashlight on the victim, who's lying face down on the pavement. Her long blonde hair is matted with grime and blood. The likely cause of death is readily apparent—the back of her head is caved in. There's a splattering of blood and gore on the brick wall behind us. It looks like someone slammed her head against the building.

Based on the state of her body—and the lack of fresh blood—I'd guess she died sometime late last night.

"Who found the body?" I ask Clements.

He nods to the rear exit of a bar. "A janitor carrying trash out to the dumpster found the body and called it in."

The victim is dressed in a white blouse, black mini-skirt, sheer black stockings, and short black boots with silver buckles. Her stockings are shredded, and her underwear is on the ground next to the dumpster. I have little doubt she was sexually assaulted.

After pulling on a pair of latex gloves, I crouch beside the body to do an initial assessment and take some pictures. I carefully brush her hair back from her face and gaze down at one lifeless blue eye. The other eye is bruised and swollen shut. There are cuts and abrasions on her cheeks and forehead. Similar wounds are visible on her arms and legs. There's blood under her nails—she fought back hard. Forensics will have no trouble securing a DNA sample.

A wave of nausea sweeps through me as I gaze down at a young woman who reminds me so much of my sister. They're close in age, and they have the same build and the same fair complexion.

I stand and peer around the scene. Since it's dark back here, Officer Clements sweeps a high-powered flashlight across the area.

"There's her purse," he says, shining his light on a small black leather bag lying beside the dumpster.

I pick it up and perform a quick search to discover a university student ID, but no driver's license, cash, or credit cards. I have a name, but no address. It will be difficult to identify her next of kin until I can talk to someone at the university in the morning.

It looks like she was robbed, in addition to being sexually assaulted and murdered. I stare down at her identification. *Addison Jenkins, twenty-two years old.* I estimate her to be about five-foot-four, one hundred twenty pounds.

And now she's deceased.

Dead before she really had a chance to live.

Clements, who is a grandfather many times over, shakes his head. "Poor kid. What a damn shame."

I take a picture of her college ID so I can begin canvassing the local bars and restaurants tonight to see if anyone remembers seeing her. This part of town is home to a slew of bars and nightclubs, so there's no shortage of people for me to interview.

Plenty of late-night activities take place in these back alleys—the homeless staking out spots for the night, drug deals, drunks passing out. But this girl? Based on her attire, I doubt she was a user, and there's nothing here to make me think she was doing tricks. It's more likely she was in the wrong place at the wrong time. She might have been followed as she left one of the local clubs.

Perhaps she fought back—hard—and wound up getting her head cracked against the wall in the process.

I continue my initial visual exam, making notes about both the scene and the victim while I wait for the forensics team to arrive.

Once forensics arrives and starts their investigation, I head back to my car. I'll visit the university in the morning to establish the victim's next of kin, but in the meantime, I can visit the clubs up and down the street to talk to the staff to see if anyone remembers seeing her.

* * *

It's almost midnight when I finally walk through my front

door, after nearly five hours of interviews that got me pretty much nowhere.

As he often does, Ian's waiting for me at the front door. His eyes are red.

"Is everything okay?" I ask him.

He nods. "I was watching a documentary about polar bears and how their ecosystem is disappearing. It got to me." He laughs as he wipes his eyes. "You know me—I cry at everything. Puppies, kittens, and now I can add polar bears to the list." His expression falls as he gets a good look at me. "What about you? You don't look so good."

"I've been better." It's not often I'm this shaken by something I see in my line of work, but tonight's definitely an exception. The victim reminded me too much of my sister, Beth. I shudder when I think about how close I came to losing her years ago, when she was just a kid. I know how fleeting life can be, how fragile.

That poor girl I saw tonight might be someone's sister. She's certainly someone's daughter. As soon as we identify her next of kin, a family is going to be heartbroken.

The downside to loving someone is that you have so much to lose.

Ian wraps his arms around my neck and pulls me in for a hug. "I'm sorry you had a rough night."

I allow myself to take solace in the heat and comfort of Ian's body. For so many years, I had to face everything alone—the good and the bad. But now I have Ian, and I have to admit, it's nice to have someone to lean on for a change.

As we stand eye-to-eye, he leans in and kisses me lightly. "I saved your dinner. Do you want me to heat it up for you?"

Smiling, I return his kiss. "That would be great, thanks. I'm sorry I ruined our plans tonight."

"It's okay. You can't help being a hero. It's in your nature."

I frown. "I'm no hero, Ian. Heroes save people. I just figure out who killed them. Big difference."

He tugs off my suit jacket and hangs it up in the front hall closet. "You give families peace of mind. And for the record, you saved my life. Both figuratively and literally."

I remove my chest holster, which holds my nine-millimeter Glock, and hang it on a hook inside the closet. Then I follow Ian to the kitchen, where I find him retrieving a covered plate from the fridge. He puts it into the microwave.

"I warn you, it probably won't be as good the second time around," he says as he programs the microwave and presses start.

I notice he only took one plate out of the fridge. "You're not eating?"

Smiling apologetically, he shakes his head. "I already ate. Sorry. I was starving."

"It's okay. I don't blame you." I head to the fridge and pull out a bottle of beer. "Whatever it is, it smells good. You want a beer?"

"Yes, please. And it's pot roast. Do you want to eat up on the roof?"

Once the food is heated, I carry my plate and beer up to the private roof-top greenhouse that is Ian's favorite place on dry land. With its glass walls, it allows him to feel like he's outdoors all year around, with unimpeded views of Lake Michigan to the east and downtown Chicago to the west. The climate-controlled space is filled with plants, from potted trees and massive ferns to a multitude of tropical flowers. There's even a three-tiered water fountain.

But the real focal point of the greenhouse is the king-size bed I had installed up here as a gift for Ian. We spend a few nights up here each week sleeping under the stars.

This late at night, the view is impressive. City lights flicker in the distance all around us. Out on the lake, moonlight shimmers on the water's rippling surface as a parade of late-night cruise ships ferry tourists up and down the shoreline.

As we sit at a small bistro table for two, Ian lights a single taper.

"That's new," I say, nodding at the candle.

He grins. "I had planned a candlelit dinner."

"And I fucked it up."

"It's not your fault, babe." He motions to my plate. "Eat while it's hot."

I don't even realize how hungry I am until the first bite of food hits my tongue. As the tender pot roast practically melts in my mouth, I moan in appreciation. "This is so much better than frozen dinners."

Ian looks horrified. "Your days of eating frozen dinners are behind you, detective." He watches me eat for a little while before saying, "Do you want to talk your new case?"

I chew my food slowly and swallow before taking a long, cold swig of my beer. I really don't want to discuss it, but Ian's being so supportive I don't want to shut him out. "The victim reminded me of Beth."

Ian reaches for my hand. "That must have been hard."

Ian has a sister, too, just a few years younger than mine. I squeeze his hand. "Forget I said anything."

I finally notice what he's wearing—a lavender T-shirt featuring a unicorn shitting out candy hearts. That makes me chuckle. No matter how rough my day might be, Ian makes everything better.

I glance at the big bed behind us. Sheer curtains and strings of fairy lights are draped over the wrought-iron canopy above the bed. "Do you want to sleep up here tonight?" I ask as I look up through the glass ceiling at the sky. "It's a clear night. We'll be able to see the stars."

"I'd love to."

After I'm done eating, I carry my dirty dishes down to the kitchen and put them in the dishwasher. Then I excuse myself to take a shower and get ready for bed. When I come back down, I find Ian tidying up the kitchen.

He must have changed while I was in the shower because now he's wearing a pair of purple flannel PJ bottoms that hang low on his lean waist. I stand in the doorway for a moment just enjoying the view—the set of his shoulders, his back, the way his torso tapers to his waist. The sight of his PJ bottoms cupping his round ass makes my cock stir.

I'm drawn to him. He's the flame that lights my way in the darkness. He warms my body and soothes my soul. I love everything about him—his tender heart, his courage, his resiliency. The way he responds to me, the way he sets my blood on fire.

Stepping behind him, I slip my arms around his waist and rest my chin on his bare shoulder. "Thank you for dinner."

He smiles. "You don't have to thank me. You know I love cooking for you."

The house is quiet and mostly dark. There's only a faint glow coming from the light fixture over the kitchen island. I turn my face toward him and press my lips to his pulse point, reveling in the feel and scent of his warm skin. My hands slide down the front of his PJs to trace the outline of his already sizeable erection.

Ian turns off the water and wrings out the kitchen rag before hanging it over the faucet to dry.

Pressing up against him, letting him feel my own erection, I wrap one arm around his chest and tease his nipple piercing. "Come to bed."

He dries his hands on a towel before turning to face me with a grin on his handsome face. His green eyes are lit with arousal.

Ian slips his arms around my waist. "I thought you'd never ask."

I run my fingers through the longer strands of brown hair on the top of his head. His undercut looks freshly trimmed. "You cut your hair."

He runs a hand over one of the short sides and to the back. "It was getting a little long."

I cup the back of his neck. "Next time, ask me. I'll do it for you."

He grins as if I just offered to blow him here on the spot. "Really? You'd cut my hair?"

I smile. "Sure." As I thread my fingers through his hair, scraping my nails over his scalp, he shivers.

It's the quiet moments like these that make me realize how lucky I am. At the ripe old age of forty-four, I thought I'd never find this kind of connection with anyone. After years of trying—and failing—to meet the right woman, I'd just about given up. I thought I was destined to be a bachelor all my life. As it turns out, I was simply looking in the wrong place.

Ian takes my hand and leads me up two flights of stairs to our rooftop retreat. The bed is already turned down, a candle lit on the nightstand.

I pull him close. "You have such a romantic streak."

For a moment, I'm overcome with emotion. I craved a relationship for so long, and now that I have one, I realize how much I'd been missing. How much I need this—how much I need *him*.

Then reality hits me hard, and I'm swamped with a sense of dread. If anything happens to us, I don't think I'd recover.

Shoving away thoughts of doom and gloom, I grasp his wrists and walk him backward toward the bed. When we reach the thick, faux fur rug beside the bed, he sinks to his knees.

Immediately, his fingers are at the waistband of my pajama bottoms. He frees my erection, and then glances up at me from beneath long lashes. As I stare down at him, I slide my fingers through his hair before tightening my grip on the strands.

His gaze darkens as he takes hold of me and licks his lips. And then his tongue glides over the head of my cock, teasing me, tasting. His fingers and lips work their magic, firm, yet nimble.

When I groan, he smiles.

2

Ian Alexander

I revel in the weight of Tyler's body on mine as he covers me. I'm lying on my belly, and he's captured both of my wrists in one hand, pinning them to the pillow above my head, while his other hand grips my chin and turns my face toward his for a kiss. I groan as his mouth eats at mine. My erection is pinned against the mattress, and it's pure torment—both pleasure and pain. I need him to touch me so badly. I need his hand working my cock.

Tyler is breathing hard, just as I am. He thrusts into me leisurely, steadily, lighting up my nerve endings and making every inch of my body tingle. His hips undulate against my ass, and the smooth glide of his cock grazes me over and over, swamping me with pleasure. The heat and the pressure steal my breath.

"Tyler." His name comes out as a breathy rasp. I deepen our kiss, giving him my tongue. "Please." I'm aching to come, but neither one of us is in a hurry. He'll draw the pleasure out for both of us. That's what he's good at.

Tyler makes me feel cherished, protected, and so well-fucked. He's naturally dominant in bed, and I love it. I *need* it. I *crave* it.

Rolling us to our sides, he wraps his long fingers around my cock and begins stroking me. The friction is exquisite, the pleasure mind-blowing.

"Tyler," I plead.

"I know," he murmurs close to my ear. "Soon." His warm breath brushes my overheated skin and sends a shiver down my spine.

As he picks up speed, thrusting faster and faster, his hand action matches the pace. My sac tightens, my balls drawing up, and I'm *so* close. I gasp. "Oh, god, please."

He chuckles. "Make it last, baby."

His lips are on the back of my neck, kissing me, taking small bites and sucking my skin. I know he's going to leave his mark on me; he always does. Suddenly, he bucks into me, pressing deep and groaning harshly as he comes. "Ian, fuck!"

He strokes me relentlessly, and with a grateful moan, I come too.

Tyler slows his thrusts, his hips bucking into me with each ejaculation. At the same time, he milks my climax, teasing me with gentle strokes and keeping me on edge. My cock is so sensitive, I shudder. Our naked bodies are plastered together, and it's almost impossible to determine where he ends and I begin. We are literally as one, and the beauty of that thought makes me tear up. As I press my hot face into my pillow, he kisses the back of my head.

When both our orgasms have waned, he withdraws and removes the condom, tying off the end. Then he kisses my shoulder. "Be right back."

A few moments later, he returns with a damp cloth and wipes the stickiness from my ass. As I lift up, he removes the towel beneath me and wipes my abs. Then we snuggle beneath the covers as Tyler spoons me, his arm secure around my waist, one of his legs slipping between mine.

"Good night, baby," he whispers, his lips in my hair.

* * *

Tyler falls asleep pretty quickly, no doubt exhausted from his long day, but I lie awake for a long time, gazing at the darkness beyond the glass ceiling as the stars flicker in the night sky.

Sleeping under the stars like this, inside the sanctity and comfort of these greenhouse walls, is the perfect antidote to my early childhood spent locked in a dark, upstairs bedroom— the windows boarded up tight—while my drug-addicted mother entertained tricks downstairs in exchange for her next fix. She tried her best to protect me from the unending parade of men that traipsed in and out of our apartment, but it was a lonely, frightening life for a child. I spent so many hours locked in that upstairs room, often hiding in the closet with little to eat or drink, and only a child's training potty to piss in.

My five-year-old imagination fantasized that someone would rescue me—Superman or Batman, or maybe a cop or a fireman. Ultimately, it was children's services that saved me from that miserable life and eventually made it possible for the Alexanders to adopt me.

Those childhood fantasies have now taken on a whole new meaning because I have my very own cop. When we met, not that long ago, he rescued me from a life of casual sex and random hookups. I'd had so many failed relationships, I'd stopped trying.

Tyler knows me like no one ever has. He knows my weaknesses, my fears, and he doesn't think less of me for them. He doesn't run when anxiety overwhelms me. He doesn't quit on me when *I* run. He loves me in spite of my deficits.

Making a quiet, sleepy sound, Tyler tightens his hold on me. Instinctively, he knows what I need.

Security.

My cop knows what I need.

When my phone screen silently lights up on the nightstand beside me, I reach for it out of habit, checking to see who's messaging me this late. I always keep my phone close by at night in case Layla needs me. I'm a light sleeper, so even the faint vibration of an incoming call or message is enough to wake me. If my sister needs me, I don't want to miss it, no matter the time.

But it's not from Layla.

When I see who's messaging me, my body switches immediately to panic mode. *Shit!* It's Brad Turner.

Brad: u awake?

I lay my phone back down on the nightstand, leaving him unread. I don't know why he keeps messaging me. Surely he's gotten the hint that I'm not interested. I was never interested in him. Besides, he knows I'm with Tyler.

When I hear the faint vibration again, I open the nightstand drawer and slip my phone inside and close it. I don't want to spend another second thinking about Brad. I want him to go away.

As if he can sense my sudden unease, Tyler shifts against me. "You okay?" he murmurs sleepily.

"Yes," I whisper.

But the truth is, I'm not okay. I'm the only one standing between Tyler and a possible prison sentence. If Brad decides to press charges against Tyler—assault charges—god, I can't even bring myself to think about the consequences.

Brad knows this, and he won't hesitate to use it against me to get what he wants.

Me.

* * *

The next morning, Tyler kisses my forehead before he leaves for work. "Bye, baby," he whispers.

He smells faintly of cologne and mint toothpaste.

It's still early—before sunrise—but he knows to wake me before he leaves for work. I need that from him—that little reminder he's coming back.

"Have a good day," I say as I stretch.

After he's gone, I wrap my arms around Tyler's pillow and breathe in his scent. Normally, I would go right back to sleep, but this morning Brad's text message from last night nags at me.

I open the nightstand drawer and retrieve my phone only to find out he texted me a second time last night.

Brad: We need to talk. call me

No. Never.

After wasting a whole hour in bed, trying in vain to fall back to sleep, I resign myself to getting up. It beats lying here and worrying about things I can't control. I pull on my PJ bottoms and head downstairs to the kitchen where I end up sitting at the table, scrolling through TikTok while I eat a toasted bagel with strawberry cream cheese and drink my coffee.

My phone rings, making me jump. When I see it's Brad calling, I let the call go to voicemail. He calls again, almost immediately afterward, and I silence the ringer.

I feel hunted, and I don't know what to do. I can't tell Tyler that Brad's harassing me. He'd lose his shit and go after Brad. But I don't want to sit here and wait for him to call again. I feel trapped. The walls are closing in on me.

I need to get out of here.

After cleaning up the kitchen, I shower and dress in jeans and a T-shirt. It's late June, and the weather is perfect for an outing.

I call Miguel Rodriquez. Ever since Tyler hired Miguel to be my temporary bodyguard, he and I have become good friends. He's on medical leave at the moment, after being grazed in the left shoulder by a bullet from Roy Valdez's gun. And even though Miguel's no longer my bodyguard, we've kept in touch.

"Hey, Ian," Miguel says. "*Que pasa*, bro?"

"Have you got plans today?"

"No, not really. I was just gonna tinker with my Mustang. Maybe take it in for an oil change, since I can't do it myself right now. Why? Whad'ya have in mind?"

"I thought I'd go downtown today, maybe walk along the river or visit Millennium Park. Take some photos. Grab some lunch. You wanna come?"

"Sure," he says. "I could use the exercise. I've been sitting on my butt too long. I'll head over to your place. See you in about thirty minutes?"

"Perfect." After I grab my camera, I lock up the townhouse and sit outside on the front stoop to wait for Miguel. I'm too antsy to sit inside.

I notice a black car in my peripheral vision, as it slows in front of my townhouse before pulling into my driveway. I glance over, expecting to see Miguel's Mustang, but it's an older model sedan with darkly-tinted windows. I can't see who's behind the wheel until the driver steps out of the vehicle.

Oh, fuck.

Brad Turner—all six-foot-two of him—stands casually by the driver's door, his arms propped on the roof of his car. His straight black hair is pulled back in a ponytail, and he's wearing a pair of dark sunglasses. He looks like a hitman.

"Why haven't you been answering your phone, Ian?" His deep voice sends a shudder through me.

My heart slams into my ribs, sending me immediately into fight-or-flight mode.

Unwelcome memories of dancing with Brad at Diego's nightclub come rushing back. Against Tyler's wishes, I'd insisted on trying to play amateur detective to find out who might have killed my friend Eric. I figured Brad had to be a suspect because he was dating Eric at the time. As it turned out, he wasn't the murderer, but he's certainly no angel.

He wants the same thing from me that he had with Eric—a sadistic, twisted sexual relationship. He wants me to be his new whipping boy.

I shoot to my feet on the top step, torn between telling him to get the hell off my property and running back inside and locking the door. I swallow hard. "What are you doing here?"

He rounds the front of his car and walks up the steps to join me. After shoving his sunglasses onto the top of his head, he glares at me. Now I can see the faint purple shadows beneath his eyes and the yellowed remnants of bruises on his cheekbones. These marks are undoubtedly remnants of the beating Tyler gave Brad when he choked me at Sapphires.

Brad's gaze narrows on me. "You didn't answer me, Ian. Why haven't you replied to any of my messages?"

As he reaches for my hand, I pull it back, shoving it into my pocket. "I have nothing to say to you." My voice shakes. "I think you said enough for both of us when you tried to strangle me."

He rolls his eyes. "You are such a drama queen. That was nothing, Ian. Choking can be rather enjoyable if you're with someone who knows what he's doing. I don't suppose your cop chokes you. Or maybe he gets off cuffing you to the bed. A little rough play, maybe?"

"You leave Tyler out of this."

Brad's eyes narrow. "That's not going to happen. After your *boyfriend* assaulted me that night at Sapphires, I spent four days in the hospital." Brad points to his head. "He cracked my fucking skull, Ian. You think I won't make him pay for that?"

"Because you were choking me!"

The smile on Brad's face is chilling. "Eric liked it when I choked him. You will, too. I guarantee it."

"Don't talk to me about Eric."

"Why not?"

"Because you got him killed."

Brad scoffs. "Hell, I'm not responsible for what Roy did. Roy became unhinged. He let jealousy drive him mad, and he paid the price for his actions. All I want from you is sex, pure and simple. You're going to let me—"

"In your dreams."

He purses his lips as if contemplating my answer. "Here's the deal, Ian. Let me spell it out for you so there's no misunderstanding. You're going to let me fuck you on your yacht. You're going to submit to me—to my every whim—until I say I'm done with you. Then we'll call it even. If you're a real good boy and beg me nicely, I won't press charges against your boyfriend. How's that?"

My pulse is pounding so hard I can hear the blood rushing. "He was just protecting me."

"No, he was out of line. I should have called the cops on him that night and had him arrested. I would have if I'd been thinking clearly and didn't have a concussion. You're the only one who can save him from getting sent to prison. Surely you know what happens to cops in there."

"He's not a criminal."

"Bullshit, Ian. He's guilty of assault and battery, and I have plenty of video evidence and eyewitnesses, not to mention the two club security guards who pulled your boyfriend off me. I've already talked to an attorney, and because of the severity of my injuries, he'd likely be charged with aggravated battery. That's a felony in this state, which means he'd get a mandatory prison sentence. He wouldn't be able to sweet-talk his way out of serving time."

The idea of Tyler going to prison makes me sick. I shake my

head. "You can't do this. He was only—"

"The law is the law, Ian. I have video evidence on my side, and he doesn't. It's that simple. Any jury in America would convict him based on that alone."

Brad pulls his phone out of his back pocket, turns it toward me, and hits play on a video of an enraged Tyler pummeling Brad with his fist. Blow after blow, he pounds Brad relentlessly.

The focus of the video shifts to show two security guards hauling Tyler off of Brad, holding him back as Brad says, "*And here's Ian Alexander, the little cunt who started it all.*"

And then the camera is pointed at me as I'm sitting on the bathroom floor trying to catch my breath.

I feel sick as I watch the video. Anyone who sees it would convict Tyler on the spot. And we have no proof that Brad tried to strangle me. It's his word against ours.

When another car pulls into my driveway, we both turn to look. It's Miguel's vintage black Mustang. *Thank god.*

"You need to leave," I say to Brad. "Now."

Brad glares as Miguel gets out of his car. "This isn't over, Ian," he says, turning back to face me. "We're just getting started. You *will* let me fuck you. You'll let me tie you up, strap you down, and gag you. And not only will you let me, but you'll *like* it. In fact, you'll beg for more." Then he jogs down the steps, passing Miguel who's on his way up.

Brad gets in his car and peels out of my driveway, his tires squealing loudly on the pavement.

Miguel joins me on the top step. "Shit, man, was that Brad

Turner? What's he doing here?"

I watch Brad's car until it disappears from sight. Then I turn to face my friend. "Nothing. Forget him." Shaking, I reach down and grab my backpack. "Let's go."

3

Ian Alexander

Miguel watches me surreptitiously as we head downtown on foot. I wish he'd forget about seeing Brad, but he's a professional bodyguard. It's in his nature to be suspicious and super observant. He also saved my life not that long ago, so I can forgive him for being inquisitive.

"Does Tyler know Brad's been in touch with you?" Miguel's tone is neutral, and I know he isn't accusing me of anything.

I shrug as I pick up my pace. "It hasn't come up."

"Are you going to tell him?"

I glance at Miguel, wishing he'd drop it. "I can't."

"Why the hell not? If Tyler knew—"

"If I tell him, he'll go after Brad, and he's already in enough jeopardy as it is. If Tyler threatens Brad again, it'll only strengthen Brad's case against him."

"What does Brad want from you?"

"Nothing."

Miguel's silent for a moment, but I can feel the weight of his stare. He can probably tell I'm flat out lying, and I hate lying to a friend.

He jogs to catch up with me. "Ian... you can't keep this from Tyler. He'll find out eventually."

Miguel's right, but if I tell Tyler, it'll only make things worse. "Don't worry. I'm not going to talk to Brad ever again. I promise." Anxious to put an end to this conversation, I charge ahead.

Miguel catches up to me, but he doesn't say another word about it.

It's mid-morning, and the sidewalks are teeming with tourists. We take Rush Street to Superior, which leads us to North Michigan Avenue.

We're both getting a lot of furtive glances from pedestrians—especially from girls. Miguel is on the receiving end of several come-hither smiles. I don't blame them. He's a good-looking guy with his midnight-black short hair, dark eyes, and gorgeous light brown skin. As always, he's dressed in black from head to toe—a look I've come to think of as *bodyguard chic*. Despite the warm weather, he's wearing a jacket—undoubtedly for the purpose of concealing the handgun that is holstered to his broad chest. I must say, he looks badass.

"Why don't you have a girlfriend?" I ask him. He should be fending off the babes. He's not just good-looking; he's an all-around great guy.

He shrugs. "When would I have time to date? I work long hours. That doesn't leave much time for a personal life."

"You have to make time to date. When was the last time you got laid?"

He laughs. "Hell, I can't even remember. Well, there was this girl I met at a bar a while back. We hooked up in the back seat of my car." He shakes his head. "It was a tight squeeze, but she was very flexible, if you know what I mean."

As we near the bridge that crosses over the Chicago River, we run into a large crowd gathered to watch a group of six guys playing snare drums strapped to their chests. Their energy is infectious as they march in a well-choreographed formation. The audience is captivated. We watch for a while, and then I drop some cash in their collection bucket before we continue on our way.

"So, where to?" Miguel asks.

"Millennium Park, if that's okay. There's a spot not far from there that I love to photograph. And later, I'll take you to my favorite Mexican restaurant. Their tacos are to die for."

"Tacos? You won't get any argument from me."

We arrive at the park and spend a few minutes observing the tourists who mill around the massive stainless-steel statue known as *The Bean*. I offer to take pics for a few groups posing in front of the iconic tourist attraction with its famous mirror-like finish. Then we move on, heading into some more run-down areas of the city.

There's something about urban decay that I find artistically fascinating. Chipped paint, rusted metal, crumbling bricks—for some reason it speaks to me. To me, there's an intrinsic beauty to be found in damage. I love photographing forsaken buildings and vintage signs that have seen better days.

Miguel claps his hand on my shoulder. "So, what's a rich guy like you doing photographing crappy old buildings that look like they should be demolished?"

I shrug as I stop to change the lens on my camera. "I spent my early childhood living in a distressed area just like this one. I guess I'm drawn to it because I can't help wondering where I'd be today—*who* I'd be—if I still lived there."

As we walk a few more blocks, I come across a number of familiar panhandlers I see on a regular basis. I greet them all by name and drop cash into their collection cups. At least I know they'll be able to eat well for a few days or get a room for the night if that's what they want.

Around noon, we head to one of my favorite restaurants, a hole-in-the-wall Mexican restaurant that makes the best tacos I've ever eaten.

"Have you ever been here?" I ask Miguel.

He glances up at the sign hanging over the restaurant's entrance and shakes his head. "Nope, and I can't wait to try it. But I warn you—I'm a tough judge of Mexican food. No one makes better tacos than *mi abuelita*."

Seated on the sidewalk right outside the restaurant is another familiar face. Jerry is dressed as always in filthy Army fatigues, with his green rucksack resting beside him and a plastic cup out in front. He's a regular fixture here.

I stick several bills into his cup. "Come inside, Jerry. I'll buy you some lunch."

Slowly, the old guy heaves himself to his feet, muttering, "Damned arthritis." Then his steely blue eyes meet my gaze. "Hello, Ian. That's mighty kind of you." He nods to Miguel.

We follow Jerry up to the ordering counter. Jerry orders his usual—ten tacos and a large Coke—and then Miguel and I each order.

"Lunch is on me," I say to Miguel as I pay the bill.

Miguel and I grab the only available booth as Jerry takes his food outside. The small dining room is packed, mostly with guys working on local construction sites. It's rare for tourists to venture this far from the shopping district.

Miguel nods toward Jerry, who we can through the front window. "Who's he?"

"I only know his first name—Jerry—and that he's a retired vet. I've offered repeatedly to get him into a shelter, but he refuses. I offered to pay his rent so he could get a room somewhere, but he won't let me. He says he prefers to be on his own. He's so stubborn."

Miguel smiles. "He's got his pride."

After a young guy brings us our orders, Miguel reaches for a taco and takes a bite.

"What do you think?" I ask him.

He swallows and smiles at me. "Don't ever tell *mi abuelita* I said this because I'll deny it, but this is the best damn taco I've ever had."

I laugh. "My lips are sealed."

"You should come over sometime and meet *mi familia*. They'd love you. Especially *mi abuelita.*"

"I'd love to. Just say when. Maybe your grandma will give me a cooking lesson. I've always wanted to learn how to make authentic tamales."

Miguel takes another bite of his taco. "She'd love to teach you. Hers are out of this world."

Just as we're about done eating, I receive a text from Tyler.

Tyler: What are you up to?

Ian: Lunch with Miguel.

Tyler: Have fun. Tell him I said hi.

I glance across the table at Miguel. "Tyler says hi."

He grins at me and shakes his head. "You two."

"What?"

"You're so cute together. I never thought I'd see Tyler Jamison acting so lovey-dovey."

"Why not? He's very romantic."

"Whatever you say. I'll take your word for it." Then Miguel winces as he carefully rotates his left arm.

"How's your shoulder?"

"It's better. I have a follow-up doctor appointment later this afternoon. I'm hoping to get the okay to return to work soon."

We leave the restaurant and after saying goodbye to Jerry, who's still working through his bag of tacos, we start walking back in the direction of my townhouse.

Another text comes in, this time from my friend Sam.

Sam: We still on for tonight? You, me, and the old guys?

Ian: yes! As long as Tyler doesn't have to work late again.

Sam: what do you want to do?

Ian: go clubbing @ Sapphires? 9?

Sam: Sounds good to me. Cooper will hate it. LOL Too bad. It'll be good for him

"What's so funny?" Miguel asks.

"Sam and I are planning a double-date tonight. We're taking Tyler and Cooper clubbing."

"Cooper's going clubbing?" He looks incredulous. "I would pay good money to see that."

* * *

After we get back to the townhouse, Miguel takes off for his appointment.

I let myself in and putz around the house for a while, doing a bit of laundry before I start thinking about dinner. As much as I love to cook, it always seemed like wasted effort when it was just me living here alone. Now that I have Tyler, I really enjoy planning meals for him. The way to a man's heart is through his stomach, right? Well, I plan to keep his stomach happy, along with other parts of his anatomy. It's more than a fair trade-off because he keeps me satisfied in every way imaginable.

After folding towels and putting away socks and underwear, I download the images I took today to my computer so I can edit the best ones to get prints made. My family has been after me for years to do something with my photography.

The art studio where I get my prints made has asked me repeatedly if they could host an exhibition of my photographs, but I haven't decided. I'm proud of my photographs of distressed Chicago landmarks, but they're not everyone's cup of tea. Maybe someday.

Late afternoon, I start on dinner. At six-thirty, right on schedule, I hear Tyler's car pull into the driveway. He parks in the carriage house and walks in through the back door, which leads directly into the kitchen. I meet him there and pull him close for a kiss.

His arms circle my waist. "Something sure smells good," he says.

"That's our dinner. Chicken enchiladas. I had tacos for lunch today with Miguel, and it got me in the mood for more Mexican food. How was work today? Any new breaks?"

He shakes his head. "I was able to ID the Rogers Park victim, and I had to perform the unpleasant task of notifying her parents. I haven't made any concrete progress yet, but there is one possible avenue I'm pursuing. There's been a rash of young women disappearing in the city over the past two months— presumed to be victims of sex trafficking. All are young women in their late teens or early twenties. I'm wondering if this girl's death is somehow connected. Maybe someone tried to snatch her, but she fought back. Her death might have been an accident. Or, she was simply in the wrong place at the wrong time and it was a random mugging that turned violent."

I follow Tyler to the front closet and watch him hang up his suit jacket and holster, his movements efficient and controlled. Sometimes I can't help staring at him—at his broad shoulders and muscular torso, his dark hair and the trim dark beard that frames beautiful lips. When he flashes those dazzling blue-green eyes at me, I feel almost dizzy.

Hello, gorgeous.

"What are you looking at?" he asks, grinning at me.

"You."

Tyler walks toward me with a heated gleam in his eye and reaches out to capture my wrists. "Did you miss me today?"

His deep voice sets me on fire. "Yes."

He steps closer, following me as I back into the wall. He pins my wrists above my head. "How much?" he says, his rough voice dropping an octave.

I love it when he teases me like this. "A lot." My chest tightens and my pulse races.

Tyler gazes into my eyes as he presses his erection against mine, aligning us perfectly. The heat and friction are incredible. All he has to do is look at me, and I want him. This man owns me—body, heart, and soul.

He transfers my wrists to one hand so he can grip my jaw. "I missed you, too." And then he kisses me, coaxing my lips open. "I think about you way too much when I'm at work. It's distracting."

My breath catches. "What do you think about?"

His hand slides down to my chest and he fingers one of my nipple piercings through my T-shirt. "This."

His touch makes my nipple tighten, and pleasure shoots down my spine. "What else?"

He smiles as his hand slides further south until he encounters my hard-on. He presses his hand against me. "This."

I smile.

And then he teases me with what he knows I crave. "And then I imagine you on your knees, sucking me off."

God, yes.

Just as I'm thinking of doing just that, the oven timer goes off, and I groan. "Dinner's ready."

Before releasing me, he kisses me once more. "Saved by the bell. But hold that thought for later."

Tyler follows me to the kitchen. I slip on my pink unicorn oven mitts and take the baking dish out of the oven. After setting it on the stove to let the enchiladas rest, I dish up the rest of our meal—a Mexican rice dish and homemade salsa with sour cream, guacamole, and tortilla chips. We carry our dinners and two beers up to the roof and eat at the little table that overlooks the lake in the distance.

Tyler takes his first bite of the enchiladas. "Mmm, these are really good. So, how was your lunch with Miguel? How's his shoulder?"

After I'm done chewing, I swallow and nod. "He's doing pretty well. He had a follow-up appointment with his doctor this afternoon. He's hoping to get the all-clear soon so he can return to work. He's getting restless."

Thinking about Miguel reminds me of Brad's visit this morning, and that ruins the moment. Miguel's right—I need to tell Tyler about Brad, but I just can't bring myself to do it.

"Hey," Tyler says, eyeing me with concern. "Is everything okay?"

"Yeah, sure." *No. I'm in way over my head and I don't know what to do.* "Everything's fine."

"You sure? You looked a bit spooked all of a sudden." Tyler picks up his beer. "So, what time are we meeting Sam and Cooper this evening?"

"Nine o'clock."

"Good. I have time for a shower. Want to join me?"

"I'd love to."

4

Tyler Jamison

D ance music blasts out of the sound system as neon blue strobe lights bounce off the black club walls. As usual, Sapphires is packed with men of all ages and backgrounds. Clubbing isn't at the top of my to-do list—I'm more of a homebody—but Ian loves to dance, and I love to make him happy. So, here we are, at a gay nightclub on our first double-date with good friends.

As I watch my boyfriend out on the dance floor, I think, *I'll never take this for granted.*

I'll never take *him* for granted.

I haven't known Ian that long, but he's already upended my life, and I'm still reeling.

Daniel Cooper, who's sitting across the booth from me, nods toward the crowded dance floor where our respective boyfriends are working up a sweat. "Ian's a good dancer."

Without taking my eyes off Ian, I nod. "He is." Smiling, I take a swig of my beer.

I'm a pretty reserved person, and I don't advertise my sexuality to the world at large. Hell, it was only recently, after meeting Ian, that I came out to my family. Ian helped me understand my own needs and desires. I'd lived my whole life thinking there was something wrong with me when there wasn't. The truth was staring me in the face—and I'd just been in denial. And tonight, on a double-date in a gay nightclub, I'm not just *out*, but out in a big way.

My gaze is glued to Ian on the floor. He's electrifying to watch, and I can't stop staring. His movements are so crisp and perfectly choreographed. He's free and uninhibited. He's in his element out there, surrounded by his usual entourage of friends, plus Cooper's much younger partner, Sam Harrison.

As usual, Ian's the center of attention.

"It's a good thing you're not the jealous type," Cooper says in his rough voice. He reaches for his beer and takes a swig, then points his bottle toward the dance floor, where Ian is at the epicenter of a crush of guys.

"I wouldn't exactly say that." I know I'm a controlling SOB, and I admit to getting jealous when I see guys fawning over Ian.

"I fine with it as long as they're not grabbing his ass."

At that moment, a bare-chested, inebriated blond joins their little group, sliding up behind Ian. The guy puts his hands on Ian's shoulders and tries to draw him back against him. *That's certainly crossing a line.* I start to get up from my seat, intending to intervene, but Sam skillfully steps between them and sends the guy on his way.

"Relax," Cooper says with a laugh. "Sam will look out for Ian."

Cooper's another late bloomer. He resisted coming out publicly until recently, after Sam left him because of it. Cooper had a choice to make—either come out and claim Sam or lose him for good. Obviously, love won, because he chose Sam. And now they're engaged to be married.

I finish off my beer. "Have you two set a wedding date?"

Cooper grins at me. "Stop changing the subject, Jamison."

"I have no idea what you're talking about." I resume watching Ian on the dance floor. As Ian laughs at something Sam said, his smile tugs at me.

I'm getting accustomed to the fact that Ian attracts a lot of attention wherever he goes. It's not just because of his looks, although he has that in spades—six feet tall, lean muscles, bright green eyes lit with mischief. His looks draw people to him, yes, but it's his personality that holds them captivated. He's brazen and charismatic. He's the belle of the ball.

And he's *mine.*

To the outside world, Ian comes across as fearless, but I

know better. I know him as the young man who, on the inside, is riddled with deep insecurities.

I'm glad Sam and Ian have hit it off well. Ian doesn't have a lot of close friends, but since he met me, he can now add Miguel Rodriquez and Sam Harrison to the list. And my sister, Beth, and her husband, Shane. I want him to have a strong support network in case something happens to me.

In case I get locked up.

I force the thought from my head. There's no use borrowing trouble ahead of time. I'll face that issue if and when the time comes.

Tonight's outing was Ian's and Sam's idea. Ever since they met, they've been nagging me and Cooper to go out. We finally agreed, mostly to shut them up.

Sapphires is Ian's club of choice now, since Diablo's closed after the owner, Roy Valdez, was shot dead on the deck of Ian's yacht. Valdez, who turned out to be the serial killer I was hunting, attempted to add Ian to his list of murder victims. He failed. Miguel and I made sure of it. We both shot him—only forensics determined it was *my* bullet that ended Valdez's life.

As far as I'm concerned, Roy Valdez got off easy. He brutally murdered—decapitated—three innocent men out of jealousy because they had the audacity to fuck Roy's ex, Brad Turner. Valdez's death was instantaneous. My bullet struck him in the heart, and he was likely dead before he hit the deck. But the men he murdered? Valdez made sure they suffered before they died.

The good-looking kid who's been waiting on us all evening returns to our table. He's dressed in a pair of tight, black leather shorts that barely cover his ass cheeks—and nothing else. He's wearing blue eyeshadow and heavy eyeliner, and his cheeks are dusted with glitter. He looks barely old enough to work here.

The kid smiles, showing a set of matching dimples as he winks at Cooper. "Can I get either of you two daddies a refill?"

Apparently, our server is into silver foxes. Cooper's in his mid-fifties—trim gray hair and beard. He's a former Marine Corps sniper and now a shooting instructor at my brother-in-law's company, McIntyre Security. When I consider the age difference between Cooper and Sam, I don't feel quite so bad for robbing the cradle myself—I'm a good decade younger than Cooper. When it comes to an age gap, Cooper and Sam have us beat by a long shot.

"I'll take a Coke this time," Cooper tells the kid.

"Bottle of spring water for me," I say.

Cooper and I are designated drivers tonight, and we've both met our limit of one beer.

After our server gives Cooper a come-hither smile, he heads back to the bar to fill our drink orders.

I shake my head at Cooper. "Did he just wink at you?"

Cooper scowls at me. "No, he did not."

"I don't know... I'm pretty sure I saw a wink, *daddy.*"

"Any word from Brad Turner?" Cooper asks, effectively changing the subject on me this time.

My smile fades. "No. Nothing. He's biding his time."

"But you think he's going to press charges?"

I nod. "He spent four days in the hospital recovering from injuries I gave him. I don't think he's going to let that slide."

Cooper scoffs. "He deserves everything he got. If someone tried to choke Sam—well, let's just say they wouldn't live to tell the tale. Turner got off lucky as far as I'm concerned."

Ironically, it was right here in this club where the altercation took place just a couple weeks ago. I've been waiting for Turner to press charges ever since.

Just as the guys return to our table, our server arrives with our drinks. Sam orders another beer, and Ian orders a Cosmo—his third for the night. Since Cooper and I are driving, the guys are free to let their hair down.

Ian slides onto the bench seat beside me and lays his hand on my thigh. It's an innocent enough touch, and yet my body responds instantly, my cock stirring.

He's a bit breathless from dancing as he leans his head on my shoulder and grins up at me. "Miss me?"

Ian's a little tipsy, and I have to bite my lip to keep from smiling. Some people are happy when they're drunk. Others get sad or angry. Ian is playful, and it's fucking adorable. I want to take him home right now and show him just how adorable I think he is.

Instead, I say, "Nah. Cooper kept me company."

Ian's lips instantly turn down in a pout. "Not at all?"

Feeling like I just kicked a puppy, I lay my hand over his and link our fingers together. Then I lean in close and whisper, "Of course I missed you. I couldn't keep my eyes off you."

He smiles, clearly pleased with my revised answer.

I wish I had the guts to kiss him, right here and now, in front of our friends and anyone else who happens to see. But I'm not quite there yet. It hasn't been that long since I admitted to myself that I felt desire for a man. I'm still playing catch-up.

In my peripheral, I catch a glimpse of Cooper sliding his arm across Sam's shoulders and drawing him close for a quick kiss on the lips. And of course that's not the first incident of PDA I've seen tonight. I've seen men groping each other, kissing, cuddling, grinding against each other on the dance floor.

As Ian notices the kiss between Sam and Cooper, he smiles wistfully and squeezes my hand beneath the table.

I'm a shitty boyfriend.

But Ian doesn't seem to mind. Reaching for my water bottle, he says, "Do you mind?"

"Go right ahead." I'm used to Ian stealing my drinks.

He chugs half the bottle before setting it back on the table.

I laugh. "Thirsty?"

He sighs, settling back in his seat. "You have no idea."

When his fingers tighten on mine, my heart contracts and my pulse quickens. I squeeze his hand in return and lean in close so he can hear me over the loud music. "How much longer do we have to stay? I want to take you home."

Ian's eyes light up. "I thought you'd never ask."

The four of us sit for a little while longer, just long enough to finish our last round of drinks. It's nearly midnight when Cooper flags our server down and asks for the check. He insists on paying the tab.

"We should do something again, real soon," Ian tells Sam as we say our goodbyes on the sidewalk outside the club.

"Absolutely," Sam says as he hugs Ian.

After the four of us part ways, Ian and I head down the street to my black BMW. I walk Ian around to the front passenger seat and open the door for him.

He pivots to face me, swaying a bit unsteadily. Besides his beloved Cosmos, he had a couple of shots and a beer. "You're such a gentleman, Tyler."

"You like that?" I know he does because he's grinning at me like a fool.

His hand slips to my waist. "You know I do. It makes me feel special."

Special? Ian has no idea just how special I think he is.

I take a step closer, just inches from him now, and we stand eye-to-eye. "Let's go home so I can make you feel *really* special."

"Oh, my god, yes," he says as he slides into the front seat and reaches for his seatbelt.

* * *

That night, as we lie in bed together, our legs intertwined, hearts beating fast and both of us short of breath, I stroke Ian's hair. As I run my fingers through the wavy strands on top, he shivers. "I'm sorry if I disappointed you tonight," I tell him.

He lifts his head off my chest. "What? No. What are you talking about?"

"At the club—you wanted me to kiss you. When Cooper kissed Sam at our table. I could see it in your eyes."

He shrugs. "Don't worry about it. It's nothing."

I trace the edge of his cheek. "It's not nothing." I lean in to kiss him. "I want to make you happy. I'll work on it, I promise."

He lays his head on my chest, right over my thundering heart. "Just being in your life makes me happy, Tyler. I don't need anything more."

* * *

I wake violently in the middle of the night, shooting up in bed as my heart slams into my ribs. For a second, I'm dazed and disoriented, my gaze frantically searching the dark room as I try to get my bearings. Then I glance down beside me at Ian, who's sound asleep in our bed.

It was just a dream.

In my dream, my boss, Jud Walker, along with two uniformed officers, comes into my office at the precinct. Jud looks gutted when he says, "I'm sorry, Tyler, but my hands are tied. You're under arrest for aggravated battery."

As the two officers approach me, I stand calmly, offering no resistance. I knew this was coming, and I'm not going to fight them. It was inevitable. Still, one of them grabs me forcibly and slams me face-down on my desk while the other one kicks my feet apart, yanks my arms behind my back, and cuffs me.

When I hear footsteps at the open door, I look up as Brad Turner walks into my office, his face bruised and bloody still, courtesy of my fists. He looks like he did that night at Sapphires, when I pulled him off Ian, as he choked him.

"You're going to prison, asshole," Brad grates out, sneering through cracked and bloody lips. "You're going to rot in prison while I pick up where I left off with Ian. That little bitch is mine."

That's when I start to fight back. "Stay the fuck away from him! I swear, if you touch him, I'll tear you apart!"

But Turner just laughs.

Then the officers haul me upright and hold me immobile as Brad slams his fist into my belly, over and over.

And that's when I wake up.

Now, I'm too on edge to lie here, so I get up and pace. I gaze down at Ian, who's sleeping peacefully on his belly, his arms hugging his pillow.

He's fine.

He's safe.

But still, my pulse pounds. Ever since the fight with Turner, I've had some variation of this same dream—or nightmare, rather. I dream I'm arrested for aggravated battery and end up behind bars, leaving Ian to deal with Turner on his own.

Or worse, I relive that night at Sapphires over again, walking into the restroom to find Ian pinned to the wall, Turner's fingers wrapped tightly around his throat. Only, in my dream,

Turner manages to crush Ian's windpipe, and Ian falls to the floor and suffocates while I try desperately to save him.

I run my fingers through my hair, attempting to slow my heart rate. I'm wide awake now and not likely to fall back asleep anytime soon, so I head to the bathroom to splash cold water on my face. When I return to the bedroom, I pull on a pair of shorts and sit in an armchair near the window overlooking the street. If I can't sleep, I'll sit here and strategize what I'll do if Turner does press charges. As I told Cooper, Turner—that manipulative fucker—is just biding his time.

One thing is clear. I don't regret my actions that night. If Turner ever puts his hands on Ian again, I'll do far worse than beat him up.

After a while, my heart rate returns to normal and I crawl back into bed. My body gravitates automatically toward Ian's, and I slide one leg between his and wrap my arm around his waist. As I spoon him, my groin nestles against his ass. He groans in his sleep and clutches my arm to his chest.

I'll never forget seeing the bruises on Ian's throat the night Turner choked him. As far as I'm concerned, Turner got off lucky with just a beating.

5

Ian Alexander

I watch with great amusement as my man sits on the side of our bed, wearing only a pair of black boxer-briefs, as he shines his perfectly-polished black dress shoes. "Relax, Tyler. They're going to love you."

Tyler raises a dark eyebrow and gives me a look I've become very familiar with. "Your father hates me, Ian. I don't think one family dinner is going to change that."

I step in front of him and cup his handsome face in my hands. "All you have to do is win my mom over, and then Dad will fall in line. And I promise my sister is going to love you."

When he finishes shining his shoes, Tyler heads into our walk-in closet to get dressed. He has already showered, trimmed his beard, and applied cologne. Now, he's deciding which one of his dozen identical white dress shirts, all fresh from the dry cleaners, he's going to wear.

"Just pick one, Tyler. They all look the same. And to think you razz *me* about taking too long to decide what to wear."

Tyler rolls his eyes at me as he pulls a shirt off the rack. "You do take too long."

Since I'm already dressed, I'm at liberty to enjoy watching Tyler get dressed. I'm mesmerized by his firm chest and his well-defined biceps. Sexy veins snake their way down his arms to the back of his masculine hands, and the sight makes me practically weak in the knees. His dark chest hair narrows to a thin line that dips below the waistband of his briefs. He reminds me of a Greek statue, all rough planes and chiseled muscles.

If we didn't have such important plans tonight, I'd already be on my knees, worshipping his cock. But we do, so the worshipping will have to wait until after we return home.

Tonight is *Operation Win Over My Dad.*

Tyler slips on his shirt and buttons it up. Then he selects a pair of black trousers, also fresh from the dry cleaners, and pulls them on. Watching him tuck in his shirt, then thread his black leather belt through his belt loops is nearly as good as foreplay. Once he's dressed, he sits on a padded bench and pulls on his black socks and shoes.

Most definitely, one of my newfound pleasures in life is

watching Tyler get dressed. It's almost as enjoyable as watching him get *undressed.*

"You know, you don't have to get dressed up to have dinner with my family. I'm not dressing up." I hold out my hands and pose for him in my ripped jeans and my favorite *Guardians of the Galaxy* T-shirt.

He raises an eyebrow. "Ian, your father's a federal judge, and your mother is a district attorney. Do you think they'll be wearing jeans to dinner tonight? I highly doubt it."

"Good point." As he reaches for his tie, I take it from him. "Let me do it." I deftly tie his tie before tucking it beneath his shirt collar and arranging it just perfectly.

I get a kick out of doing the simple things for him, like tying his tie or picking up his clothes from the dry cleaners. Tyler is a domineering, controlling force of nature, which I love—especially in bed—so when he indulges me, it's extra sweet. Plus, I enjoy taking care of him. God knows he does a great job of taking care of me.

Tonight's a big deal for him. He and my dad got off on the wrong foot initially. When my father discovered Tyler and I were dating, he threatened to get Tyler fired if he didn't stop seeing me. My dad means well, but he has a tendency to be overprotective.

Tyler wants to get on a better footing with my dad. He wants my family to like him. I already have his family's blessings—his mother and sister both welcomed me with opens arms.

I smooth the fabric of his shirt over his chest, delighting in the feel of his firm muscles beneath the fabric. "You have nothing to worry about."

His hands come up to cup my face, and he pulls me in for a kiss, his lips warm as he teases mine open. I wrap my fingers around his wrists, holding onto him and relishing his strength. He's my anchor.

"I hope you're right," he says as he grabs his Rolex off the dresser and straps it on. Then he grabs his suit coat. "Okay, let's go. I don't want to be late to my first Alexander family dinner."

"The first of many," I say.

"Let's hope so."

The thought that he's actually nervous about tonight makes me smile. Tyler investigates murders for a living. I didn't think anything fazed him. I reach out to brush his sexy bottom lip. "I promise, they're going to love you."

He laughs. "I appreciate your optimism. The last time we talked, your father threatened to have my badge if I didn't stay the hell away from you. He said he'd make sure I never work in law enforcement again."

I find it hard not to laugh. "Don't let him intimidate you. He's not your boss. He doesn't have *that* kind of control over your career."

"Ian, in addition to being a federal judge, your father is a very wealthy man. Don't underestimate his influence in this city."

I tug gently on Tyler's tie. "I'm an adult. I make my own decisions, and I choose *you*. He'll just have to accept that."

Tyler caresses the back of my neck. "My little ray of sunshine." And then he drops a quick kiss on my lips. "Come on. Let's get this over with."

* * *

As Tyler drives us to my parents' house, I find myself preoccupied by the sight of his long fingers gripping the leather steering wheel. I love watching him drive. The confident way he navigates Chicago's crowded streets, negotiating bumper-to-bumper traffic with ease, is a total turn-on. My gaze lingers on the backs of his hands—his sexy, rugged hands.

Tyler pulls the car around to the access lane behind my family home and parks next to my dad's Mercedes. He shuts off the engine and turns to face me. "Ready?"

Grinning, I nod. The truth is, I'm excited about tonight. This is a big deal for me because I've never brought someone home to meet my family. "Absolutely. Let's do this."

He smiles at my eagerness. "Let's just hope you're right about tonight."

My reply is interrupted by the screech of tires as a cherry-red Fiat comes tearing around the corner and zips into the parking space beside us.

As Tyler glares out my window at my sister's new bodyguard, Sean Dickerson, who's behind the wheel, he doesn't bother to hide his irritation. "Sean should be more careful when he's driving your sister."

Layla's just twenty-one, a sophomore at the University of

Chicago, and an heiress with a sizable fortune—hence the need for a bodyguard. She can never leave the house without protection. My sister is featured on Forbes' list of the wealthiest young adults in the US, along with me. And like me, she's adopted. We're not biologically related, but we couldn't be closer. And like me, she has her share of issues.

Layla, dressed in ripped jeans and a burgundy UC hoodie, hops out of the Fiat and races around to my car door. Her long black hair is pulled back in a ponytail, and she's wearing large silver hoop earrings.

After opening my car door, she leans in, ignoring me to peer at Tyler. She's practically bouncing with excitement. "Hi. You must be Tyler."

Tyler returns her smile. "And you must be Layla. It's a pleasure to finally meet you."

"I know, right?" she says. "I've been bugging Ian to bring you by." Layla tucks some loose strands of hair behind her ear and nudges my shoulder. *He's hot*, she mouths to me.

Tyler gets out of the car and walks around the front of the vehicle to join us.

"Layla, this is Tyler," I say as I step out of the car and make proper introductions. "Tyler, this is my sister, Layla."

I practically hold my breath as the two most important people in my life meet for the first time. I'm desperate for them to like each other.

Tyler offers Layla his hand, and she shakes it eagerly, her gaze bouncing from him to me and back again.

Tyler then turns his attention to Layla's bodyguard, who's now leaning insolently against the Fiat beside us, his arms crossed over his chest.

Tyler levels his gaze on Sean. "Do you always drive like a maniac when your client is in the car?"

I have to bite my lip to keep from laughing. That's my man—he never minces words. And I love that he's already sticking up for my sister.

Sean whips off his dark sunglasses and hangs them on the neckline of his T-shirt. "I don't see how that's any of your business." He rolls his eyes toward my sister. "I don't see Layla complaining."

Tyler's expression darkens, but before he can reply, Layla butts in with a shaky laugh and grabs my hand. "Come on, guys, let's go inside. Mom's dying to meet Tyler." Then she glances at Sean. "I'm in for the rest of the evening, so you can take off if you want. I'll see you in the morning."

As Layla pulls me toward the rear entrance to our house, I glance back at Tyler, who's still engaging in a pissing contest with Sean. He can't help it—he's a protector. It comes naturally. "Tyler? Are you coming?"

Tyler turns to face me, his expression transforming instantly. "I'm right behind you."

6

Tyler Jamison

Ian's young and exuberant sister leads us through a sprawling, early twentieth-century Chicago mansion that takes up, quite literally, an entire city block. I know Ian comes from old money, and lots of it, but this home is beyond anything I could ever have imagined. There are exquisite oriental rugs on the polished dark wood floors, pristine pieces of antique furniture, oil paintings covering the walls—landscapes and portraits. I feel like I'm walking through a museum.

Layla is a bit of a surprise. I'm not sure of her ethnicity, but her hair is a deep black and her wide, kohl-lined eyes are as dark as obsidian. If I had to guess, I'd say she perhaps is of Mediterranean descent. One thing is certain… she's stunning. I imagine Sean has his work cut out for him as I'm sure the college boys are all over her.

I follow Ian and his sister into a spacious living room, where we find their parents seated on a dark green velvet sofa, sipping red wine.

Judge Martin Alexander is dressed in a navy-blue, pinstriped suit. He probably just got home from the courthouse. His expression is stern as he meets my gaze, his jaw tightly clenched. His wife, District Attorney Ruth Alexander, is dressed in tailored black slacks and a white silk blouse, a string of pearls around her throat. But whereas Ian's father appears anything but friendly, his mother is all smiles.

Ruth jumps to her feet the moment we enter the room. "Hello, detective. Welcome to our home." She sets her wine glass on the coffee table and comes to greet us, first hugging her two children before directing her attention to me. "Detective Jamison." She offers me her hand. "I'm so happy to meet you."

I nod. "It's a pleasure to meet you, Mrs. Alexander. Please, call me Tyler."

"Of course. There's no need to stand on formality. I'm Ruth." She glances back at her husband. "And I believe you've already met Martin."

"I have." I tip my head toward the judge. "Good evening, Your Honor."

Martin sets his wine glass down and rises to his feet, coming forward to offer me his hand. "Detective."

Martin hugs Ian, then draws Layla under his arm and kisses the top of her head. "Hello, sweet pea."

"Daddy, please," she complains, pulling away with an embarrassed grin.

And then we're called to dinner by an older woman wearing a starched gray uniform.

Not surprisingly, the meal is beyond reproach—filet mignon, roasted baby potatoes, steamed vegetables—followed by Crème Brulee in fancy little ceramic dishes for dessert. I notice Layla is having fresh strawberries for dessert.

Ian told me Layla was born a type one diabetic—it was primarily the reason her teenage parents gave her up for adoption shortly after birth. She was labeled *medically fragile*, and I guess they couldn't handle the responsibility of meeting her needs.

Even now, as a young adult, her blood sugar levels have to be closely monitored. Modern technology has made that task a lot easier. Between her insulin pump and her continuous blood glucose monitor, a lot of it is automated. But it's not foolproof. Her previous bodyguard was fired because he slept through her monitor signaling an alarm in the middle of the night when her blood sugar levels crashed dangerously low.

I sit back and listen to the conversation at the table. Martin asks his daughter how her classes are going at school. Ruth asks me about my family. Layla grills me on my career.

How long have you worked in law enforcement?

Do you like being a homicide detective?

Why did you want to become a cop in the first place?

What's it like to see a dead body?

"Layla, darling, please," Ruth says. "Let's not discuss dead bodies at the dinner table."

I don't mind her questions. "I always wanted to follow in my father's footsteps. He was a cop, too. He died in the line of duty when I was eighteen." I pause a moment to sip my coffee and lock down my emotions. Talking about losing my dad is still painful, even more than two decades later. Sometimes the pain is so fresh, it feels like it happened just yesterday.

After that somber moment, Ruth skillfully steers the conversation in a different direction. Layla tells us about her current load of courses at UC, where she is majoring in psychology. Then the conversation turns to boating, and Ian talks about some high-tech navigation upgrades he wants to make to his yacht.

I sip my coffee and take it all in.

Ian's father is reserved, sitting back quietly and listening, but not contributing much. His mother, on the other hand, is friendly and engaged.

The four of us polish off a bottle of Chianti, while Layla sips sparkling water.

After everyone has finished eating, Martin rises from his chair at the head of the table and nods toward the door. "Tyler, come join me in my study for a drink."

It's not so much an invitation as it is a command. Not wanting to risk pissing him off any more than I already have, simply by being here, I stand and lay my white linen napkin on the table. "Of course."

Ian shoots to his feet as well, clearly not wanting to be left out, but his father says, "Stay, Ian. I know you have a lot of catching up to do with your mother and sister. We won't be long."

Ian's worried gaze shifts to me, and I can tell he's torn between visiting with his family and coming with me. Knowing Ian, he probably sees it as his duty to act as a buffer between me and his father. But I can hold my own with Martin Alexander. My guess is Martin doesn't want Ian to hear what he's about to say to me.

"It's okay," I tell Ian. "Stay and visit."

Ian frowns, but he doesn't argue.

I follow Martin out of the dining room and down a hallway to his home office, a dark-paneled room dominated by a large mahogany desk and walls lined with bookcases. He takes a seat behind the desk and motions me toward a chair beside it. "Have a seat, detective."

Detective. I wonder if this is going to be a personal or professional conversation. I suppose I'll find out soon enough.

As I take a seat, the judge reaches for the crystal decanter sitting on his desk and pours us each a shot of whiskey. He hands me a glass and takes a sip of his. "Any word yet on charges?"

He certainly didn't waste time getting to the point. I had assumed he wanted to resume threatening me for daring to date his son, but no, this is about Brad Turner. "No. Nothing yet."

He shrugs. "He has time. The Illinois statute of limitations for battery is two years." He levels his gaze on me. "He could hold this over your head for quite a while."

I nod. "Unfortunately, yes."

"How bad were his injuries? Because if the injuries were bad enough, the charges could amount to aggravated battery, which is a class three felony. Of course, you acted in defense of another—my son. That fact could be enough to exonerate you, depending on the charge. Still, if it goes to trial, Ian will be called upon to testify. And let me tell you, if Ian takes the stand, the prosecuting attorney will do everything he can to rip my son apart and destroy his credibility as a witness."

Martin tosses back the rest of his whiskey and grimaces. "I think it goes without saying that Ruth and I don't want our son to testify."

"I don't want that either."

Martin leans back in his creaking leather chair. "How can I impress upon you the importance of keeping Ian off the witness stand? My son is emotionally fragile. His early formative years—living with his drug-addict of a birth mother—did profound damage to him. His sense of self-esteem was shattered. His sense of security nonexistent. When Ruth and I first got him, the slightest thing would set him off. Later, he was the perfect target for bullies at school. Kids can be mean, Tyler. They saw his fragility, and it was like sharks sensing blood in the water. Ian was the poor little rich kid the other children

loved to torment. He was hounded to the point that he attempted to hurt himself. More than once. There were times
when he required twenty-four-hour supervision, for his own
safety. We had to pull him out of school and educate him at
home, just to keep him safe. That was his darkest period—his
teenage years. He's in a much better place now, as an adult, but
his mother and I still worry about him. We're afraid that, if he's
put on the witness stand, the prosecution will tear him apart.
We already know he feels responsible for you getting into a
fight with Turner. If the prosecution drives that notion home,
it could trigger him and put him right back in that dark place
he's worked so hard to escape."

Listening to Martin describe Ian's tormented childhood
chills me to the bone. In some ways, Ian reminds me of a but-
terfly—beautiful, captivating, and yet also fragile. One dusting
of his wings, and he'd lose his ability to fly. I don't ever want to
be the reason he suffers further damage.

I feel the impact of Martin's weighty gaze. "I'll do everything
in my power to keep your son off the witness stand."

Martin nods in relief. "Thank you." He opens an engraved
wooden box on his desk, removes a cigar, and offers it to me.
"Care for one?"

"No, thank you."

He cuts off the cap and lights the cigar. "Cigars are one of
my few vices. Ruth's been after me for years to quit." He puffs
on the cigar and blows out smoke. "From what Ian has told me,
Turner has video evidence that shows you beating him. You

have nothing. It's your word—and Ian's—against Turner's. And in addition to the video evidence, I understand that Turner has multiple eyewitnesses who saw you beating him. It sounds to me like the evidence is stacked against you."

I maintain a neutral expression. I'm not sure where he's going with this, but I won't let him rile me. "I'm well aware of the facts, Your Honor. I was there."

Martin chuffs with amusement as he pours himself another shot. "Don't take it personally, detective. My wife and I are just looking out for our son."

"So, what do you recommend I do?"

"Simple. Plead guilty, thereby avoiding a trial altogether, and hope the court shows you mercy. You have an excellent history with Chicago PD. I hope the judge presiding over your case will see that and be lenient."

"If I'm convicted of a felony, then what?"

Martin frowns. "For a felony, the mandatory minimum sentence is two years. But, if you can get a plea deal—offer to plead guilty in exchange for getting the charge reduced to simple battery, then based on your work history, you would get either probation or at most a short jail sentence—a week or two in the Cook County jail. I think that's your best option."

"But there's no guarantee."

The judge polishes off the last of his liquor. "No guarantee, I'm afraid. But if you plead guilty, it'll save Ian from being called upon to testify."

My chest tightens. None of us wants Ian testifying in court, but I also have to consider what it would do to him if I went to prison. He already blames himself. "Understood."

As much as I dislike the idea of pleading guilty, I don't blame Martin for wanting to protect his son. On that score at least, we're on the same page.

On the upside, he hasn't repeated his threat to me for dating his son. I think we're making progress. "I love your son, Mr. Alexander. I'll do whatever is necessary to protect him."

The man nods. "I believe you will. In fact, his mother and I are counting on it."

* * *

Martin and I rejoin the others, who've moved back to the living room. Ruth is seated on the sofa, with Ian beside her. Layla is seated on an adjoining sofa.

When she spots me, Layla jumps up, grabs my hand, and pulls me to the sofa to sit beside her. "So, tell me about how you and my brother met."

All eyes are on me, and I definitely feel like I'm on the hot seat. I glance at Ian, who's eagerly awaiting my answer. His mother looks just as interested.

"There's not much to tell," I say. "We met in a bar."

Layla frowns. "And then?"

"And then we ran into each other again later that night at a crime scene."

Layla sighs. "What are the odds of that happening? I mean,

meeting twice in one night? Come on, Tyler, it had to have been fate."

The conversation continues as we talk about everything from boating on Lake Michigan to Chicago baseball to a lively debate on who serves the best pizza in Chicago.

After a while, I notice Layla zoning out on us, her gaze drifting away as she stares at a blank wall. She pulls a pair of earbuds out of her hoodie pocket and slips them into her ears, then fiddles with her phone. She leans her head back on the cushion and closes her eyes.

Ian glances at his sister, then at me. He doesn't say anything, but I can surmise what's going on. I know Layla suffers from paranoid schizophrenia—specifically from auditory hallucinations. *Mean girls*, she calls them. They chide and deride her, putting her down and decimating her self-esteem. Ian says listening to music helps her block them out and redirect her thoughts in a more positive direction.

I notice that both Martin and Ruth are observing their daughter's withdrawal. When Ruth catches my gaze, she gives me a sad smile.

* * *

"Layla was having hallucinations tonight, wasn't she?" I ask Ian on our drive home.

He nods. "Auditory hallucinations are pretty common in people who suffer from paranoid schizophrenia. She takes medication, which helps her to manage it pretty well. She's getting really good grades in school—all A's and B's. She hasn't let her mental health issues stop her from going after her goals."

"She's an amazing young woman."

"She asked me if she could come over and have dinner with us sometime. I told her *yes*. I didn't think you'd mind."

"Of course not. She's welcome anytime."

Ian lays his hand on my thigh. "So, what did you and my dad talk about tonight? Did he threaten you again?"

I laugh. "No, he was actually quite civil. He wanted to talk about Brad Turner."

The judge's advice keeps reverberating in my head.

Plead guilty.

Hope for leniency.

Don't subject Ian to a trial.

I clasp Ian's hand and link our fingers. "It was a good talk. He was very supportive."

Ian looks skeptical. "Really?"

"Yes, really." As I pull into our driveway, I lift his hand to kiss it. "I told you, there's nothing to worry about."

"That's easy for you to say," he says. "It's not your fault."

Ian pulls his hand from mine and gets out of the car without a word. I fully expect him to bolt into the house. When the going gets tough, Ian has a tendency to run. In his mind, running away is better than being pushed away or, worse yet, abandoned. But this time, he doesn't bolt. He waits for me.

I skirt around the car to meet him at the passenger door.

"Talk to me, baby."

It's dark out, but not so dark I can't see the glitter of tears in his eyes.

"It's nothing," he says. But his throat muscles are working, and his jaw is taut. His gaze is everywhere but on me.

I reach for his hand. "Let's go inside."

He nods, and we walk together through the back door of the house.

He didn't run this time. I'd definitely call this making progress.

7

Ian Alexander

Once we're inside, Tyler leads me into the living room and sits me down on the sofa. "Now talk."

I try not to smile. *He knows me so well.* "Have you heard anything from Brad?"

He gives me a look. "Don't you think you'd be the first to know if I had?"

"Not if you're trying to protect me." I turn to face him. "That's mainly what you and Dad talked about tonight, wasn't it? Brad?"

Tyler nods, but he doesn't elaborate.

I try desperately to shove aside any thoughts of criminal charges, but of course it's impossible. I only just found Tyler. I can't lose him. But then I realize I'm being a selfish prick. His career is at stake. Maybe even his freedom.

And it's all my fault.

I gaze directly into Tyler's eyes, and all I see is concern for me. And that scares me more than anything because it means my fears aren't far off the mark. "I'm so sorry, Tyler."

He cradles my hand in both of his. "You have nothing to apologize for."

I've lost count of how many times he's said that. But it doesn't change reality. "You're in trouble because of me. I can't let you go to prison."

His grip on my hand tightens. "No. I protected my boyfriend. That's my right. And it's no one's *fault*, Ian, least of all yours. If I could go back and do it all over again, I wouldn't change a single thing."

Then he kisses me so sweetly, so reverently, my heart aches.

There are so many things I want to say.

I can't live without you.

I'm scared.

Please tell me everything's going to be okay.

But I don't want to be that clingy boyfriend. I want to be strong and stoic, like Tyler. So instead, I say, "I love you." And then I pull free of his hold and drop to my knees on the thick rug in front of him.

His gaze heats as I position myself between his legs.

"Ian." His voice is low and rough, and just the sound of it makes me hard. I'm not sure if he's chastising me or encouraging me.

Watching his reaction, I unbuckle his belt and release the fastener before carefully lowering the zipper.

With a sound that's part sigh and part groan, he leans back and raises his hips so I can tug his trousers and boxer-briefs down his legs. His erection springs free, already thick and hard as steel.

He wants this.

I wrap my hand around the base of him and run my fist up his shaft. Groaning, he throws his head back against the cushions. I catch a drop of pre-cum on my thumb and spread it over the crown.

Just the sight of his impressive erection makes my belly clench in anticipation. As I draw him into my mouth, he watches me intently.

I absolutely love going down on Tyler. I love submitting to him. I love pleasuring him. And I love the satisfaction I feel from seeing to his needs. As I take him to the back of my throat, he groans roughly as he grips my head and positions me where he wants me. I lick and suck and tease him until his muscles tighten and his chest heaves as he draws in breath.

Finally, he gives in to his need to thrust, not holding back as he lets himself go. Arching his back, his muscles straining, he comes with a hoarse shout.

After I swallow every drop and lick him clean, he pulls me up onto his lap so that I'm straddling him. Crushing his mouth to mine, he unfastens my jeans.

* * *

The next morning, just as sunrise peeks through the trees outside our bedroom window, I feel Tyler's lips on my forehead.

"Shh," he murmurs when I stir. "I'm heading to work. Have a good day."

"Mmm. You, too."

And then he slips out the bedroom door. I listen to the receding sound of his shoes striking the wood floors as he walks down the hall toward the stairs.

A short while later, when I hear the front door open and close, followed by the turn of the deadbolt, I roll over and hug his pillow close so I can breathe in his scent.

Later in the morning, after a quick shower and breakfast, I toss some water bottles and protein bars into my backpack and head toward the marina. Whenever I'm stressed, I escape to my boat, a sleek, forty-foot yacht named *Carpe Diem*. She's moored not far from my townhouse at the private St. James Yacht Club, located off Lake Shore Drive. Miguel is meeting me there this morning, and we're going to take my boat out for the day.

Miguel is still on medical leave—his doctor advised one more week of rest before returning to work—and that means he's free to hang out with me.

I arrive at the marina a few minutes early. There's no sign of

Miguel's Mustang, so I grab my backpack, lock up the Porsche, and make my way to the boardwalk. When I head out onto the dock that leads to my slip, I stop at Eric Townsend's yacht, *Sassy Pants*, which is moored next to mine. The bright yellow crime scene tape is long gone, and there's not a single indication that a horrific murder took place on that boat just weeks ago. Now, there's a FOR SALE sign attached to the hull. Eric's parents are selling it.

Eric and I had so many good times on his boat, staying up all night to talk, drinking cocktails and doing shots, dishing about the guys we were crushing on. He and I were close. And now he's gone.

Memories of that traumatic night come flooding back—how I walked into the stateroom on Eric's boat and found his body on the floor, his throat sliced nearly clean through. My stomach churns at the thought of it.

It was one of the worst nights of my life. But it was also the night I met Tyler. Maybe Layla is right, and it was fate that we met.

I smile when I remember how uptight Tyler was in the beginning. He insisted on keeping things strictly professional between us, demanding that I call him *Detective Jamison*. I had to tease him mercilessly just to get him to call me *Ian* instead of *Mr. Alexander*. I wasn't about to let him keep me at arm's length. As soon as I saw him, I wanted him. How could I not? He was the most exciting, sexiest man I'd ever met. Just being in his presence sent my pulse racing.

After taking one last look at Eric's boat, I move on to mine.

"Ian, wait up!"

I freeze, and my skin crawls at the sound of that familiar voice. I hear the heavy pounding of feet on the wooden boards as someone jogs toward me.

Brad rushes up, almost breathless, and smiles down at me. His black hair is loose today, brushing his shoulders.

He smiles as if we're the best of buddies. *We're not.*

"Fancy meeting you here," he says with a laugh.

I find it impossible to believe his presence here, at this exact moment, is a coincidence. "Did you follow me?" My stomach twists at the thought he might be watching the townhouse.

He laughs dismissively. "No. Of course not. I just thought I'd pay a visit to the marina. You know how much I love boats." He glances at Eric's yacht. "Too bad about Eric."

Too bad? I don't understand how Brad can be so nonchalant about Eric's death. He was dating Eric at the time of the murder. In fact, at one point he was the primary suspect during Tyler's investigation.

Without saying a word, I turn toward my boat, wanting to put some distance between us.

Brad follows me. "Ian, wait."

I pause before stepping aboard. "I have nothing to say to you."

He lays a hand on my shoulder. "Sweetie—"

"Don't call me that," I say, pulling away. As I step on board, the boat rocks gently beneath my feet.

When he follows me onto the swim platform, I turn to face him, my heart hammering. "Get off my boat."

Brad drops his pretense of a smile. "You'd better lose the pissy attitude, Ian."

I point toward the dock. "I said *get off.*"

He takes a step forward, looming over me, and grips my shoulders hard. I wince as his fingers dig hard into my muscles.

As the deck rocks beneath our feet, Brad struggles to keep his balance. I'd like to toss him overboard.

He gets in my face, his expression tight. "We're going to fuck on your boat." He glances over my shoulder at the steps leading up to the main deck, which leads to the stateroom below. "Let's go inside, right now, just the two of us. We can have a little fun." He brushes his hand against one of my nipples, teasing my piercing. "Eric told me you're pierced. I wanna see. Come show me."

He reaches for my hand, but I pull back. "You're crazy if you think I'd go below deck with you. You're the last man I'd ever—"

He grasps my jaw firmly and forces me to look him in the eye. "Don't play games with me, Ian. You want this just as much as I do."

His gaze drops to my mouth, and he starts to lean in to kiss me. I wrench out of his grasp, stumbling backward, and narrowly escape falling on my ass. Brad steps forward, but before he can reach me, we both hear someone shout, "Ian!"

Miguel.

Relief rushes through me as I turn to see Miguel striding

purposefully toward us. For the first time since Brad showed up, I begin to relax.

Brad frowns. "We're not done, Ian," he says as he jumps back onto the dock.

"Oh yes, we are," I say.

Glaring at me, Brad jabs a finger in my direction. "That's where you're wrong, sweetie."

As Brad walks back toward the parking lot, Miguel steps in his path, blocking his way.

Oh, shit.

When Brad shoves past Miguel and walks on, Miguel turns to go after him.

"Miguel!"

Miguel stops to look at me. Then he glances back at Brad, clearly torn.

"Let's go," I shout, motioning for him to join me.

After hesitating, Miguel resumes walking toward me. "What the hell?" he says when he steps onto my boat, clearly upset. "What's he doing here?" Miguel watches as Brad gets in his car and drives away.

My pulse is still pounding, and I feel a little sick. "I think he followed me here. He might be watching the townhouse."

"Have you told Tyler?"

"No."

Miguel gives me an incredulous look. "Ian, you have to."

"I know! Trust me, I know, and I will. There just hasn't been a good time to tell him. He's gonna lose his shit." I turn to climb up onto the main deck. "Let's get going. I'll prep the engines while you take care of the lines."

As I head up to the cockpit, Miguel releases the lines and tosses them on board. I go through my routine, checking the fuel gauges and battery levels. While I prep the boat to cast off, I try not to think about Brad. It can't be a coincidence that he just happened to show up when I did. *No way.*

"All ready down below," Miguel says as he steps into the cockpit. He drops down into the co-pilot's chair beside mine.

I back the boat slowly out of its slip. "Thanks."

"Ian." He hesitates as he chooses his words carefully. "Look, I hate to ask, but I have to. Are you and Turner—"

"No!" I shudder. "God, no. Of course not."

"I didn't think so, but—"

"Absolutely not. I'd rather die than let him touch me. Please, just forget you saw him."

Miguel leans back in his seat and crosses his arms over his chest, regarding me with concern. "You know I can't do that."

"You're here as my friend, not as my bodyguard," I remind him.

"Yeah, but that doesn't mean I automatically stop looking out for you. If Tyler knew Brad was here, he'd go ballistic, and you know it."

"And that's why you're not going to tell him. He has enough on his plate to worry about. Brad's gone, and that's the end of it."

"Is it?" Miguel doesn't look convinced.

Hoping to change the subject, I turn my attention to the controls and navigate us into the channel that leads to open water. Once we're past the no-wake zone, I open up the throttle and move us away from the harbor and into deeper water.

We spend the rest of the morning motoring up the shoreline, passing the heavily-populated public beaches, restaurants, and parks. It seems everyone is out today enjoying the summer weather—joggers, cyclers, and families.

Miguel seems to have snapped out of his mood and has returned to being his usual cheery self.

When my phone vibrates in my pocket, I pull it out and quickly skim a new text message.

Brad: Meet me @ ur boat tmrw at 1 pm. ALONE. If u don't show, I promise u will regret it

I shove my phone back into my pocket.

Miguel watches me out of the corner of his eye. "Who was that?"

"My sister." The lie burns like acid on my tongue. I bring the boat to a stop and drop anchor. "I'm going down to the fridge. You want anything?"

8

Tyler Jamison

I spend the morning interviewing possible witnesses in the Addison Jenkins case. I manage to find a bartender who remembers seeing her the night she was killed. He said she came in with a group of girls, but he didn't see her leave, so he has no idea if she left alone or with someone. It's possible she might have hooked up with someone that night. Still, it's not much help.

I continue down the street, visiting one establishment after another, but no one else remembers seeing her. I haven't made much progress on this case yet, and that's frustrating. I keep remembering the look on Addison's parents' faces when I appeared at their front door. Needless to say, the news of their daughter's death was a crushing blow.

I love my job—providing closure for families who've lost loved ones and identifying the guilty—but sometimes I wish I could do something to *prevent* deaths, instead of investigating them.

There's still been no word from Turner, but I'm not fooling myself that he'll just go away quietly. What's been eating at me for days now is what the fallout will be when news of the fight makes it back to the precinct. *Me*—a Chicago homicide detective—caught brawling in the bathroom at a gay club during my off-duty hours. I'll be outed for sure.

It's not that I'm against coming out publicly—although, to be honest, I'm still coming to terms with the idea. I know it's going to happen eventually. It's just that I have no idea how my colleagues will take the news. Some of them will be fine with it, I'm sure, perhaps even openly supportive. Others won't be so accepting. I'm prepared to find hate mail shoved under my office door. I can handle whatever they throw at me. My real concern is for Jud.

Yes, he's my boss, and as such, his opinion matters a hell of a lot to me. But he's much more than that. He was my father's best friend. They went through the police academy together, and they joined the department at the same time. They were partners for years.

Jud was there for me after my father was killed. He was there for my family. I don't want him finding out about my sexuality through the department grapevine or on the evening news. He should hear it directly from me. I owe him that.

My stomach knots at the thought of coming out to anyone at work, but especially to Jud. He'll be the first person I've told outside of my extended family, and I have no idea how he'll react. If I'm being honest, I'll be devastated if he responds badly. He's the closest thing I have to a father, and I don't want to lose that connection.

I hate having my hand forced like this. It should have been my choice, on my timeline, but that's not possible. No matter the risk to me, personally or professionally, I have to tell him.

So, I leave my office and walk down the hall to his. As usual, his door is ajar. I stand outside it for a moment as I muster the courage to knock. Figuring I might as well get it over with, I rap my knuckles on his door.

"Come in," he bellows in his gruff voice.

I step inside and close the door behind me. "Do you have a minute, Jud?"

He leans back in his worn office chair and waves me forward. "Come on in, Tyler. Have a seat."

I do as he says, taking a seat in one of the chairs in front of his desk.

He watches me expectantly. "What's on your mind, son?"

In private, he calls me *son*. He has ever since my dad died, as if he knew I needed someone to try to fill that void in my life. He doesn't show me favoritism at work, which I appreciate, but

I've always known he's here for me.

"There's something I need to tell you," I say, tamping down my fears.

His dark eyes widen. "That sounds rather ominous."

I guess he'll have to be the judge of that. "I met someone recently."

It takes him a minute to catch my meaning, but when he does, he grins. "Hell, that's good news. It's about time. I'd just about given up on you ever settling down."

"We're... *together*."

He nods. "Good, good. I'm sure Ingrid is pleased. Do I know the lucky lady?"

My heart starts pounding, and I feel like the walls are closing in around me. There's no going back now. "Well, yes and no."

His smile fades as he picks up on my guarded tone. "Okay, I'm listening."

In this moment, I feel like I'm leaning over the side of a cliff with one foot in the air. The slightest shift could topple me over, sending me crashing and burning.

Is it always going to be this hard?

There's no point in delaying the inevitable, so I just lay it out there. "It's Ian Alexander."

His brow furrows as he processes the information. "Ian?" Then his dark eyes widen in shock. "The judge's kid?"

"Yes."

Jud practically reels back in his seat. "You and Ian? You mean, romantically?"

His careful choice of words makes me smile. "Yes, romantically."

"Well, I'll be damned," he says as he crosses his arms over his big barrel of a chest.

"I wanted you to hear it from me before the information becomes public."

He nods. "I appreciate that, Tyler. To be honest, if I'd heard it from someone else, I doubt I would have believed it. You've never struck me as... um... you know...."

"As *gay*? It's not one-size-fits-all, you know."

I take a deep breath because I'm not done yet. I have to tell him about the fight at Sapphires. I have to tell him I might be looking at battery charges. For me, the possibility that I might be facing criminal charges and even jail time is the most difficult admission of all. "There's more."

He nods. "Go on. I'm listening."

* * *

When I arrive home from work that evening, I hang up my jacket and holster in the hall closet and go in search of Ian. I find him in the kitchen, bent over as he peeks inside the oven. Whatever he's making smells amazing. "Please tell me that's our dinner I smell."

As he straightens and closes the oven door, he says, "Roasted chicken with rosemary." He props his hands on his hips, looking pretty damn proud of himself. "Baked potatoes and hot rolls. Dinner will be ready in about thirty minutes. You have just enough time to change."

He's dressed in ripped blue jeans and a pale-blue T-shirt, but it's the apron he's wearing that takes the cake. The words *LICK MY BUNS* are printed above a picture of a cinnamon roll.

I meet him halfway and pull him into my arms. "I think I've died and gone to heaven."

He grins. "It does smell good, doesn't it?"

I press a kiss to the side of his neck. "Actually, I meant coming home to you."

For the past two decades, I came home every night to an empty condo, faced with the prospect of heating up a frozen dinner or eating take-out leftovers. On the rare occasions I had a date—with a woman—the outcome wasn't much better. After dinner at a restaurant and, what was for me at least, an emotionless fuck, I still ended up coming home alone.

I kept hoping things would change, that I'd meet a woman I could connect with, one who would make my heart pound and my blood burn, but it never happened.

And then I met Ian. This guy lights me on fire.

I've moved in with Ian, but I still own the condo. I wonder if it's too soon to sell it. I certainly don't need it anymore. I don't *want* it. My home is here, with Ian.

"I thought we'd eat up on the roof," Ian says as he grabs a bottle of white wine and an opener.

"Here, I'll do it." I take the bottle from him and remove the cork with a resounding pop. I set the open wine bottle on the kitchen island to breathe. "I'll grab a quick shower while dinner's cooking. Then I'll help you carry everything up to the roof."

"That sounds—" Ian flinches at the sound of his phone ringing. He makes no effort to answer it, and that's not like him. He's usually attached to his phone.

"Is everything okay?" I ask him as the ringing stops.

He shrugs. "I've been getting tons of spam calls lately. It's so annoying." Then he turns me toward the hallway and gives me a push toward the stairs. "Go take your shower. Dinner will be ready soon."

I turn back to gaze into his eyes. *Something's off.* "Are you sure everything's okay?"

He smiles. "Of course. Now hurry, or our dinner will get cold."

I still think something's bothering him. I cup the back of his head and kiss him. "It's good to be home. I missed you today."

He smiles. "Me too."

His phone starts ringing again.

"You should check that," I tell him as I loosen my tie and head for the stairs. "It could be Layla."

* * *

After a quick shower, I put on a pair of drawstring flannel bottoms and a T-shirt and return to the kitchen just as Ian is about done plating our dinners. He carries our plates up to the roof, and I bring the silverware, napkins, bottle of wine, and glasses.

While I pour the wine, Ian lights the candle in the center of the table.

"Why the special treatment tonight?" I ask him.

He smiles. "No reason. I just wanted to make you a nice dinner."

I take a bite of the chicken and groan in appreciation. "You've outdone yourself, babe. This is fantastic."

He raises his wine glass, and we toast.

"To us," he says.

He's smiling, but I detect a hint of something else in his gaze. "Is something bothering you?"

"No," Ian says quickly. Too quickly. He looks away, lowering his gaze as he focuses on his meal.

Perhaps I'm reading too much into his behavior tonight. I know I have a tendency to be suspicious and skeptical. I can't help it—I'm a cop. Usually, when I come home from work, Ian talks my ears off, but tonight he seems more interested in his supper.

I extend my arm across the linen tablecloth, my hand palm up. Ian sets his glass down and lays his hand in mine. I don't say anything more—I'm not about to interrogate him—but instead I stroke the back of his hand with my thumb.

As the meal progresses, Ian continues to pick at his food. He's going through all the right motions, cutting and shuffling bits of food around his plate, but I don't see him put much of it in his mouth. He has, however, downed two glasses of wine without any problem.

As he becomes increasingly preoccupied, I find myself having to tamp down a growing sense of unease.

I manage to polish off my plate, while he's barely touched his food. "You're not hungry?"

He shakes his head. "No. I ate a big lunch."

He's lying. "Ian, if something's wrong—anything—you know you can tell me, right?"

"Of course," he says, and then he looks down at his plate.

I don't know what I'm supposed to do here. Should I tell him I believe he's lying to me? But I'm afraid if I push him, he'll think I don't trust him.

Ian picks up my empty plate. "I'll clean up the dishes and take a quick shower. Then maybe we can relax and watch a movie or something."

I take the plate from him. "You go take your shower. I'll clean up here."

After Ian disappears, I carry our dirty dishes down to the kitchen and load the dishwasher. Then I transfer the leftovers to glass containers and store them in the fridge.

A buzzing noise attracts my attention. When I turn to look for the source, I notice Ian left his phone face down on the kitchen table. And apparently, it's on silent. The vibration stops, and a moment later it starts up again. Someone's in an awful hurry to get in touch with him.

As I stand there staring at his phone, I contemplate checking to see who it is.

Should I look? Or would that be an invasion of his privacy?

Here I am, at my age, with my first serious relationship—hell, my first relationship of any kind—and I don't know the rules.

I'm dying to pick up his phone. But relationships are about trust. And I do trust Ian, completely. That means I need to mind my own business.

I head upstairs to our bathroom where I find Ian in the shower. I lean against the bathroom wall and watch him through the foggy glass. "Someone's blowing up your phone, babe. You should check it."

"It's probably Layla," he says as he shampoos his hair. "We might get together tomorrow."

I watch as he ducks beneath the spray and rinses out the shampoo. When he turns off the water, I hand him a towel.

I can't help admiring his body as he dries himself. He's as tall as I am but leaner, not quite as muscular. I outweigh him by at least thirty pounds. My gaze follows the trail of brown hair that runs from his navel to his groin.

Ian wraps the towel around his waist and steps out of the shower. He comes to stand in front of me, his eyes glittering with heat. Yeah, he's noticed I'm staring.

"See something you like?" he asks me, grinning as he presses his hips into my growing erection.

"Maybe." I reach out and brush my thumb against one of his piercings. As his nipple puckers tightly, my belly clenches, and

I find it increasingly difficult to breathe. "I told Jud about us today," I tell him before I get even more distracted.

Ian's eyes widen. "You did?" Then he gives me a blinding smile. "Seriously? You came out at work?"

"Just to Jud."

"How did he react?"

"He was surprised at first. I told him I'd met someone, and he asked me who. He assumed I meant a woman, but then I told him it was you, and of course he knows who you are because of your dad. I think he reacted pretty well."

Ian links our fingers together. "I'm so proud of you. I know that wasn't easy."

"I wanted him to hear it from me. I also told him all about the fight at Sapphires. I didn't want him to be caught off guard if Turner brings a complaint against me."

Ian's smile falls. "It's good you told him. He should be prepared."

He walks to the bathroom counter and retrieves his comb from a drawer. I watch him comb his hair and brush his teeth.

We end up lying in bed together, watching a movie. Ian is still uncharacteristically quiet, and it worries me.

Should I leave him alone, or keep trying to get him to talk to me?

Near the end of the movie, Ian falls asleep on me.

I run my hand up and down his back but he doesn't stir. I guess our talk will have to wait until tomorrow.

❧ 9

Ian Alexander

The next morning, my phone buzzes repeatedly with incoming texts from Brad.

Brad: don't forget. your boat @ 1 or you'll regret it

Brad: Ian?

Brad: You'd better be there

Brad: Answer me dammit

I have two choices. I can either let this sadistic monster fuck me, or I risk Tyler facing criminal charges that could put him in prison. Neither option is acceptable.

I honestly don't know what to do. I won't be the reason Tyler goes to prison, and yet there's no way I can give in to Brad. He gets off on administering pain. Eric used to tell me about the ball gags and cock rings, about the whips and the spreader bars. I shudder. And this sick prick wants *me* to be his new plaything.

Honestly, I'd rather die than let him touch me. But it's not that simple. Tyler's freedom is at stake.

My phone rings, and I glance at the screen. It's Brad again. This time, I pick up. "Stop calling me." And then I end the call.

Immediately, my phone rings again. Jesus, he doesn't know when to quit. I answer the call. "I mean it. Stop calling me."

"Or what? Are you going to call the police?" He laughs. "Why don't you just tell your *boyfriend*, Ian?"

When I don't reply, he scoffs. "You're not going to tell him, and we both know it. No, you're going to do whatever the fuck I tell you, and you're going to enjoy it. Aren't you? Because if you don't, I'll file a police brutality report against your cop. Is that what you want?"

I don't answer him because it's pointless. He's never going to back off.

"Do you *want* him to go to prison, Ian? Is that it? Surely you know what happens to cops in the prison system—he'll have a target painted on his ass. A *gay* cop? He'll end up being some-one's bitch. So look at it this way... he's going to end up fuck-ing around on you. So you might as well beat him to it. Meet me at your boat this afternoon. If you don't show, I'm going straight to the police station to file a complaint. This is your last warning."

As the line goes dead, I drop down onto the sofa, feeling sick to my stomach. I can't bring myself to give in to Brad's demands. I wouldn't be able to live with myself, and it would break Tyler's heart if he found out. And he would find out. He's so perceptive, he'd realize something was wrong.

It's almost noon, and I know I can't sit at home all afternoon and worry about whether or not Brad will follow through on his threat.

I call my sister, who picks up right away. It's her early day. She should be done with classes by now.

"Hey, Ian." She sounds breathless. "What's up?"

"Why do you sound so winded?"

She laughs. "I just jogged down three flights of stairs. I'm at school."

"Will you be done soon?"

"I just finished my last class for the day. Why?"

"Do you wanna go see a movie with me?"

"Right now?" She sounds both surprised and excited. "Sure! I'd love to. I'm heading home now. I'll meet you there."

Yes, I'm a coward.

I'm going into hiding—at a movie theater. Someplace where Brad won't find me.

I grab my keys and wallet and head out to the carriage house.

* * *

Layla and I decide on a rom-com because we're both suckers for romance movies with happy endings. I drive us to the theater in my Porsche, and we make Sean sit in the cramped rear seat.

We park and enter the movie theater, a disgruntled Sean trailing behind us. I think he resents the fact that I insisted on driving, but there was no way I'd ride in the Fiat with Sean behind the wheel.

Before we reach the ticket counter, I tell Sean he doesn't have to come in with us if he doesn't want to. "You can sit in the lobby if you want or see a different movie."

"No way," he says. "I'm sticking with Layla."

"Suit yourself."

I purchase our tickets and we walk into the auditorium. As it's still early afternoon, there aren't a lot of people here, so we find great seats.

Sean parks himself in the next row back, directly behind Layla. Then he ignores us while he plays games on his phone.

Normally, I'd applaud him for his professional dedication—for refusing to leave Layla—but the truth is, I'm not impressed. And neither is my sister.

While we're waiting for the movie to start, Layla catches me up on the latest in her classes. One o'clock is fast approaching, and my phone continues to vibrate with reminders from Brad.

Brad: You'd better be here

Brad: I'm at the marina. Where r u?

The messages keep coming.

Even with my phone silenced, Layla can hear the vibrations. "Who keeps texting you?"

I shrug. "Nobody important."

Just as the movie is about to begin, I turn off my phone and stick it in my pocket. For the next two hours at least, I can try to forget about Brad.

10

Tyler Jamison

After spending the entire morning working on the Jenkins case, I return to the office to write up my notes and see if anything new has come back from forensics. They did get a partial set of prints from the scene, but so far, no matches have materialized.

As I enter the precinct building, Rose, our receptionist, flags me down and hands me a sealed white envelope. "This just came in for you, Tyler. Some guy dropped it off about twenty minutes ago."

"Thanks."

As I continue to my office, I glance down at the envelope, which has my name scrawled across it in heavy black ink, all caps. Once I'm inside my office, I tear open the envelope and pull out a folded slip of paper bearing a single sentence written by hand.

DO YOU REALLY THINK YOU'RE THE ONLY ONE FUCKING HIM?

As my vision narrows to the slip of paper in my hand, there's a deafening roar in my head. I stare at the writing, at the words, as my brain tries to process them. My objectivity has flown right out the window, because this is personal. This is about Ian. And it's a direct threat.

The note isn't signed, but my gut tells me I know exactly who sent it. It's utter bullshit, of course. I have no doubt of that. Turner's just trying to get to me. Yes, he's been interested in Ian for a while—no secret there—but Ian has never shown any interest in Turner. They danced a couple of times at Diego's when Ian was trying to help me find out who Eric Townsend had been dating at the time he was murdered.

But, that's all.

They danced. Nothing more.

In fact, the night Turner came on to Ian at the club, Ian escaped out the back door of the club with me. He told me he was repulsed by Turner.

No, Ian would never let Turner touch him.

Immediately, I start to worry about Ian's safety. If Turner is fixating on him—that's not good.

I pull out my phone and call Ian, but my call goes straight to voice mail. I try again and get the same result. I wait a few minutes and try several more times. Straight to voice mail each time. Either Ian's phone battery is dead, or his phone is turned off.

It doesn't make any sense. I've never known Ian to let his battery die. The guy charges it religiously every night before he goes to bed. But the alternative is that he intentionally turned his phone off, and that makes no sense either. He never turns his phone off.

My gaze drifts back to the note in my hand.

DO YOU REALLY THINK YOU'RE THE ONLY ONE FUCKING HIM?

"Yes, I do," I say aloud, because I need to say the words.

The thought of Ian betraying me cuts like a knife. When Ian and I first confessed our feelings for each other, I made it clear that I'd never share him with another man, and he readily agreed we'd be exclusive. I have never once doubted him.

And I'm not going to start now.

I pick up my phone and try his number again.

Nothing.

Come on, baby. Answer your phone.

I start pacing as I contemplate my next move.

This is exactly what Turner wants—to sow distrust between me and Ian. He would love nothing more than to get Ian in his bed. Or, to make me think he'd already done so.

I pick up my phone again, but this time I call Miguel. He's been spending a lot of time with Ian lately. He might know something.

"Hey, detective," Miguel says when he answers. "How's it going?"

"Do you know where Ian is?"

"At the moment, no. Why?"

"He's not answering his phone. It's either dead or turned off. That's not like him."

"Do you want me to track him down? I'd be happy to."

"No. You're on medical leave. You're not supposed to be working."

"I have a bum shoulder, detective, but I'm perfectly capable of tracking your boyfriend down. I don't mind, really." Miguel hesitates a moment, and then he adds, "Maybe I should."

I don't miss the sudden shift in his tone. "Why? Is there a problem?"

"I'm sure he's perfectly fine. It's just that—yesterday—I saw Brad Turner at the marina."

Immediately, the hairs on the back of my neck rise. "Where, exactly?"

"He was on Ian's boat when I arrived. But as soon as Turner saw me, he took off."

"Jesus." Ian never said a word to me about seeing Turner. The roaring in my ears gets a bit louder. "Thanks, Miguel."

"Do you want me to look for him?"

"No. That won't be necessary. I'll do it."

"Tyler, wait."

"What?"

"I—look, you should know. Turner had his hands on Ian. Ian looked uncomfortable, to say the least. I think he was scared. After Turner left, Ian and I took the boat out, and he seemed a bit shaken all afternoon. When I tried to get him to talk to me about it, he clammed up, said it was nothing."

"Thanks, Miguel."

After I end the call, I shut down my computer, strap on my holster and gun, grab my jacket, and I'm out the door. I can't sit here for the rest of the day worrying about Ian and not do something. Not when I know now that Ian's been keeping things from me.

I head straight home and race up the front steps and into the townhouse. "Ian! Are you home?" I check the kitchen, our bedroom, and the roof, but he's not there. I go down to the lower level to check the fitness room, but it's empty.

He's not home.

I go out back to check the carriage house and find that his Porsche is gone. So I head to the marina. I don't see his car in the parking lot, and he's not on his boat when I search it.

I drive by his parents' house to see if the Porsche is parked in the back, but it's not. Layla's Fiat is here, though.

Great. Now I've turned into a stalker.

I try his phone again but get nothing.

Not knowing where else to look, I go back home to wait for

Ian to show. The house is dark and quiet, and it makes me realize how much of a presence Ian has. I can physically feel his absence.

After hanging up my jacket and holster, I head to the kitchen to grab a cold beer. It's a little early to be drinking, but it's Friday afternoon. I tell myself it's the weekend and I'm just getting an early start.

I head to the front parlor, where I have a good view of the street, and I pace. And the longer I pace, the more agitated I become. My blood pressure is skyrocketing, and my pulse is pounding.

Ian would never betray me.

He just wouldn't. There's no way the man who trembles and cries in my arms would turn to another. We've got something really good between us—hell, what we have is amazing. I love him. And I know he loves me.

But I also know how manipulative Turner is—that sadistic son of a bitch. If he has some kind of leverage over Ian, then there's no telling what—and then it hits me.

Fuck.

Of course he does. *Me*—I'm the leverage. Turner's manipulating Ian with the threat of pressing charges against me.

What does Turner want more than revenge on me for beating the shit out of him? *He wants Ian.*

Ian's words come back to me. *I can't let you go to prison.*

Shit.

Would Ian betray me? *No.*

But would he do something stupid, like sacrifice himself—trade his body—to protect me?

Maybe.

There's no telling what Ian would do if he felt cornered and thought he had no choice.

Feeling sick, I walk to the bar and grab the bottle of Glenfiddich from the top shelf. My hands shake as I pour myself a shot.

I feel so god-damned helpless. All I can think about is Turner getting his hands on Ian. I know what Turner's capable of. I saw the photographs of the men he's fucked and hurt in the process.

Jesus, Ian, where are you?

I knock back my drink and pour another. I pace, and I worry. What the hell good am I if I can't protect the one person who means the world to me?

And then my fear and anxiety morph into something ugly, into anger. Why in the hell didn't Ian tell me Turner was pressuring him? I would have taken care of it. I would have put an end to the harassment real quick.

But no, my obstinate little ray of sunshine thinks he has to protect *me*, when I'm the one who should be protecting *him*.

I pour another shot, hoping liquor will make this pain go away. God, I'm so out of my element here. My mind is torturing me with images of Ian with Turner. Images of Ian on his knees. Of Turner fucking Ian. Or worse—*hurting him.*

My eyes burn as tears well up. As I reach for my glass, I hear a key in the front door lock. I suck in a deep, shuddering breath, overcome with relief.

He's home.

Quiet footsteps hesitate outside the parlor door, and then it's dead silence.

When I turn to face the door, Ian is standing there looking shocked. The guilt on his face hits me like a physical blow.

Dear god, what has he done?

"Tyler, what are you doing home so early?" he says, his voice shaking.

I knock back the contents of my glass. "Where in the fuck have you been?"

Ian recoils as if I slapped him. "I—" He falters as he stares at me, dumbfounded.

I swipe my hand across my burning eyes and grind out the words I can't keep bottled up. Words driven by my own fears. "Did you let him fuck you?"

Ian pales. "What are you talking about?"

"Don't play dumb, Ian." I pull Turner's note out of my breast pocket, unfold it, and hold it out to him. "Turner. Did you let him fuck you?" My heart is breaking into pieces, and I'm not sure if I'm ready to hear his answer.

Ian stares at the slip of paper. He shakes his head, but when he opens his mouth to speak, nothing comes out.

"Answer me, damn it!" Impulsively, I hurl my glass across the room. It hits the brick hearth, shattering on impact and sending shards of glass raining down on the floor.

Ian flinches, and as his eyes tear up, he shakes his head. "I didn't, Tyler, I swear. I didn't."

"Did he touch you?"

"No!"

My fear for Ian's safety has morphed into fury, and I'm so wired I want to beat Turner all over again. Through gritted teeth, I say, "Tell me exactly what happened yesterday at the marina. All of it."

"He followed me onto my boat," he says shakily. "He wanted us to go below. I said no, Tyler. He grabbed me and tried to kiss me, but Miguel showed up then, and Brad took off. He didn't actually do it—kiss me. I swear."

"Why didn't you tell me this yesterday? Jesus, Ian, how could you keep this from me? You could have been hurt."

"I was afraid to tell you because I knew it would only make things worse. If you found out he was pressuring me for sex, you'd go after him."

"So, instead you *protected* him?"

"No! I was trying to protect *you*."

Growling like an animal in pain, I slam my fist down on the bar, rattling the bottle of whiskey.

Eyes wide, Ian stumbles back.

Fuck.

I'm scaring him.

He wraps his arms around his torso, closing in on himself. "I was scared, Tyler. I didn't know what to do."

Closing my eyes, I take a deep breath and struggle to rein myself in. I believe Ian. I believe him one hundred percent, and he doesn't deserve this kind of response from me. I'm furious at him, yes, but I'm angrier at myself for losing control. "Ian, you should have told me. What if Miguel hadn't shown up when he did? Turner's bigger than you are, stronger. He could have easily overpowered you. He could have dragged you below deck and raped you."

"I know," Ian says quietly. "I'm sorry."

∼ 11

Ian Alexander

Tyler turns to face the window, his shoulders taut, his back rigid. His hands are balled into fists as he struggles to regain control.

My heart hammers in my chest, and my lungs billow as I try to breathe. I'm fighting the urge to run—to the roof, outside, to my boat—anywhere away from here. But I don't. This is too important. There's too much at stake.

Calmer now, Tyler turns back to face me. "Where were you this afternoon? I tried to reach you, but my calls went straight to voicemail."

"I went to see a movie with Layla, and I turned off my phone." I reach into my pocket and pull out our crumpled movie ticket stubs. He's a cop. He'll want evidence. My hand shakes as I offer him proof. "Here."

As he stares at the ticket stubs, his expression softens, and then he crosses the room and pulls me into his arms. "Jesus, I'm sorry."

"You believe me?" Overcome with relief, I melt against him.

"Yes." He cups the back of my head and holds me close, his mouth near my ear. "I'm a shitty boyfriend, aren't I?"

I slide my arms around his waist. "No, you're not. I hid all afternoon in a movie theater with my little sister, so I didn't have to face Brad. I guess that makes me a shitty brother."

He chuckles, and then he kisses my temple. "No, you're a wonderful brother. Now tell me, what did Turner want from you?"

"He told me to meet him at my boat at one o'clock this afternoon. He said if I didn't, he'd go straight to the police and file a complaint against you."

Tyler scowls. "Promise you'll let me know if he contacts you again. He's dangerous, Ian. I'm afraid he might try to hurt you. After reading that note, all I could think about was finding you and making sure you were all right. I looked for you everywhere, and when I couldn't find you, I didn't know what to think."

"You didn't know what to *think*?" Pain lances through me. "Did you really think I'd let him touch me? That I'd betray you?"

Tyler tightens his hold on me. "God, no. I was just afraid you might feel like you had to give in to him—to protect me."

As the pain of his accusation swamps me, I pull away from him, putting space between us. "How could you think I'd betray you, Tyler? I love you."

Tyler winces. "Damn it, Ian. That's not what I meant. I'm sorry."

He reaches for me, but I step back as I rub the excruciating ache in my chest. "I've never given you any reason not to trust me."

"I do trust you. I—"

When my phone chimes with an incoming message, I flinch. I pull it out of my back pocket and glance at the screen. My stomach drops. "It's him."

Brad: I warned u. Now ur bf's going to prison

Tyler holds out his hand. "Give it to me."

I hand him my phone, and after he reads the message, he hits redial and puts the call on speaker.

"Ian," Brad says, his voice smug. "It's about time you called me back. Where the fuck were you this afternoon? I waited for you."

"Leave Ian the hell alone," Tyler warns through clenched teeth. "If you continue to harass him, we'll get a restraining order. And if you *ever* lay a finger on him again, you will answer to *me*. Is that clear?"

Brad growls in anger. "You son of a—"

Tyler ends the call abruptly and hands the phone back to

me. "Let me know if he contacts you again."

Realization hits me like a ton of bricks. Brad's going to do it. "He's going to press charges against you."

"He was always going to do that, Ian. He's just stringing you along and using me as leverage. Nothing you do, or don't do, is going to change the outcome." He pulls me into his arms. "I'm not afraid of Turner," he says quietly. "The only thing I'm afraid of is losing you."

I stand stiffly in his arms, my emotions still stinging from his insinuation that I might have betrayed him.

"Ian." He pulls back and looks me in the eye. "I'm sorry." His hands come up to frame my face and his thumbs brush gently across my cheeks. He leans in and kisses my forehead, then the bridge of my nose, and lastly my lips. As he presses his forehead to mine, I feel the force of his apology, of his love, and even his fear. "Please, forgive me," he says. "I let doubt get the best of me. The idea of that sadistic monster hurting you made me go a little crazy."

"Did we just have our first fight?"

"That wasn't a fight. It was just me being an ass. And I'm sure it won't be the last time." He brushes my cheeks with his thumbs, his eyes suddenly full of heat. "Come upstairs with me. Let's shower and change, and then we'll think about dinner."

Tyler takes my hand and leads me up the stairs and into our bedroom. Without saying a word, we both strip and walk into the bathroom. Tyler turns on the water in the shower while I grab some towels.

He pulls me with him under the spray of hot water and kisses me. "I'm sorry," he says again.

"Apology accepted," I say as I lay my hands on his pecs. His
dark chest hair is crisp beneath my fingertips. His torso is a feast
for the eyes, and just looking at him makes me hard. When I
lean in to lick one of his nipples, he arches his back with a cry.

We take turns washing each other, soapy hands caressing
long limbs, muscles, abdomens, shoulders, biceps, and backs.
Neither of us is in a hurry—this is more therapeutic than anything else. We need this time to reconnect after the emotional
shitstorm we just experienced.

Where the fuck have you been, Ian?

Did you let him fuck you?

It hurts that he even had to ask those questions. But then
I think how devastated I would have felt if the situation were
reversed.

"I'm sorry I scared you," I tell him. "I was just trying—"

"To protect me. I know."

I admit it stings—that Tyler thought even for a split second
that I would let Brad touch me. We both know what Brad did to
Eric—the pain and the degradation he put Eric through. Brad
might not have killed Eric, but he abused him nonetheless.
Even if it was consensual.

Tyler pulls me into his arms beneath the hot spray. "I
shouldn't have come down on you like that. I didn't even give
you a chance to explain. I was just so scared, Ian. If he ever hurt
you, I'd never forgive myself."

I watch the water drip down his face, running into his beard. The concern in his eyes floors me. "I love you."

He closes his eyes in relief. "I love you, too."

* * *

Tyler and I crash in the living room, lounging on the sofa while we decide what we want for dinner. We end up ordering Chinese food. And then we lie back on the couch together and snuggle as I cue up my favorite YouTubers on the TV.

My phone rings in the other room, where I left it after Tyler talked to Brad. I hear my sister's ringtone—*Let It Go* from *Frozen*. "That's Layla," I say, jumping up from the sofa and racing across the hall to grab my phone. "Hey, sis."

"Hey. Whatcha doing?"

"Watching TV with Tyler. What's up?"

"Oh, nothing. I just thought I'd call and say hi."

But I can tell from the tone of her voice that it's not *nothing*. "Layla, what's wrong?"

She exhales a frustrated breath. "Everything. Mom and Dad are smothering me more than ever, and it's driving me crazy. Talk about helicopter parents! There's this guy at school I like, and I thought he was going to ask me out, but then Sean scared him off by being an ass to him when he tried to talk to me after class this morning."

I bite back a laugh. She doesn't like her new bodyguard any more than Tyler and I do. "So, in other words, it's the same old, same old."

She sighs. "Yeah. I just need a break, you know?"

I check the time—it's still early, not even six. "Why don't you come over and join us for dinner? We just ordered Chinese."

"Can I?"

The excitement in her voice makes me realize I haven't been spending enough time with her lately, ever since Eric's murder investigation, meeting Tyler, and then the shooting on my boat. I've been so wrapped up in my own life that I haven't been paying enough attention to hers. Layla doesn't have a lot of friends. The other girls shy away from her when they learn of her schizophrenia. I'm probably her only real friend. "We'd love for you to join us. Come on over."

"You don't think Tyler would mind?"

"Of course not." I return to the living room and put the call on speaker so Tyler can hear us. "Hop in the car right now and come join us. Is Chinese okay with you? We ordered plenty."

Lying stretched out on the sofa, Tyler motions me closer. "Yes, Layla, come have dinner with us."

"Awesome, you guys. Thank you so much." I can hear her rushing around to get ready. "I'll let Sean know we're leaving in five."

Ugh. Of course she has to bring her bodyguard with her. "Fine," I say, meeting Tyler's amused gaze. "But Sean stays in the car."

She laughs. "Got it!" And then she ends the call.

I lie down in front of Tyler, both of us on our sides, and

there's barely enough room for the two of us. "I hope you don't mind that she's coming over. She sounded a bit stressed."

"Of course I don't mind." He runs his fingers through my hair, twirling a lock around his index finger. "I like your sister."

I lean back to kiss his cheek. "Thank you."

I play the newest video from one of the gay couples I follow on YouTube.

After watching a few of their videos, Tyler shakes his head at the TV. "I can't imagine filming my life for the whole world to see."

"Maybe we should start a channel of our own. You're a hot cop. Viewers would love you. What's not to like? A sexy gay homicide detective and... well, me. I could be your sidekick. Like, Robin to your Batman."

Tyler laughs. "You're far more interesting than I am—a hot, wealthy playboy on his yacht? Not to mention, a great dancer... absolutely."

"You think I'm a good dancer?"

"Not good. I said *great*. You're an amazing dancer, and you know it. Even Cooper said so."

That makes me smile. "He did? Really?"

"Yes, really." Tyler grabs the remote and mutes the TV. Then he turns me to face him and begins playing with one of my nipple piercings, sending a shiver through me. He leans down to flick the barbell with the tip of his tongue, then smiles up at me. "Your piercings alone would draw a crowd."

I run my hands over his shoulders and arms, marveling at his rock-hard muscles. When he draws one of my nipples into his mouth and teases the barbell with his tongue, I arch my back with a loud moan.

He trails kisses down my torso to the waistband of my drawstring pants and palms my dick through the fabric, tracing the outline as I begin to harden. Just as Tyler's about to slip his hand beneath the waistband, the doorbell rings.

Tyler presses his forehead to my abs and groans. "Damn it."

"It's Layla." I hop up from the sofa and adjust my pants to accommodate my erection. "Sorry. Rain check. I'll get the door."

Tyler sits up. "And I'll run upstairs to get us some shirts."

I'd forgotten we're both shirtless after our shower.

12

Ian Alexander

As Tyler runs up the stairs to grab us some shirts, I unlock the door for my sister. She's standing on the top step, ear buds in, dressed in jeans, sneakers, and another UC hoodie. Her hair is pulled back in a messy ponytail.

I glance over at the driveway to see Sean sitting in the driver's seat of Layla's Fiat. I wave, attempting to be polite, but he ignores me.

Layla she steps inside and gives me a hug.

"Hey, sis," I say, mussing her hair.

She ducks out from beneath my hand and removes her earbuds. "So, where's your handsome cop?"

"I'm right here," Tyler says as he jogs down the stairs.

He's wearing a plain black T-shirt that hugs his chest and arms. In his hand is one of my graphic boating tees, which he tosses to me. I slip it on.

Tyler glances into the living room, then back at Layla. "Sean's out in the car?"

"Yes," Layla says. "Frankly, I'm happy to have him wait outside."

"Still don't like him?" I ask.

She shakes her head. "He gives me the creeps. I'm not sure why, but he does. I swear, sometimes he acts like he owns me, telling me what I can and can't do, who I can talk to at school and who I can't. It's weird."

"Tell Mom and Dad you want a replacement," I say.

She shrugs. "I don't want to cause a fuss. Besides, I might end up with someone even worse. First Rob, and now Sean. I seem to attract losers."

"Your parents need to use a different security company," Tyler tells her. To me, he says, "Shane's company offers personal protection."

Before I can respond, there's a sharp knock at the door. Layla jumps.

"It's just our food," I tell her as I open the door. There are two sacks from our favorite Chinese restaurant sitting just outside the door. "Dinner has arrived." I pick them up and bring them inside.

We set up in the living room, spreading the food out on the coffee table. While Tyler and I grab plates, silverware, and drinks from the kitchen, Layla makes herself comfortable on the floor.

"You can join us on the sofa," I say as I hand her a chilled bottle of her favorite sugar-free lemonade. I make sure to stock plenty of sugar-free snacks and drinks for my sister.

She takes the bottle from me. "Thanks. But I'm fine on the floor."

We dish out the food. Layla opts for the beef and broccoli, sans rice. Tyler has his favorite—a spicy Kung Pao chicken. And I have some of the beef and broccoli and some sweet and sour chicken.

"Should we send some food out to Sean?" I ask Layla. I don't like the guy, but I feel bad that we're eating when he's been relegated to the car.

She shakes her head as she chews. "He's fine," she says after she swallows. "He picked up something on the way here." Then she gets a devilish gleam in her dark eyes. "So... tell me more about how you two met—the whole story."

I look to Tyler, who's looking at me.

He nods. "Go ahead. You tell her."

I grin at the memory. "I already told you, we met in a bar."

"I know that," she says. "But I want the tea. Come on, Ian! Details! The juicier the better."

"All right." I sigh. "I was coming out of the men's room just as Tyler was about to go in. I'd had my eye on him all evening long from across the bar. I watched women coming onto him, giving him fuck-me eyes, but he didn't take any of them up on their offers. That kind of gave me hope. When we crossed paths in the hallway, I waited outside the restroom for him."

Layla grins at Tyler. "When you first saw Ian, did you think he was hot?"

Tyler suppresses a smile. "No comment."

Layla balls up a napkin and throws it at Tyler. "Oh, come on! Be honest."

Tyler shrugs. "I might have thought he was a good-looking guy, yes. You know, in an objective way."

She laughs, then looks to me. "And what did you think when you first saw Tyler?"

I lean back on the sofa and eye Tyler, who's looking a bit uncomfortable being put on the spot like this. "I thought he was the hottest guy I'd ever seen. He gave me goosebumps. He still does."

Layla bounces up onto her knees. "I knew it! It was love at first sight, wasn't it?"

Now it's my turn to laugh. "Are you kidding? He was such an uptight stick in the mud, I didn't think I had a chance with him. But I wasn't willing to give up so easily. I worked my ass off to get him to notice me." I lay my head on his shoulder. "Isn't that right?"

"Oh, I noticed you all right. But I was trying to be professional." He grins at me. "You loved pulling my chain, didn't you?"

"Yep. I still do." I tilt my face up and kiss his cheek.

Layla is beaming at us. "You guys are so cute." She takes a sip of her lemonade. "I envy you. It's obvious you're really into each other." Then her smile fades. "Not everyone's so lucky."

My sister has trouble making friends. She finds it difficult to trust people, and when you're so wealthy you have to have a bodyguard following you around everywhere, you start to question everyone who pays you any attention. She's been burned so many times by girls who are just using her, and by guys who see her as a conquest. Her health issues only exacerbate the problem.

"Layla," Tyler says, drawing her attention. "Earlier you said Sean gives you the creeps. What makes you say that?"

She sits back down and shrugs. "I don't know. He just does."

"Has he done or said anything to you to make you doubt him?"

"Not exactly. It's just, I don't know. The way he watches me, for one thing. I'll catch him staring at me, and it makes my skin crawl. And, honestly, I'm pretty sure he's doing drugs. He comes and goes from the house at weird hours, and sometimes when he comes back his eyes are really glassy. I just don't trust him."

"In the middle of the night?" Tyler says. "Why is he around you at night?"

"Her bodyguard has a separate apartment in my parents' house," I explain. "So he's close by and can monitor her blood sugar in the night."

Tyler frowns. "I really think you should tell your parents

how you feel, Layla. A bodyguard should never make you feel uncomfortable."

She stares down at her plate as she pushes food around with her chopsticks. "I don't want to get him in trouble. It's probably just me, you know? Maybe I'm being oversensitive." Then her voice drops. "It could be my paranoia."

The shame I see in her dark eyes makes me sad. If I could take my sister's mental health issues from her, I would. I'd gladly suffer them in her place. "I don't think it's that, sis." Her hallucinations are primarily auditory. She hears voices that aren't there—mean, critical voices. She doesn't go around suspecting people in general.

Tyler drops the issue, but I can tell he's not happy about it. Maybe I should say something to Mom and Dad, but I hate going behind Layla's back. She already feels like she doesn't have any control over her life. If I take what little control she does have, it would just make things worse for her.

Layla's head snaps toward the living room window as if she heard something outside.

I turn to look, but there's nothing there. "Layla?"

She's lost in thought, a frown on her face, and no longer paying us any attention.

Tyler glances at me, then back at my sister. "Layla?"

But she still doesn't respond.

"She's hallucinating," I say quietly. I lean across the coffee table and tap her shoulder.

Layla jumps, turning back to face me. "I'm sorry, what?"

Then she must notice it's starting to get dark outside. "I should get going. I have homework." She jumps to her feet and comes forward to give me a hug. "Thanks for asking me over tonight."

Tyler stands and opens his arms to her. "What about me? Don't I get a hug?"

Smiling, my sister launches herself at Tyler. "Of course you get a hug."

As Tyler envelops her in a bear hug, he meets my gaze over the top of her head and smiles. "If you need anything, Layla, we're here for you. All you have to do is ask."

She beams at the both of us. "I love you guys."

We walk her out to her car and wait until she's safely buckled into the front passenger seat.

As Sean starts the engine, Layla sticks her earbuds in her ears, leans back in her seat, and closes her eyes. I'm not sure if she's doing it to block out the voices or so she doesn't have to talk to Sean.

"Hello, Sean," Tyler says, peering inside the car. "Good to see you again."

Sean barely glances at Tyler. "Yeah, sure." And without another word, he puts the car in reverse and backs out of the driveway way too fast, the tires squealing as he hits the gas pedal and tears down the street.

Tyler scowls at the car's retreating taillights. "There's definitely something off with that guy."

"You're such a cop," I say, smiling as I slip my arm around his waist and we walk up the front steps to the door. "Come on.

Let's clean up our dishes, and then we can Netflix and chill."

"Isn't that a euphemism for something?"

Smiling, I grab his hand and pull him inside. "You bet it is."

* * *

When we go to bed that night, Tyler rolls me onto my belly and begins massaging my back. His touch is perfect—firm, but not too hard. The pressure is enough to make my muscles melt and my nerves tingle.

As he gently digs his thumbs into my shoulders, I groan. "God, that feels good."

"That's the plan." He chuckles as he drops a light kiss on the side of my neck, right behind my ear where I'm ticklish. I shiver.

Tyler moves methodically down my body, kneading my arms next, all the way down to my palms and fingers. Then he massages my back, running his knuckles firmly down my spine. His hands are soon replaced by his mouth, and he trails kisses down my back, to my waist, then lower. My body heats, my dick hardening. I have to shift my position to make room for a growing erection.

His mouth is everywhere, hot and hungry. Playfully, he bites my left butt cheek, then soothes the spot with his tongue. Then he bites the right one. He rolls me onto my back and leans over me as he takes my erection in hand and starts stroking me.

"I'll tell you what I thought when I first saw you," he says, his voice low. "My body lit up like fireworks. My chest was on fire, and I had trouble breathing. I didn't know what to think. I'd never had such a physical reaction to anyone before. To be honest, it was unsettling."

I smile, thinking back to that first night. He seemed so unsure of himself. When I touch his face, he turns his head to plant a kiss in the center of my palm. "You know what I thought?" I ask him.

"What?"

"I wanted you more than my next breath. And later that night, when you came to the marina to investigate Eric's murder... as upset as I was over Eric's death, when I saw you, I just *knew* you were the one. Fate wouldn't put us together twice in one night if we weren't destined to be together." Smiling, I sit up to kiss him.

"I don't believe in fate or destiny," he says. "But when I saw you that night at the marina... knowing how close you'd come to a murder scene—it shook me. The case became personal because I couldn't bear the thought of anything happening to you."

Tyler urges me to lie back down. I watch in fascination as he runs his tongue up the length of my erection and swirls it over the head. He teases me to the point that I'm gasping before he takes me into his mouth. Mesmerized, I watch him. The sight of my cock disappearing into his mouth, his lips caressing me as moves on me... it's mind blowing.

I throw my head back onto the pillow and close my eyes just so I can feel how good it is.

He cups my sac in one hand, gently tugging and massaging my balls, while he practically swallows my dick to the root. The heat and pressure build until I fist the sheets. My back bows off the mattress. "Fuck, Tyler!"

He works me until my body is on fire and my nerves are screaming. I'm throbbing and desperate to come. I climax so hard I see stars. I grip the back of his head and hold him close as I thrust into his mouth with each pulsing release.

Tyler rolls me onto my side to spoon me. I hear him tear open a condom packet, and after he sheathes himself and lubes up, a slick finger slides between my butt cheeks to tease my hole.

I sigh as I feel the pressure of him sinking slowly into me. "Tyler."

His lips graze the back of my neck, my shoulders, my throat. He sinks deeper into me, slowly, gently, swamping me with pleasure as the glide of him inside me teases my nerve endings.

Once he starts thrusting, his arm comes around my waist, and he holds me close. He buries his face in my hair.

This isn't fucking. This is making love.

And it feels so damn good I could cry.

13

Ian Alexander

When I awake Saturday morning, I stretch long and hard before turning to the man beside me. Tyler's sitting up in bed, leaning against a pile of pillows propped against the headboard, reading on his tablet. He's got a pair of black reading glasses perched on his nose. Very Clark Kent.

"I didn't know you wore glasses," I say as I slip my arm across his lap and lean in to kiss his firm bicep.

"Yeah, middle-aged eyes. I need them for reading."

"They look good on you. What are you reading?"

He peers down at me over the top rim of his glasses. "Jamie McIntyre's new release. It just came out yesterday."

"McIntyre? Shane's brother?"

"Yes. Jamie's a former Navy SEAL, now an author. He writes military thrillers."

"He's the blind brother, right? Is he any good?"

"Yes, very," Tyler says. And then his stomach lets out a growl.

"Someone's hungry." I sit up and finger-comb my hair, trying to tame my inevitable bedhead. After placing a quick kiss on his cheek, I swing my legs to the floor. "I'll start on breakfast."

He sets his tablet aside. "I can make breakfast. Do we have any frozen waffles?"

I groan. "Oh god, nothing from the freezer, please. If you want waffles, I'll make some from scratch."

"Actually, waffles sound really good."

"How about Belgian waffles with homemade whipped cream?"

"Those are the thick ones, right?"

"Yes, those are the thick ones. What else would you like?"

"Bacon?"

"Okay. How about eggs?" I squeeze his bicep. "These muscles require lots of protein."

He laughs. "That sounds perfect."

I hop out of bed and visit the little boys' room. Then I pull on a pair of gray sweats and head downstairs to get started on breakfast. Once I have the coffeemaker going, I gather the ingredients for breakfast.

Tyler joins me in the kitchen and sits at the table reading. When the pot is ready, I set a cup of plain black coffee in front of him. The man has no imagination.

"Mm, thanks," he says after taking a sip.

I pour batter into the preheated waffle iron. While the waffles are cooking, I whip heavy cream until it's thick and fluffy. Bacon is frying in one pan, while eggs are cooking in another.

While I plate our breakfasts, Tyler takes the trash out. It's all very domestic.

As we sit down to a weekend breakfast, I gaze at him from across the table and feel ridiculously happy.

Tyler looks up from his plate. "This breakfast is amazing. Thank you."

"My pleasure."

"I'm planning to go to my mom's house in a little bit to mow the grass. Would you like to come with me?"

"Oh, my god, yes. I'd love that." I met his mom just recently at his nephew Luke's first birthday party. I'm dying to get to know her better.

After breakfast, we clean up the kitchen together, then change into jeans and T-shirts.

Tyler drives us in his BMW to a gated community that his brother-in-law, Shane McIntyre, bought and turned into a private family compound. He slows as we approach the gate, and when the guard on duty recognizes Tyler, he waves us through.

In addition to the small cluster of existing houses, there are two homes under construction, with building crews hard at work. The air is filled with the echo of pounding hammers and nail guns.

"Who's building?" I ask him.

He points to one of the new houses under construction. "That one is Shane's wedding present to his sister Sophie and her new husband, Dominic. The other house... I'm not sure, but I think it's for Shane and Beth. With a second child on the way, they decided it would be best for them to move to the suburbs so their kids can play outside and be near their cousins and grandparents. Shane's parents live here, as does my mom. Everyone in the family is planning to live here except Jamie and Molly, who prefer to stay in Wicker Park close to Molly's art studio, and Shane's middle sister, Hannah, who lives out west in the Rockies."

We park in front of a charming, one-story white cottage. Tyler's mom, Ingrid, is out front pulling weeds from a flower garden. She's dressed in a pale gray linen skirt and a sleeveless white blouse.

In her early sixties, Ingrid Jamison is a beautiful woman, with long, silver-blonde hair, bright blue eyes, and a peaches-and-cream complexion. She's lovely and soft spoken, with just a hint of a Swedish accent.

As Tyler shuts off the engine, I release my seatbelt. "Why didn't your mom ever remarry after your dad died?"

Tyler shakes his head. "I've tried encouraging her over the years to date again, but she just isn't interested. She says my dad is the love of her life, and no one could ever take his place."

"That's so sad."

"She's been alone a long time. I wish she'd found someone years ago. I know what it's like to be alone." Tyler reaches for my hand. "And now that I know what it's like to have someone, I want that for her. I want her to love and be loved."

As we approach, she greets us with a smile and open arms.

She hugs me first. "Welcome, Ian. It's so nice to see you again." And then she releases me to hug her son. "Hello, darling. Thank you for coming."

While Tyler gets the lawn mower out of the garage, Ingrid invites me inside. She gives me a quick tour of her cozy two-bedroom cottage. We end up at the back of the house, where the kitchen and sitting room look out over a pretty patio. There's a duck pond not far away.

"Can I get you something to drink?" she asks me. "Coffee, tea? I made fresh lemonade this morning."

"Ooh, I'll have lemonade, thank you."

She invites me to sit on a stool at the breakfast counter, and I watch her pour for both of us. While I'm sipping mine, she brings over a plate of iced lemon bread.

"I was in the mood for lemon this morning," she says, laughing. She has a lovely, lilting accent. She winks at me. "I made the lemon bread especially for Tyler. It's one of his favorites."

I had no idea. "What else does he like?"

She sits on the stool beside me and nibbles on a slice. "Let's see. His favorite sweets are chocolate chip cookies—"

"Crispy or chewy?" I ask.

"Definitely thin and crispy, and not too many chips."

Why did I not know this already? "What else?"

"Hmm, what else? Snickerdoodle cookies for sure, banana bread, and pumpkin bread. Anything with pumpkin, really—pumpkin pie, muffins, rolls—especially if it has cream cheese."

I'm just now realizing what a fount of information Ingrid is when it comes to all things Tyler. Of course, who would know him better than his own mother? "What were his favorite foods growing up?"

She laughs. "Oh, that's easy. Chicken and dumplings, fish sticks, macaroni and cheese, anything pasta related, and he prefers red sauce over white. Oh, and chicken nuggets and French fries with lots of ketchup." She smiles at the memory. "He was such an easy child."

"Would you mind sharing your recipes with me? I'd like to make his favorite dishes."

She looks surprised. "You cook?"

"I love to cook. Especially for Tyler. You know what they say..."

She smiles. "The way to a man's heart is through his stomach."

"Exactly."

"It was the same with Tyler's dad. On our third date, I invited him to my apartment for dinner. After he tasted my homemade chicken and dumplings, that very evening, he proposed. I swear it was because of my cooking."

I can hear the love and longing in her voice. "You had a

match made in heaven."

She nods. "It truly was."

The faraway, bittersweet smile on her face makes my heart hurt. She lost her husband over two decades ago, and it seems like the pain is still fresh.

I reach out and squeeze her slender fingers. It doesn't escape my notice that she's still wearing a slim gold wedding band. "I'm very sorry for your loss, Mrs. Jamison."

Teary-eyed, she gives me a grateful smile. "Call me Ingrid, please. And thank you, Ian. I appreciate your kind words very much." She squeezes my hand back. "Would you like to help me make some chocolate chip cookies for you and Tyler to take home with you?"

"I'd love that."

"So would I. You know, when Tyler was in high school, I always hoped he'd bring home someone special for me to do things with. Someone to go shopping with, someone to bake cookies with. But that never happened. I guess he just wasn't ready."

While Ingrid gets two mixing bowls down from the cupboard and grabs a cannister of flour, she says to me, "Would you mind getting the butter and eggs from the fridge?"

Then she opens a cupboard drawer and pulls out two aprons, handing me one and slipping the other over her head.

I'm awed by the way this woman has so graciously welcomed me into her life. "You're okay with me?" I ask her. Because I really need to know. "With Tyler and me?"

She gives me a curious look. "Of course, dear. Why wouldn't I be? You make my son happy, and that's all that matters."

I feel myself choking up. "It is."

She starts adding the dry ingredients to a large bowl. "Tyler's father and I suspected he was gay by the time he was a young teenager. He never really paid any serious attention to girls, not like his friends did. His friends would go on and on about this girl or that, but he never did. Later in high school, he started dating girls. His dad and I assumed we must have been wrong about him. But he never stayed with one girl for long. And he never brought anyone home." She smiles as she reaches out to brush my hair back from my forehead. "Not until you."

About the time we slide the first tray of cookies into the oven, there's a knock at the door.

A moment later, we hear a female voice call out. "Mom? It's me."

Ingrid's eyes light up. "Beth! We're in the kitchen, sweetheart."

Beth McIntyre—Tyler's much younger sister—comes strolling into the kitchen, her one-year-old, blond-haired baby boy perched on her hip, despite the fact that she's seven months pregnant.

Right behind her is Sam who, in addition to being her full-time bodyguard, is most likely her best friend in the world.

"Hey, Ian." Sam offers me a fist bump. "Good to see you again."

When Luke catches sight of his grandmother, he squeals as

he reaches for her. Ingrid wipes her hands on a kitchen towel before taking the baby from her daughter.

"Hi, Ian," Beth says as she gives me a hug. "It's so good to see you again."

"What brings you here, dear?" Ingrid asks her.

"Tyler texted to let me know that he and Ian would be stopping by your place this afternoon. I didn't want to miss out on a chance to visit with my family, so here we are."

"Did Shane come, too?"

"Yes. He's outside talking to Tyler."

Then we hear another knock on the door.

"Come in!" Ingrid calls.

A moment later, a mountain of a man walks into the kitchen, his broad shoulders practically filling the doorway. He's big—not just tall, but also muscular. This must be Joe Rucker, the retired heavyweight boxer who is now Beth's driver. His buzzed cut white hair and trim white beard contrast dramatically with his brown skin and dark eyes.

Ingrid's eyes widen and her cheeks flush. "Joe." She's speechless for a second before her impeccable manners kick in. "How lovely to see you. Welcome."

"Hello, Miss Ingrid," he says, in a deep southern drawl. "I hope I'm not intruding."

"No, of course not. It looks like today is my lucky day, with my family and so many friends stopping by."

Sam helps himself to a slice of the iced lemon bread. Then he takes Luke, who's jabbering eagerly as he points at the back door. "I'll take the little guy out back to see the ducks."

"Can I get either of you anything to drink?" Ingrid says to her daughter and the chauffeur, who's standing awkwardly in her tiny kitchen. With his hands stuffed into his pockets, he looks uncomfortable and a bit out of place.

"I'll get myself some lemonade, Mom," Beth says as she retrieves a glass from the cupboard.

"Joe, what about you?" Ingrid says. "I have lemonade, tea—"

"I'll take some lemonade, ma'am, if it's not too much trouble."

"Of course not," she says, grabbing him a glass. "It's no trouble at all."

After thanking Ingrid profusely, Joe takes his glass out back as he joins Sam and Luke at the duck pond, leaving me and Beth in the kitchen with Ingrid.

Ingrid watches out the back window at the threesome standing by the pond. From the other side of the kitchen, Beth watches her mother. And I watch the both of them.

I sidle up next to Beth. "I think your mother has an admirer," I whisper, nodding out the window at Joe.

Beth grins. "I think you're right," she whispers back.

* * *

While the cookies are cooling, I go outside in search of my man. I find him deep in conversation with Shane McIntyre and another guy. This one, tall and dark-haired, looks like he could easily give the former boxer a run for his money. What is it with these guys and their massive arms?

Tyler waves me over. "Ian, you remember Jake McIntyre, Shane's brother. And you've met Shane."

Jake and I say our hellos.

"Are you done mowing?" I ask Tyler.

"Yes, all done."

"Good. Your mom and I made chocolate chip cookies, just the way you like them."

Tyler's smile lights up his eyes. "Really?"

"Yes. Come inside and have some."

Later, as we're driving back to the townhouse, I ask Tyler, "Does your mom know that Joe Rucker is crushing on her?"

"You think he is?"

"I know he is. Beth thinks so too. The man couldn't keep his eyes off your mom. And who could blame him? Your mom is seriously hot."

Tyler laughs. "This, coming from a gay man?"

"Just because I'm gay doesn't mean I can't appreciate a beautiful woman when I see one."

14

Ian Alexander

Later that afternoon, Tyler gets a call from Shane, inviting him to stop by his penthouse apartment to meet with Troy Spencer, Shane's lawyer.

"You told him?" I ask. "About Brad's threat to press charges?"

Tyler nods. "Shane offered me the services of his personal attorney."

"You should go," I tell him. "So you can be prepared if Brad follows through on his threat."

"Come with me. You can visit with my sister and Luke. Ever since Luke's birthday party, she's been asking me to bring you by."

I jump at the chance to hang out with Beth. His mom and sister mean the world to him, and I want to be part of their family.

That evening, Tyler drives us to their apartment building, and as we pull into the parking lot, I glance up at the impressive glass and steel structure overlooking Lake Shore Drive and Lake Michigan. "This has to be one of the nicest apartment buildings in Chicago," I say. "It's certainly one of the most expensive properties."

Tyler nods as he parks in a reserved spot in the underground garage. "Shane owns the building. He and his family use the top floor as their private residence, as well as the roof. The next several floors down are reserved for McIntyre Security employees, and the rest of the apartments are leased to the public."

After Tyler punches in an access code, we take the private elevator up to the penthouse. When the doors open, we're greeted by Luke, who is bouncing excitedly on his feet as he holds the hand of his very pregnant mom.

As we step out of the elevator, Luke walks over to Tyler and begs to be picked up.

Tyler picks up his nephew and kisses his cheek. "Hey, little guy."

When I step out of the elevator, Beth hugs me. "I'm so glad you came, Ian."

Luke reaches for me, his little arms outstretched, and Tyler transfers the kid over.

"He loves the toy camera you two gave him for his birthday," Beth says. "It's become one of his favorite toys, second only to his stuffed kitty cat."

I elbow Tyler, grinning. "I told you he'd like it."

Tyler puts his arm around his sister and pulls her close to kiss the top of her head. "How are you doing?"

"I'm fine," she says, smiling up at him as she pats her rounded abdomen. She slips an arm around Tyler's waist and leans into him.

"I'm here for you," he tells her quietly. "Anything you need. Just call me."

"I know. Thank you."

Luke starts squirming in my arms, wanting to be let down. When I set him on the floor, he runs back to his mama, who picks him up and kisses his cheek.

* * *

While Tyler disappears down the hallway with Shane and his attorney, I join Beth and her son in the living room.

"Come sit with me, Ian," Beth says, patting the sofa cushion beside her.

As soon as I sit, Luke tries to pull himself up onto the sofa. I reach down to give him a hand, and he climbs into my lap.

"He really likes you," she says. "He's usually shy around new people, but he's definitely taken to you."

Luke stands up on my thighs, facing me, his legs wobbling as he tries to keep his balance. He clutches my shirt tightly as he pats my cheek and says, "Dada."

"He likes beards," Beth says. "Shane has one."

"Dada," Luke repeats, glancing around as if he's looking for his father. He climbs down off the sofa, crawls over to a basket of toys, and pulls out the little camera Tyler and I gave him for his birthday. He holds the toy out to me and says something in gibberish.

"So, how many words can he say?" I ask her.

"He says *mama* and *dada* and that's about it."

I scoot off the sofa and join Luke on the rug. Clutching his toy camera, he crawls into my lap and hands it to me.

I hold the toy up to my eye, squinting as I look through the viewfinder and click the button that makes the pretend flashbulb light up.

"I think you've made a friend," Beth says. "Have you ever thought about having kids?"

I glance up at her. "Not really. It always seemed so unlikely. I never had anyone special in my life before."

Absently, she smooths her hands over her baby bump. "But you like kids?"

"Sure, I love them."

Luke lunges forward all of a sudden, sliding off my lap, and crawls toward the toy basket. He pulls out a gray-and-white stuffed kitty that looks very well loved and brings it back to me.

"That's his kitty—his other favorite toy." She smiles at me. "You'd make a great dad, Ian."

I can feel myself blushing. "Tyler would be a great dad."

She nods. "I can attest to that. He practically helped my mom raise me."

"Speaking of kids, when's your new baby due?"

She nods as she glances down at her rounded belly. "Not until the end of September." She pats her abdomen. "You hear that, pumpkin? You still have some time to go. Don't be in a hurry." She smiles at me. "Luke was born prematurely. Shane and I are hoping that won't be the case with this baby."

The elevator chimes and, a moment later, Sam and Cooper walk into the penthouse. Cooper is juggling three grocery sacks, and Sam is carrying two cases of beer.

"Hey, Ian," Cooper says when he spots me on the floor with Luke.

While Cooper puts the groceries away, Sam carries the beer to the bar across the room and stows some of the bottles in the fridge beneath the counter.

Sam and Cooper join us. Sam sits beside Beth and Cooper sits on the sofa opposite theirs.

Luke immediately abandons me and crawls over to Cooper, who scoops him up.

"I see where I stand," I say, laughing.

"Don't take it personally," Beth says. "Luke idolizes Cooper."

"We all do," Sam says as he winks at me. Then he pulls Beth's feet onto his lap and starts massaging them.

Beth groans as she lies back against a pillow. "Oh, thank you." She looks at me and wiggles her toes. "Sam knows all the right pressure points."

"Is Tyler here?" Cooper asks, looking toward the kitchen.

Beth nods. "He's in the office with Shane and Troy. They're strategizing."

Cooper looks to me. "Have you heard anything from Turner?"

I shake my head. "Nothing yet, but I'm afraid it's coming."

Cooper sets Luke on the rug near his toys and extends his hand to me. When I take it, he hauls me to my feet. "Come on, I'll buy you a drink. What would you like?"

"Do you know how to make a Cosmo?" I ask as I follow him to the bar.

"Coming right up. Sweet or dry?"

"Sweet, please." I sit on a bar stool and watch Cooper mix my drink, adding citrus-flavored vodka and cranberry juice to the shaker.

After shaking it, he pours the mix into a martini glass, tops it with a fresh lime wedge, and slides it across the bar to me. "Don't worry, Ian. Everything will work out okay."

I take a sip of my drink. "Mm, perfect. Thank you. That's what Tyler keeps telling me. Just have faith. But that's easier said than done."

"You've met Tyler, right?" Cooper says, cocking an eyebrow at me. "The man is a force of nature. If he says something, he means it."

"Hey, what about us?" Sam hollers from across the room. "We're thirsty, too."

Cooper shakes his head at his boyfriend. "Let me guess... a virgin strawberry daiquiri for Beth, and you want a beer."

"You're a mind reader, babe," Sam says as he rises from the sofa and joins us. He walks behind the bar, slips his arm around Cooper's waist, and winks at me.

15

Tyler Jamison

Troy Spencer sits beside me with a legal notepad propped on his lap and a pen in his hand. He's also recording our conversation on his phone. "Why don't you start by telling me exactly what happened that night," he says in a smooth, cultured voice.

Troy's a polished professional. It's Saturday night, and he's wearing a suit and tie. This guy has represented more McIntyres in court than I can count—including bailing Shane out of jail after I arrested him for assaulting an officer—admittedly not cool on my part as I was the one who threw the first punch.

Troy prosecuted the asshole who terrorized Lia McIntyre by leaking a video of them having sex—it was her first time—broadcast for the whole world to see. It was a federal crime, as Lia was underage when the video was shot—it amounted to distributing child pornography.

He also represented Beth McIntyre in the case against Andrew Morton, the medical student who beat Beth unconscious in her office at the medical school library. He prosecuted Luciana Morelli, the bitter ex-girlfriend who tried to break up Shane and Beth right before their wedding.

Fortunately for me, Troy's good at what he does.

Shane sits behind his desk, listening for the most part. Part of me feels like a delinquent teenager who's been called to the principal's office.

I hate rehashing that night, but I realize I don't have a choice. Taking a deep breath, I launch into my recitation. "I walked into the restroom at Sapphires to find Brad Turner choking Ian. He had Ian pushed up against the wall, his fingers around Ian's throat. Ian was turning all shades of red as he struggled to get a breath."

Troy makes a note on his legal pad. "So, it was self-defense?"

"Yes," I say, struggling to rein in my temper. "He was *choking* my boyfriend."

Troy nods. "I get it. I'm sorry, Tyler, but we have to go over everything. We have to cover all angles."

I nod. "I know."

"Was anyone else in the bathroom at the time? Besides you,

Turner, and Ian?"

"Yes. Ian's friend Chris."

He asks me a slew of additional questions, and I answer everything as precisely as I can.

I pulled Turner off Ian.

I beat the hell out of Turner.

Two security guards showed up and pulled me off him.

Yes, several witnesses in the hallway saw me beating Turner, but no one besides Chris saw Turner choking Ian. It's our word against theirs.

Yes, Ian had bruises around his throat for days. Yes, we took pictures.

I level my gaze on Troy. "The bottom line is, the evidence is stacked against me. He has objective eyewitnesses and video. I have nothing, other than the pictures of Ian's bruised throat."

Troy writes something on his pad. "I see. Still, Ian is an eyewitness."

I shake my head. "My primary goal is to protect Ian."

Troy stops writing. "What does that mean?"

"It means I don't want him testifying. I don't want to put him through that."

Shane speaks up for the first time. "Shouldn't your aim be to stay out of prison?"

I shake my head. "Ian comes first. The prosecution will rip him to shreds, and I refuse to put him through that."

"How does Ian feel about it?" Troy asks.

"It doesn't matter. I won't let him do it."

Troy raises an eyebrow. "Don't you think Ian should have a say in the matter?"

"No."

Frowning, Troy says, "You won't have a say in the matter if the prosecution calls him as a witness. And let's face it, Tyler, Ian is the *key* witness."

"He won't have to testify if I plead guilty."

Troy does a good job of hiding his surprise. "We don't even know the charges yet, Tyler—in fact, we don't know for sure that charges are forthcoming. Even if Turner files a complaint, the DA's office may not take up the case. But if they do—and if they charge you with a *felony*, and you plead guilty, you're looking at a mandatory prison sentence."

"I know," I say. I hate even thinking about what might happen. I stare out the window at a view of downtown Chicago. Darkness has fallen, and the city is lit up. "The only thing that matters is protecting Ian." I turn to Shane. "If I do end up incarcerated, you've got to promise me Ian will be protected. If I'm locked up, there will be nothing to stop Turner from getting to him."

Shane frowns. "He's still harassing Ian?"

"Yes. That sadistic bastard is pressuring him for sex."

"You won't need to worry about Ian's safety," Shane says. "I guarantee it."

* * *

When we wrap up our discussion, Troy returns to his own apartment in this same building, just two floors down. Shane and I join the rest of the family in the great room.

The lights have been dimmed. Beth is asleep on the sofa, her feet in Sam's lap. Cooper's in the kitchen. Ian is seated on the other sofa with Luke asleep on his chest.

At the sight of Ian holding a sleeping baby, my chest tightens. It floors me to think that one day we might have a child.

Ian smiles as he waves me over. "He likes me," he whispers as I sit beside him. Ian pats Luke's diapered bottom. "I changed him earlier. He had quite a blowout."

I lay my arm across the back of the sofa and run my fingers through Ian's hair. He shivers visibly and leans closer.

I never in my life contemplated having kids of my own— it just never seemed in the cards for me. I figured I'd have to settle for being an uncle to my sister's kids. Having Ian in my life opens up new possibilities—marriage, kids. Ian would be a wonderful father. He's loving, nurturing... he'd be amazing.

But all of that will have to be put on hold because I don't know what the future brings for us, or if I'll even be at liberty to have a future with him.

"Tyler, can I get you a drink?"

I glance behind me to see Shane standing at the bar, pouring a shot of whiskey. I leave Ian to his baby-cuddling and join my brother-in-law.

"What can I get you?" he asks.

"Beer would be great."

Shane reaches into a fridge beneath the bar counter, pulls out a cold bottle, pops the cap, and hands it to me.

"Thanks," I say before I take a long swig.

He takes a sip of his whiskey, then sets his glass down. "You know, if things go bad at the precinct, you can always come work for me."

Shaking my head, I laugh quietly. "I appreciate the offer, Shane, but I don't think being a bodyguard is in my future." Then I glance back over at Ian and smile. "Unless I'm *his* bodyguard."

Shane nods. "No problem. I just wanted you to know you have options."

* * *

That night in bed, Ian rests his head on my chest and wraps his arm around my waist. "Beth asked me if I've ever thought about having kids."

It sounds like a casual question, but I suspect it's not. It looks like I'm not the only one with babies on the brain. "What'd you say?"

"I told her sure, I love kids." He draws a pattern on my chest with his index finger. "What about you?" he asks.

I stroke his arm lightly, contemplating how to answer his question. I guess honesty is the best policy. "I've been single my entire adult life, so I never gave it much thought."

"If you weren't single, how would you feel?"

Right now, I'm finding it hard to think past tomorrow, let alone think about the future. I know what Ian's getting at, and I know how I want to answer him.

If you were in my life, yes. I'd want kids with you.

But I don't want to make him a promise I might not be able to keep. I also don't want to hurt him.

In the end, I tell him the truth. "I'd love to have kids with you."

"That's what I said." He burrows closer. "I told Beth you'd be a great dad."

❧ 16

Tyler Jamison

Monday morning, after I dress for work, I stand beside our bed and gaze down at Ian, who's sound asleep in his usual position... on his belly, hugging his pillow. For a moment, I allow myself to simply watch him and fight the desire to undress and crawl back into bed. I could call in sick... but no. Addison Jenkins deserves better. She and the other cases I'm working on deserve all the attention I can give them.

Resisting temptation, I lean down and kiss the nape of his neck. "Bye, baby. Have a good day."

I hate waking him this early, but I learned the hard way never to leave without saying goodbye. The first time I made that mistake, the morning after the first time I slept over, he assumed I had simply walked out on him. Thanks to his abusive formative years, he has a deep-seated fear of abandonment. Knowing this, I've been more careful.

He stirs sleepily and rolls onto his back, stretching like a big cat. "You too."

I lean down to speak softly to him. "If you go anywhere today, take Miguel with you, all right? He's still on medical leave, so he's probably got some free time. I'd feel better if you didn't go out alone. Promise me."

"Kay," he mumbles as his eyes drift shut. "I promise."

* * *

For most of the morning, I'm out in the field working on my current caseloads. When I'm done with serving a search warrant and conducting some interviews with eyewitnesses, I grab something at a fast food drive-thru window, eat in my car, then head back to the office to check e-mails and process some DNA and fingerprint reports that have come in.

Midafternoon, my desk phone rings. "Jamison," I say, not bothering to look at the caller ID.

"Tyler, can you come to my office?"

It's Jud. Something about the tone of his voice puts me on alert. "Sure. Is something wrong?"

"I—just come to my office. We need to talk."

After hanging up, I head down the hall, past the reception desk, toward the police captain's office. His door is ajar, and as I approach, I hear quiet voices inside. He's not alone.

My heart rate picks up as I push open the door and walk inside to find Andrea Davis from Internal Affairs and Bill Lesko, our union rep, standing in the room, eyeing me expectantly. I nod in greeting to Andrea and Bill. I've known them both for years, and we've always had a good working relationship.

Jud is seated behind his desk, his expression flat, his dark eyes filled with something that looks a lot like regret.

Shit. This is it.

My pulse kicks into high gear. In this moment, I don't see my *boss* seated behind that desk. I see my father's best friend, a man I've looked up to my entire life. And now, he's a man who's facing what has to be an unbearable task.

"You wanted to see me, sir?" My voice is strong as I meet his gaze head on.

Jud glances out his office window, his throat muscles working as he collects himself. A long moment later, he turns back to me and, with a heavy sigh, says, "I'm sorry, Tyler."

I can only imagine how hard this is for Jud. Ever since my dad was killed, Jud's been there for me, advising me. And he's a big reason why I worked toward a promotion to detective. I stare at the lines on his dark, weathered face, at his severe buzz cut that gets thinner and whiter every year.

"It's okay, sir," I tell him. "Just come out and say it."

"Tyler—" He closes his eyes for the briefest moment. When he reopens them, they're directed at me. He squares his shoulders and takes a breath. "Brad Turner has filed a complaint against you. It's been turned over to the prosecutor's office, and they see cause to bring charges." He waves toward the other two in the room. "I called Andrea and Bill in so we can talk before the assistant DA arrives."

"Do you have an attorney?" Bill asks me.

I nod. "I do. I had a feeling this would happen."

"Then call him," Bill says. "Right now. He should be here when the ADA arrives."

I pull out my cell phone and send Troy a text, asking if he can come to the precinct. He texts back almost immediately.

Troy: Just need to wrap up a meeting and then I'm on my way.

"He's coming," I say as I pocket my phone.

Jud frowns, shaking his head. "Damn it, Tyler, my hands are tied. Based on the circumstances, I have no choice but to suspend you while there's an investigation. I'm sorry, son."

"I understand." As much as it kills me, I retrieve my badge from my jacket pocket and lay it on Jud's desk. For a long moment, I stare down at the shiny star, a symbol that represents the totality of my professional career. My entire identity is wrapped up in being a cop. It's the only thing I ever wanted to do—the only thing I know how to do. If I lose that, I won't know who I am.

I feel bereft without my star, but at least I can take solace in the fact they won't take my gun. It's a personal firearm, not department-issued.

And then it hits me—I won't be able to follow through on my current investigations, including the murder of Addison Jenkins. These are *my* cases. "What about my caseload?"

Jud frowns. "I'm reassigning your cases. I'm sorry, but you'll need to turn over your notes, reports, anything you have to the investigating officers."

Jud gestures to his door. "The assistant DA is on her way, so we'll need to move this meeting to the conference room. Your attorney can join us there." He smiles sadly. "Let's get this over with."

I follow Jud and the other two down the hall to one of the larger conference rooms.

"Have a seat, Tyler." Jud motions to the chair at the head of the table. He sits to my right.

Andrea and Bill take the two seats next to Jud.

"I've been contacted by the assistant DA," Andrea says. "Brad Turner has filed a complaint against you, detective, alleging police brutality. Apparently, you beat him in a nightclub restroom?"

"I did." There's no point in denying it. "Although I was off-duty at the time. It was a private matter between us, not official police business. Is there any word yet on what the exact charges are?" The charge will make a big difference in how this plays out.

Andrea shakes her head. "No. But given the fact that the

plaintiff—Mr. Turner—was in the hospital for four days, we can assume battery. Maybe even aggravated battery."

"Any specifics on his injuries?" Jud asks.

Andrea checks her notes. "A cracked left eye socket, broken nose, and numerous lacerations. Oh, and a concussion." She lifts her gaze to mine. "The security guards on duty at the club that night reported that, and I quote, 'you hammered the hell out of him with your fists.'"

Everyone looks my way, as if they expect me to either deny or corroborate the account. "Yeah, I hammered him all right. He was *choking* my boyfriend." And now I've just outed myself to the whole room.

The room goes silent as everyone digests that little bomb.

"So, it was self-defense," Bill says.

After I give them a detailed rundown of the events that night and answer all their questions, Andrea reviews her notes. "Based on witness interviews, there's plenty of video evidence from the scene. Three bystanders in the hall took video, as did Turner himself." She turns her phone to face the rest of us and plays a short clip. "Turner took this. That's his voice you hear."

The video is jerky, as presumably Turner's hand was shaking as he recorded it. The camera is focused on Ian, who's collapsed on the floor, hand to his throat as he coughs and wheezes. He looks shaken, his face flushed. Turner's voice is strained as he grates out, "And here's Ian Alexander, the little cunt who started it all!"

Then the camera turns to me, as I'm being physically restrained by two nightclub security guards. With a growl, I break free of their hold and rush Turner, slamming my shoulder into his abdomen, pushing him back into the wall. He drops the phone, and we hear it clatter as it hits the floor. There's no picture now, but we hear the distinct sound of a fist hitting flesh, accompanied by Turner's grunts and cries of pain.

"The incident took place at Sapphires?" Andrea asks, confirming her notes.

"Yes," I say.

"If I'm not mistaken, that's a gay nightclub, isn't it?" she asks.

"It is."

"I see." Andrea writes something on her notepad.

"Tyler's sexual orientation has nothing to do with this case," Jud says, sounding more than a little defensive.

"You're right. It doesn't," Andrea says. "But it's going to come out, one way or another, and it will be an issue in the court of public opinion. It's inevitable. We have a Chicago cop beating a gay man in the bathroom of a gay nightclub. I'm assuming the plaintiff is gay—please correct me if I'm wrong. Either way, it's not a good optical."

There's a knock at the door.

"Come in," Jud calls.

The door opens and a young officer pops her head inside. "Excuse me, sir. Assistant DA Lydia Franklin is here."

"Send her in," Jud says.

A few moments later, a tall African American woman with a trim afro walks into the room. She's dressed in an emerald green business suit and white blouse, with matching heels. "I'm sorry I'm late," she says. "I came straight from the courthouse." She takes the seat at the far end of the table, directly opposite me, and quickly surveys the room.

Jud makes the introductions, starting with himself before going around the table. He ends with me. "And this is Detective Tyler Jamison."

Ms. Franklin nods to me. "Thank you for coming, detective. Your cooperation in this matter is greatly appreciated."

I smile, but I don't say anything. *It's not like I had a choice in the matter.*

"Do you have representation?" she asks me. "Besides the union, I mean." She nods to Bill Lesko. "Hello, Bill."

"My attorney is on his way," I say. "Troy Spencer."

She smiles. "Ah, yes. I know Mr. Spencer well."

Before she can say anything else, there's another knock at the door.

"Come in," Jud says.

The door opens and in walks Troy, dressed in an Armani suit and carrying a leather briefcase. He walks up behind me and clasps my shoulder. "Hello, Tyler." Then he takes the seat to my left.

"Perfect timing, Mr. Spencer," Lydia Franklin says. "I was just about to address conditions for the arraignment."

"My client has a sterling reputation with the Chicago PD," Troy says as he opens his briefcase and takes out his notepad. "In fact, he has one of the highest case success rates in the department. He has no priors, and he's not a flight risk. There-fore, I—"

"Calm down, counsel," Ms. Franklin says with an amused smile. "No one is suggesting Detective Jamison be detained. I agree he should be released on his own recognizance. He'll be expected to show up at the courthouse for arraignment tomor-row afternoon, along with counsel, of course."

As they hash over the details, I check the time. It's already half past six, and the way Troy and Lydia are posturing, this could go on for a while. I told Ian I'd be home at six. He's going to worry when I don't show.

"Do you mind if I make a personal call?" I ask, addressing the room at large.

"Go right ahead, Tyler," Jud says.

I step away from the table, turning my back on the discus-sion, and call Shane. I debated calling Ian first, but I don't want him to be alone when he gets the news. He's going to be upset when he finds out, and I want someone there with him. Some-one like my sister.

"Tyler," Shane answers on the second ring. "Troy's already notified me. I know charges are in process."

"I don't know how long I'll be at the station. Ian's going to worry when I don't come home."

"It's already taken care of. Sam and Beth are on their way to your place now. Don't worry about Ian. They'll stay with him until you get home."

I'm flooded with relief. "Thank you."

I return to the table just in time to hear Troy's question to Lydia Franklin. "So, what are you thinking?"

Lydia clasps her hands in front of her and eyes Troy first, then me. "Given the severity of Mr. Turner's injuries, and the length of his hospitalization, I'd say we're looking at *aggravated* battery."

"That's bullshit," Troy says, shaking his head. "My client—"

I tune the rest out. Aggravated battery is a felony in the state of Illinois. That means I'd be facing, at minimum, a two-year prison sentence, with no chance for probation. My stomach drops. The prospect of serving real time behind bars has suddenly gotten more likely.

I feel sick, and all I can think about is Ian.

ᦰꙠ **17**

Ian Alexander

Tyler's late.

He's never late.

And he hasn't called or texted.

I pace the living room, periodically glancing out the window that overlooks the driveway, watching for his BMW. He should have been home forty minutes ago. We have plans to grill steaks tonight on the roof. If he were going to be late, he would have called me.

As my anxiety soars, I keep telling myself to calm down.

So what, he's late. It's no big deal.

Maybe he got stuck in traffic.

Maybe he was assigned to a new case and hasn't had a chance to call.

Or, maybe he's been arrested.

Feeling lightheaded, I drop down onto a chair by the window and work on controlling my breathing. Hyperventilating won't help. And the last thing I need right now is a full-blown panic attack.

As I run through the list of reasons why he might be late, I hear a car pull into the drive. "Oh, thank god."

I jump to my feet expecting to see Tyler's car in the driveway. But it's not his car. It's a shiny black Escalade. I stand frozen in place as I watch Sam help Beth step down from the rear passenger seat. Together, they walk up the steps to my front door. A moment later, I hear a knock.

I swallow hard as my ears start ringing.

This is bad.

Deep down, I know Tyler sent them to break the news to me that he's not coming home.

Because he can't.

Because he's probably sitting in a jail cell right now.

There's a second knock, louder this time.

Feeling numb, I head to the foyer, turn the deadbolt, and open the door.

Beth's eyes are red, her lashes wet with tears. Nevertheless, she pastes a smile on her face. "Hi, Ian." She glances at Sam. "We thought we'd stop by."

"Tyler sent you," I say in a choked voice.

Sam nods as he ushers Beth inside and closes the door. "Mind if we come in?"

I step back and point toward the living room.

Beth steps forward and throws her arms around me. With her big belly in the way, it's a bit of a challenge. "He's being charged," she says through her tears.

I tighten my arms around her. She and I share a powerful bond—we both love Tyler.

Sam watches us, his brown eyes radiating pain and understanding. Then he steps close and wraps his arms around me and Beth. "Have faith, guys. It's going to be okay."

My mind is racing, my heart pounding, and I can't stop shaking. It's happening. Everything I dreaded—my worst fear—is coming true.

All I can think about is Tyler in prison, locked in a cage like a common criminal. And I didn't even get to say goodbye.

Anxiety is choking me. "This is my fault," I say, my voice breaking. "I did this to him."

"No, you didn't," Sam says. "Tyler's a big boy. He makes his own choices."

We all end up sitting on the sofa, Beth to my left and Sam to my right. I haven't known them very long, and yet they're here with me—like family. "Do you know what's happening?"

Sam shrugs. "Not exactly. Just that there's some big meeting taking place at the precinct. Troy was called in. He gave Shane a heads-up on his way to the precinct building, and here we are to keep you company."

I stare straight ahead at the fireplace. "Are they going to arrest him? Put him in jail?"

Sam shrugs. "We don't know."

As Beth reaches for my hand and links our fingers together, she gives me a sad smile. I can tell she's struggling not to cry. "Don't worry. Troy knows what he's doing."

My throat closes up as tears blur my vision. "Tyler can't go to prison. He just can't."

* * *

As the evening drags on, I'm drowning in a sea of pain and agony. I can't think straight. My chest hurts, and my lungs struggle to get enough air. I want to get drunk, but I can't because I have two house guests. *Babysitters* is probably a more accurate description.

I lose all track of time. Sam and Beth do their best to keep the conversation going, but I hardly register anything they're saying. Beth's phone rings a couple of times—her husband keeps checking up on her. Cooper calls once to check in with Sam.

"Does your mom know?" I ask Beth.

She shakes her head. "I want to wait until we know something concrete before we tell her."

I nod. "There's no point in worrying her prematurely."

It's getting late, nearly ten o'clock, and it's obvious Beth is exhausted.

I glance at Sam. "You guys should go. It's getting late, and Beth is worn out."

Beth straightens her spine. "I'm fine. Really. I'm fine."

But judging by the concern on Sam's face, I know he agrees with me.

As a car pulls into the driveway, headlights shine into the living room. I'm on my feet and racing to the window. My heart is in my throat when I see a black BMW pull up next to the Escalade. "It's Tyler. He's home."

I watch until he's out of the car, across the driveway, and heading toward the front steps. His tie is loosened, and the top button of his shirt is undone. He looks exhausted.

A moment later, I hear the key in the front door, and then it swings open. I'm there waiting for him, my heart about to burst out of my chest.

I don't know which one of us reaches out first, but a moment later, we're in each other's arms, and he holds me tight and secure against him. His hand cups the back of my head, and we just hold each other.

I bury my face in the crook of his neck. "Thank god." My voice is barely more than a whisper. "I was afraid they put you in jail."

"No. I'm free on my own recognizance. I have to report to court tomorrow afternoon for the arraignment." He steps back and looks me in the eye. "Are you okay?"

I nod, too choked up to say anything.

Tyler's gaze travels over my shoulder. "Thanks for coming,

you two."

I realize Beth and Sam are right behind us. Tyler holds out his arm and his sister joins us in a three-way hug.

She's crying, and I realize my cheeks are wet too. Even Sam's eyes are glittering. We're a mess—all of us.

After Sam and Beth say their goodbyes, Tyler closes the door and locks it. He hangs his jacket and holster in the closet.

He turns to face me, and a heartbeat later, we're in each other's arms once more, locked in a tight embrace. His mouth crushes against mine as he walks me back into the wall. My hands are all over the place, grasping his arms, his shoulders, his face. He grabs my hands, stilling their frantic movements, and after linking our fingers, he pins my hands to the wall.

"We'll get through this," he says with so much conviction there's no room for doubt.

And then his mouth is on mine again, hungry and demanding. He swallows my cries and our heavy breaths mingle, our chests colliding as we both suck in air. His hands grip mine hard, holding me in place, and his strength makes my knees weaken. This is what I need from him—this all-consuming power and confidence that makes me feel like he's invincible. With him, I can let go of my fears because I trust him to catch me when I fall.

Tyler releases one of my hands to run his hand down my torso to my groin. His fingers trace the length of my erection, and then his palm presses hard against me. The pressure feels so good, I whimper into his mouth, needing more.

With a growl, Tyler pulls me into the darkened parlor and walks me over to the bar. He turns me so I'm facing the counter, and his hand goes to the back of my neck as he bends me forward.

I moan. "Oh, fuck, yes."

I hear his belt buckle loosening, followed by the smooth slide of leather. As his belt falls to the floor with a thud, I hear the tell-tale sound of him unfastening his trousers and lowering the zipper.

Tyler tosses his wallet onto the counter. "Grab the condom and lube," he orders in a gruff voice.

While he reaches around me to unfasten my jeans and lower them and my boxer-briefs to my ankles, I open his wallet with shaky fingers and pull out a condom and a packet of lube.

He grasps the hem of my T-shirt, pulls it over my head, and tosses it aside. Knowing he's still mostly dressed, while I'm practically naked, is such a fucking turn-on. I want his hands on me so badly I'm shaking.

His warm hands are on my hips, stroking my skin. One hand reaches around me to grasp my cock, while his other slides down my ass and slips between my thighs to cup my sac. He cradles my balls in his hand, gently massaging and tugging.

"Get the condom," he says, his voice rough.

I tear open the condom packet and hand it to him.

He quickly sheathes himself. Then he reaches for the lube packet and tears it open. A moment later, his finger slides between my ass cheeks, slippery and cool. He teases my opening before he works his finger inside. I hear him applying more lube, and then he's there—the head of his cock pressing into me.

Blowing out a breath, I will my body to relax. My muscles soften for him, and he slides in. The feel of him pushing into me, the pressure, his hands gripping my hips—it's incredible.

I drop my forehead onto my arms. "God, Tyler."

He moves slowly at first, giving me time to adjust to him. As he picks up speed, I brace myself on the counter. He grips my shoulders to hold me steady.

It's fast and a bit frantic, but it's what we both need. Today was a wakeup call. Brad pulled the trigger. Now, neither of us knows what's going to happen.

Tyler drives into me, his pace fast and steady, almost punishing. He's breathing hard; we both are. He slides one hand around my waist to grip my erection and starts stroking me. I'm already hard as a rock and aching for his touch.

Between his hand and his cock, my nerve endings are on fire, my blood surging. My arousal climbs, along with his. His harsh grunts in my ear, his breath on my back, only turn me on more.

With a cry, he burrows deep inside me and holds himself there. I can feel his body tense as he comes with a hoarse shout. I follow a moment later, my cries mingling with his.

As I collapse onto the bar, he follows me down, his chest pressed against my back. We're still joined, both of us shaking in the aftermath.

Tyler presses a kiss to the nape of my neck. After withdrawing, he pulls me upright and slides his arm across my chest to hold me steady. I barely have the strength to stand.

As the clock in the foyer chimes eleven, Tyler says, "I need a stiff drink and a hot shower."

I laugh shakily. "Same."

While Tyler zips up his trousers, I pull up my briefs and jeans.

Tyler steers me to a barstool. "Sit, before you fall down." Then he walks behind the bar and gets out two glasses. He doesn't need to ask what I want—he makes me a Cosmo. He hands it to me, and then he pours himself a shot of whiskey.

"I have to appear in court tomorrow at two for the arraignment," he says, and then he takes a sip of his liquor.

"What does that mean, exactly?"

"The charges will be read in court, in front of a judge, and I'll enter a plea."

"Not guilty, right?"

Tyler tosses back the rest of his liquor and pours himself another shot. "Right."

But something in the tone of his voice gives me pause. "What does Troy think?"

"I'm being charged with aggravated battery, which is a felony. Troy says he can get the charge reduced to a misdemeanor because it was essentially an act of self-defense, and I have no prior convictions."

"It counts as self-defense?"

He nods. "I was defending *you*."

Tyler walks around to my side of the bar and turns me to

face him. He steps between my legs, cups my face in his hands, and kisses me lightly. "Have you eaten?" he asks me.

"No. I don't have any appetite."

"Me neither."

"Then let's skip it," I say.

"Fine with me." Tyler takes my hand. "Let's go upstairs."

We head up to the bedroom. Tyler disappears into the closet to undress, and I stand in the open doorway, watching him.

As he passes me on his way to the bathroom, he says, "I was suspended this evening. I had to surrender my star."

"Oh, my god, I'm so sorry." My heart breaks for him. I know how much his badge means to him. "But they didn't take your gun?" I ask him, surprised. I saw him hang his gun and holster in the closet when he arrived home. On TV, they always take the officer's badge and gun.

He shakes his head. "Just my star. Here, our firearms are personal property, not department-issued." He shrugs like it's nothing. "It's standard procedure, Ian. Until the case is resolved, I'm off the job. It looks like you're stuck having me around the house."

As I follow him into the bathroom, he turns back to me. "You're overdressed."

I let him unfasten my jeans and tug them down, along with my Calvin Kleins. I kick off my sneakers and remove my socks. Once naked, I stand before him and let him look his fill.

There's an edginess about him tonight, an urgency I'm sure has been fueled by this evening's events. He cups my face as we stand eye-to-eye. His nostrils flare, his chest rising and falling hard. He's upset.

"I'm sorry about your job," I say past the knot in my throat. But the words feel so inadequate. "It's only temporary, right?"

He leans closer, his mouth locking onto mine, and it's a rough kiss—demanding. One of his hands slides around to the back of my head, gripping me hard. "You have nothing to apologize for, Ian," he says. "I made my choice."

"But your job—"

"Stop." His voice is sharp. "What's done is done." And then he turns on the water and pulls me with him into the spray of hot water.

* * *

"So, you're suspended," I say much later when we're lying together in bed. We're both wired, neither one of us ready for sleep.

"Yeah. I'm off duty until further notice. Think of it as house arrest. There are strict rules. I have to be home during regular business hours—essentially eight to five. There are a lot of restrictions on what I can and can't do. I can't perform any law enforcement activities."

"I'm sorry they took your badge from you. I know that hurts." He nods. "It does."

"But you'll get it back, right? It's only temporary?"

He doesn't answer right away, and that makes me nervous.

"Tyler?"

"I guess that depends on the outcome."

"Surely this will blow over. You're a good cop. You were defending someone you love from harm. They can't convict you for that."

"I guess we'll have to wait and see what happens."

His guarded words chill my blood. "What do you mean?"

"I'm being charged with *aggravated* battery. That's a felony."

I sit up in bed. "That's ridiculous! You're not a felon!"

"Under the definition of the law, I might be." He pulls me back down beside him and wraps me in his arms.

"What's the penalty if you're found guilty?"

"A minimum of two years."

"In prison?"

He nods.

I tighten my arms around him. "No, you can't go to prison. That's insane. I'll tell the judge Brad choked me. I'll tell the jury—"

"You're not going to testify."

"Of course I am. I'm not going to let them convict you of a felony."

Tyler turns my face to his and kisses me. "No more talk about charges and courts." He runs his fingertips up and down my spine, gently stroking me. "Try to sleep, baby."

I press my forehead against his shoulder and try not to cry.

How can he take this so calmly when I'm falling apart?

ᨀ 18

Tyler Jamison

It's nearly seven the next morning when I awake. For the first time in my life, I didn't set an alarm on a weekday. Ian is still asleep, his backside nestled against me. I turn toward him and wrap my arm around his waist so I can hug him to me. I need to take advantage of every second I have with him because there might come a time when we're forced to be apart.

I try not to think about what could happen. If the assistant DA is successful in making the felony charge stick, I'm going to prison, at least for a couple of years. I can't fathom that. I can't imagine being separated from Ian for that long. I'd miss two years of my sister's life, and her son's. I'd miss the birth of Beth's new baby. I wouldn't be around to help my mother out. Others would step in to do it, but that's not the point. She's *my* mother.

I press my lips to Ian's shoulder and breathe in his scent—warm male skin, a hint of cologne. He's become an addiction I can't live without. I want to memorize everything about him—the sound of his voice, his laughter, his touch, the way he tastes, the sounds he makes when he comes. God forbid I'm in a position where memories are all I have to sustain me.

Our story can't end here. Life can't be that cruel. I waited my whole life for him, and I'm not about to lose him now.

No matter what he says, though, I won't let him testify. I'm pleading guilty—no matter the consequences.

* * *

When Ian wakes, we take a quick shower and then head downstairs to make breakfast. Well, he does the making, while I do the fetching. In some ways, it feels like any ordinary weekend morning—the two of us at home together. But we both know better. It's a Tuesday, when I should be at work.

Just as we're sitting down to eat, I get a text from Troy Spencer.

Troy: I'm coming over at eleven so we can prepare for the arraignment.

Me: That's fine

Troy: Shane's coming with me.

Troy and Shane aren't going to be happy when they learn I still plan to plead guilty.

I lay my phone down and reach for my fork.

Ian's sitting across the small table, watching me intently. "Was that work?"

I shake my head. "Troy."

"What does he want?"

"He's coming over later this morning to discuss the arraignment."

"What's there to discuss?"

"The charge and my plea."

Ian frowns in confusion. "You'll plead *not guilty*, right? What else is there?"

I sip my coffee. "Right." I'm not ready to tell him anything different.

Ian stabs his food with his fork, more than a little agitated. "I mean that's your only choice, Tyler. I don't see why you guys need to discuss it."

"We're just going over the procedures for today's hearing. It's nothing to worry about."

By the way he's staring at me, I suspect Ian doesn't believe me.

He shoots to his feet, dropping his fork onto his plate. His gaze is filled with hurt. "This is bullshit. You're not telling me everything." Then he shoves his chair back from the table and stalks out of the kitchen.

And there he goes.

* * *

I find Ian up on the roof, seated on the bench in the greenhouse. It's an overcast, rainy day, the sky gray like my mood and his. It's quite windy, and blowing rain lashes against the glass panes, making them rattle.

As I stare down at Ian, I notice his hair is sticking up in places, probably from running his fingers through it. My chest constricts. I'm doing my best to protect him, but I'm failing miserably. No matter what I do, Ian's going to get hurt.

I sit beside him on the bench. "I know this is difficult."

He stares out at the lake in the distance. "You can't plead guilty, Tyler."

"Ian." I let out a heavy breath as I slide my arm around him. "I promised your dad you wouldn't have to testify."

Furious, Ian turns to me. "But I want to testify. I'll do anything to help you. This is about your freedom, Tyler. It's about your future. It's not about me. And leave my parents out of it. This is between you and me."

He's angry, his chest rising and falling as tears well up in his eyes. And he's so damn beautiful I could cry. He's like a magnet, drawing me to him, and I'm unable to resist the pull.

I cup one side of his face and brush his cheek with my thumb. "Ian, you have to trust me."

He shakes his head, tears spilling. "Not if you're just going to roll over without a fight. Don't you dare sacrifice your freedom for *me*. Don't you dare let Brad win."

I hate this tension between us. Impulsively, I lean in and kiss him, and the feel of his lips trembling against mine is enough to do me in.

But he pulls back, clearly not ready to be distracted. "And what about your sister? She's having a baby soon. And your mom—it would kill her if you went to prison. If you won't fight this for me, fight it for them, Tyler. Please. You can't just abandon us."

Abandonment.

His greatest fear.

His birth mother abandoned him, time after time, because of her drug addiction. It left a wound on his soul that has never fully healed.

As I pull him into my arms, he resists at first, angry and hurt. "Shh," I tell him, holding on tightly. "I'll never abandon you, Ian. If I have to go away for a while, it'll only be temporary. I promise I'll come back. You'll be okay, I—"

He starts sobbing then, his hot tears soaking my T-shirt.

My breath catches as I struggle to maintain my composure. "You have to trust me, Ian. Please."

* * *

Right on time, Troy Spencer arrives, accompanied by my brother-in-law.

Dressed in a dark suit and tie, briefcase in hand, Troy looks ready to storm the Cook County courthouse. Shane is dressed more casually.

"Hello, Tyler," Troy says. When we hear Ian slamming pots and pans in the kitchen, Troy lowers his voice and asks, "Is there somewhere private we can talk?"

I nod toward the parlor. "Let's sit in there."

I follow them into the room and close the door behind us. The less Ian hears, the better.

The two men take their seats at the bar, while I stand across from them. "Can I get you guys anything?"

Troy shakes his head. "No, thank you."

"Nothing for me, thanks," Shane says. "How is Ian holding up?"

"Not very well," I say, remembering how he cried in my arms. I would give anything for this fucking nightmare to be over.

Troy gets right to the point. "At today's arraignment, after the charges are read, you'll be asked to enter a plea. You'll plead *not guilty*. It's a quick procedure, very routine. We should be in and out in less than fifteen minutes."

"You didn't come over here just to tell me that."

Troy purses his lips. "No. I came over here to talk some sense into you."

I shake my head. "My mind's made up. I'm pleading guilty."

"Don't be an idiot, Tyler," Troy says. "You're being charged with a class three felony. As long as you're facing a mandatory sentence, I won't be able to get you probation."

"I don't want Ian testifying, so that means no trial. I have to plead guilty."

"Out of the question, unless I can talk Lydia Franklin into reducing the charge. We can try for a plea deal. If she lowers the charge to simple battery, then we're looking at a misdemeanor. You can plead guilty to a misdemeanor, and I can probably get you probation. Worst-case scenario, you'd spend a week in the Cook County jail, ten days at most. We can all live with that, can't we?"

My heart stutters at the solution Troy is presenting. Yes, I can live with a week behind bars. Even Ian could survive that. It's almost too good to be true. "Do you think she'll go for it?"

He nods. "I do. You're not a criminal, Tyler, and she knows it. You're just a guy who was protecting someone he loves. It would be different if you had a history of abusive conduct as a police officer, but you don't. Your reputation is solid."

I glance at Shane, whose expression is perfectly neutral as he listens and observes. He doesn't fool me, though. I know he has an opinion on the subject. "What do you think, Shane?"

Shane crosses his arms over his chest. "My primary concern is how this affects Beth. Any option that keeps you out of prison is a win as far as I'm concerned."

"Then it's settled," Troy says. "You'll plead not guilty today. That will give me time to negotiate a plea deal."

* * *

That afternoon, Troy returns to give me a ride to the courthouse. Just as he said, the hearing is brief. In front of a judge, I acknowledge the charge: aggravated battery. And I plead *not guilty*. I'm trusting that Troy will be able to get me that plea deal, and then I'll change my plea to guilty.

Just as Troy predicted, it's all very by-the-book, and we're out of there in fifteen minutes.

"I'll talk to Lydia about making a deal," Troy says once we're back in his car. "If she goes for it, you'll be facing a misdemeanor."

I nod. But I'm not going to let myself get too excited that this will work. "If she doesn't go for it, I'm still changing my plea to *guilty*."

Troy frowns. "That's one hell of a gamble, Tyler. If you're found guilty of a felony, you're going to serve time in prison. As your counsel, I can't in good conscience advise you to—"

"Let's just hope she agrees, then," I say.

Sighing, Troy leaves it at that.

When he drops me off at the townhouse, I thank him as I get out of his car. "I appreciate everything you're doing."

He nods. "My pleasure. As soon as I get back to my office, I'll e-mail Lydia to see what we can come up with. In the meantime, sit tight and try to relax. We've got this, trust me."

"That's what I keep telling Ian."

* * *

When I let myself into the townhouse, I expect Ian to greet

me at the door like he usually does, but there's no sign of him. "Ian?"

There's no response.

I race up the stairs to check our bedroom, but he's not there. I go up to the roof and downstairs to the fitness room in the lower level.

My heart is pounding as I step out onto the back patio. "Ian!"

"I'm here," he calls back.

I find him seated on a swinging bench in the backyard. "Hey," I say as I join him. "You okay?"

He nods. "How'd it go?"

"I plead not guilty."

Ian closes his eyes and sucks in a deep breath.

"Troy's going to contact the assistant DA and see if we can get a plea deal that will lower the charge."

Staring straight ahead, Ian nods.

I reach for his hand and link our fingers together. "I know you're scared, but everything's going to be okay, I promise." I'm actually starting to believe it myself. "Troy knows what he's doing."

∽ 19

Ian Alexander

I've been a wreck all day, trying to stay busy around the house and not hover over Tyler. Since he's stuck at home under house arrest, I don't want to leave the house either. I don't want to leave *him*. But I'm on edge. I have been all day. I can't throw off this sense of impending doom. I know he has faith that Troy Spencer will somehow orchestrate a miracle with the DA's office, but I'm not so optimistic. There's too much at stake here, and something could easily go wrong.

I'm in the kitchen washing out the coffee pot when Tyler appears in the open doorway and watches me with a pained expression. He's more worried about me than he is about himself.

I shut off the water and set the pot on the drying rack. "I can't bear the thought of you behind bars." My fingers tighten on the edge of the sink. "You put killers behind bars, Tyler. You don't belong there yourself. It's not right."

Tyler sighs. "Go pack a bag, Ian. We're going away for the night."

I turn to face him. "Where are we going?"

"Just pack what you'll need overnight."

"I thought you were under house arrest."

"I have to stay at home during business hours, but that doesn't mean we can't go somewhere overnight. Don't worry, we'll be home before eight tomorrow morning."

Tyler steers me toward the stairs and follows me up to our bedroom and into the closet. He grabs a large duffle bag off the floor and hands it to me. "Start packing. We're getting out of here. I think a change of scenery will do us both good."

"What should I bring?"

"Whatever you need for one night. For starters, how about lube and condoms?"

That certainly gets my attention. "Yeah?"

Tyler winks at me. "I'm pretty sure we'll need those. And bring a pair of swim trunks."

So we pack one overnight bag with just the basics—toiletries, swim trunks, and one change of clothes each, and of course condoms and lube—and at five o'clock, we lock up the townhouse and climb into Tyler's BMW.

Tyler is driving, obviously, since I have no idea where we're going.

"You won't even give me a hint?" I ask as we head north on Lake Shore Drive.

Grinning, Tyler flexes his fingers on the steering wheel as he gets comfortable in his seat. "Nope. Sit back and relax, baby. Enjoy the scenery."

It's not long before we've left the city behind us and we're in the suburbs.

"You're really not going to tell me anything?" I say, laughing.

"If I told you, it wouldn't be a surprise."

When we pass a sign that says WELCOME TO KENILWORTH, Tyler makes a turn and follows the road that leads up the shoreline.

"Kenilworth?" I'm vaguely familiar with the small, upscale town, but I've never actually been here before. The houses we pass are stately and picturesque, many of them with large, sweeping yards and ornate private gates.

Tyler slows the car and turns right onto an unmarked lane that takes us through some woods.

"Where are we?" I ask as I sit up straight.

"Shane owns an estate here, right on the lake."

The lane eventually leads us to a secured gate. Tyler stops, lowers his window, and enters a passcode into an electronic keypad. The gate swings open, and we drive through. A few minutes later, we stop at a second gate.

I laugh. "Good grief, are we breaking into Fort Knox?"

"This place is about as secure as Fort Knox," Tyler says as he lowers his window.

"Good evening, detective," says a booming male voice over the intercom. "Welcome to Shangri-la."

Tyler grins as he replies over the intercom. "Open the gate, Charlie. I know you're expecting us."

"What's the password?" the mysterious voice asks.

"Charlie—" Tyler begins.

I lean toward the open window and say, "Open sesame?"

"That works," says the disembodied voice.

The gate swings open, and Tyler drives through.

"What is this place?" I say.

"Shane's high-profile clients stay here occasionally... celebrities, politicians, foreign dignitaries. The house has twenty-four-seven, on-site security."

As we continue on, the trees give way to grass. We pass a pond on the left side of the road and a pasture on the right. There's a small herd of horses grazing on a low hill.

As we come around a bend, an enormous two-story structure comes into view.

I peer out the window. "Niiice."

Tyler pulls the car up to the front entrance and turns off the engine.

The front doors open and an older couple walks out. The man—tall and built solid—is dressed in a blue plaid flannel shirt, khaki overalls, and mud-splattered boots. His gray hair is buzzed short, and his face is heavily weathered and lined with wrinkles. The woman wears her long silver hair in a braid. She's dressed in riding gear, complete with dusty brown riding pants and boots.

"That's George Peterson and his wife, Elly," Tyler says. "They manage the property. He's the groundskeeper, and she runs the house."

As we step out of the car, George and Elly come down the steps to greet us.

George offers his hand to Tyler. "Welcome, detective."

Elly hugs Tyler fiercely. "Hello, Tyler. It's so good to see you again." And then she turns to me with a curious smile and opens her arms wide. "You must be Ian."

After giving me a bear hug, she says, "Come inside, you two. George will take your bag up to your suite. Dinner's almost ready. It's such a nice evening, I thought you'd enjoy eating outside on the back patio so you can enjoy the lake view. Ian, I hear you like the water."

"I love it," I say, surprised. Oh, my god, Tyler must have told her about me—about *us*.

"Then you've come to the right place," she says. "Follow me."

As we follow her inside, she says, "We haven't seen much of the family lately, not with Beth being so far along. Shane's leery of letting her travel right now, in light of what happened when Luke was born. So, your presence is a very welcome distraction."

"What happened the last time?" I ask.

Elly's eyes widen. "You don't know the story? Good lord, the poor girl went into labor in a convenience store during an armed robbery. Thank goodness Lia was with her and managed to hide her and keep her safe until Shane and his men could rescue her and the baby. It was awful. Luke was born premature, and his lungs weren't fully developed, and he had to be hospitalized. It was a harrowing experience."

Shocked, I glance at Tyler. "Why did you not tell me this before?"

He lays his arm across my shoulders. "I'll tell you all about it later, I promise."

Elly pauses inside the foyer to point up a grand, curving staircase. "The suites are up on the second floor. I'll show you to your room after dinner." Then she gives us a quick tour of the main floor—the library, a huge dining room that seats a dozen, the kitchen, and a great room. "There's a movie theater downstairs, as well as a swimming pool, if you're so inclined."

Now I know why Tyler told me to bring my swim trunks.

Next, she leads us through the great room, with its soaring ceiling and massive stone hearth that extends up to a second-floor balcony. The exterior glass wall provides a sweeping view of the back lawn, which slopes down to a private beach and a dock, where several boats are moored.

We step through a pair of French doors onto a rear patio that includes a number of small bistro tables. One of the tables is already set with a white linen tablecloth, a candelabra, and a glass vase holding freshly-cut daisies. A bottle of red wine is sitting out, along with two glasses.

"Have a seat and relax," Elly says as she lights the candles.

"I'll bring your dinners out shortly."

Tyler pulls a chair out for me, and I sit. Then he takes his seat and pours us each a glass of wine. "Think of this as a mini vacation. While we're here, none of the worries back home exist."

"That's easier said than done," I say.

"I know, but let's try. After we eat, we can walk down to the beach and look at the boats."

I glance toward the private dock, where a small yacht is moored, along with a pontoon boat, and a small speed boat.

The back patio is decorated with outdoor lighting, and solar lights illuminate the path that leads down to the water.

"This place is magical," I say as I lift my glass for a toast. "Thank you for bringing me here."

"My pleasure," Tyler says, as he touches his glass to mine. "How about a toast? To us."

I smile. "To happy endings. Please, Tyler, tell me we'll get our happy ending."

Tyler's smile falls. "We have to have faith in the process."

Before I can reply, Elly walks out of the house carrying two dinner plates. "Chicken parmesan over linguine, with my own homemade marinara and freshly-baked bread." She sets our plates in front of us. "And I made Tiramisu for dessert. I hope you enjoy it."

"Thank you, Elly," Tyler says.

The food looks and smells amazing. On impulse, I reach out and squeeze her hand. "Thank you, Elly. This is divine."

Beaming, she goes back inside and leaves us to our meal.

As soon as I taste the food, I moan in appreciation. "This is as good as a five-star restaurant."

Our delicious dinner is followed by dessert and a second glass of wine. "You're not trying to get me drunk are you?" I ask Tyler.

He grins. "If it means I get lucky tonight, then yes."

When we're through eating, we walk down the path that leads to the lake. It's quiet down here and very private as there aren't many boats on this section of the lake tonight. I sit on a fallen log and take off my shoes and socks, then roll up the legs of my jeans so I can walk barefoot in the surf.

Tyler removes his shoes and socks and joins me on a stroll along the shoreline. We step over pieces of driftwood and strands of greenery that have washed ashore, and we manage to stay just out of the reach of the chilly waves as they roll in.

I reach for his hand. "When everything's over and done, let's go on vacation. Have you ever been to Key West?"

Tyler links our fingers as we walk. "I haven't. I've been to Miami, though."

"You've got to see the Keys—there's nothing like it. When we're free to do what we want, let's go there. I promise you'll love it."

"All right. I'm long overdue for a vacation."

I stop and pull him to me. "Promise me. I want to go somewhere with you, somewhere beautiful and fun, where we can play in the sun and surf without a care in the world."

"I promise," he says as he takes me in his arms. His beautiful blue-green eyes, so reminiscent of the waters off the Keys, fix on mine. "I know this is hard on you. It's hard on both of us. When it's over, we'll go anywhere you want to go."

When it's over.

That's just the problem. Neither of us knows when that will be... or even if.

A wave surges over our feet, the frigid water making me jump.

"Do you want to go swimming?" Tyler asks. "The house has an indoor pool."

"I'd love to."

We return to the patio to collect our dirty dishes and carry them to the kitchen.

"Thank you for a wonderful meal," I tell Elly.

She smiles. "You are very welcome, Ian. Your bag is upstairs in your suite, third door on the right. I gave you the room with the best view of the lake."

By the time we make it upstairs to our room, darkness has fallen, and the stars are coming out. We walk out onto a private balcony and stare up at the night sky.

As Tyler wraps his arms around me, I wonder if he's thinking the same thing I am. *Is this one of the few nights we have left together?*

"How about that swim?" he asks as he pulls me back inside our room.

I open our duffle bag and locate two pairs of swim trunks. I toss him his pair, and we both change.

We walk down the grand staircase, and I follow Tyler through a door that leads to the lower level. We pass a movie theater and a fitness room, and then we come to an enormous pool behind a glass wall.

"Whoa," I say. "I am majorly impressed."

Tyler opens the door for me, and I step into a warm, humid room that smells of chlorine. The rectangular pool is huge, its surface perfectly still, like polished glass. There is a zero-entry wading area to the left, and diving boards tower over the deep end to the right.

I grab a beach towel off a cart, drape it over a reclining lounge chair, then make a run for the pool, diving in head-first near the deep end. The water is the perfect temperature—refreshingly cool, but not so cold it steals my breath. I swim up to the surface and tread water.

Tyler's standing at the edge of the pool, his arms crossed over his sexy AF chest, just watching me.

"Come on in," I say, splashing him with water. "The water's fine."

Tyler surprises me by executing a perfect dive, hitting the water right next to me and disappearing below the surface.

I watch him swim the entire width of the pool before he surfaces. "You didn't tell me you were part dolphin," I say, laughing as I splash him.

Tyler swims over to me and nods toward the shallow end. "Come on. I'll race you."

We swim to the other side of the pool, where we stand in a

few inches of water as I do a countdown. "Ready? Three, two, one."

We run until the water is deep enough to swim in. Then Tyler dives, taking a big lead. He quickly leaves me far behind as his long arms cut cleanly through the water in a perfect breaststroke.

"Damn." I swim down to the deep end to join him. "Where did you learn to swim like that?"

"I was on the high school swim team," he says as he treads water beneath the high dive. "I worked summers as a lifeguard. And I attended university on a swimming scholarship. So did Beth."

"Aren't you full of surprises," I say as I swim up to him, sliding my arms around his shoulders.

He wraps his arms around me and kisses me, and we both drift below the surface of the water, our lips locked as we sink. When we touch bottom, we kiss until we can't hold our breath any longer. Then we kick back up to the surface.

We race twice more, Tyler beating me by a long shot both times. Then we head for the diving boards.

"Show me what you can do," Tyler says, nodding toward the low dive.

I make an attempt to do a front flip off the board, trying to show off, and I completely blow it and end up doing a belly flop. Laughing, Tyler climbs the ladder to the high dive.

"Show off," I say, as he executes a perfect backward flip. "Why didn't you tell me you're a merman?"

He swims toward me and wraps his arms around my waist as we tread water. "I guess it never came up."

I cling to him like a monkey, my legs around his waist and my arms around his neck, and he manages to keep us both afloat. When I feel his cock stirring against me, I lean in and kiss him. "Wanna make out in the pool?"

He nods toward the ceiling. "You see those video cameras placed strategically throughout the room?"

"Yeah?"

"Those aren't just for decoration. They're monitored by the security staff, just out of precaution, in case a guest gets into trouble in the water."

"Oh."

"Yeah, so if we're gonna make out, we should definitely do it in our suite."

I slip my hand beneath the water and stroke the outline of his growing erection. "That sounds like an excellent idea."

ℰ 20

Ian Alexander

After our swim, we head back up to our suite. I strip and walk straight into the shower to wash and prep. I'm getting laid tonight.

When I finish, I dry off, finger-comb my hair, brush my teeth, and without bothering to put anything on, I walk into the bedroom to find Tyler sitting at the foot of the bed in just his black boxer-briefs. His hair is still damp from our swim. I glance out onto the balcony and see both pairs of swim trunks hanging over the railing to dry.

I allow myself the luxury of simply looking at Tyler. As always, my eyes are drawn to his chest—the man's chest is sexy AF. My gaze follows the trail of dark hair that leads to his groin, disappearing beneath the waistband of his underwear.

"You're overdressed," I say as I approach the bed. I want to fall to my knees and worship him.

Tyler rises to his feet and heads my way, toward the bathroom, but I stop him with a hand to his chest and push him back toward the bed.

"I should shower," he says with a laugh.

I shake my head as I tug his briefs down, dropping them to the floor. Then I push him back so he's sitting on the bed. "No, you look like a fucking god, and I'm here to worship at your feet."

He smiles. "Ian—"

Before he can say another word, I drop to my knees and ease between his legs so I can take his cock in my mouth.

Tyler cries out, gripping my head and groaning loud. "Baby, this isn't about me—*fuck*."

Tyler takes my hands in his and carefully withdraws from my mouth. Then he pulls me up onto the bed and rolls me onto my back. He leans close and whispers, "Lie back, baby."

He motions for me to scoot back until my head reaches the pillows. His warm hands run up my legs, to my thighs, and then he wraps his fingers around my erection, which is straining wildly for attention. As he settles in beside me, he strokes me firmly from root to tip. Then he licks me, his tongue swirling over the head of my cock. He takes his sweet time, running his lips and tongue along the length of my throbbing shaft.

As I close my eyes with a groan, my back bows off the mattress and my head digs into the pillow. He's gotten so good at giving head. I think I've created a monster.

"You love torturing me," I say, my breathy voice barely audible.

When he chuckles, I feel the vibration travel down my shaft to my balls.

"I just want to make you feel good," he says, still leisurely licking me.

He rises up on his knees, crouching over me, and continues this slow, methodical torment. My cock is throbbing now, my balls heavy and aching for release. But just when I feel I'm getting close, he backs off. *The bastard.*

I groan with frustration. "Tyler, please."

"Patience, baby."

He reaches for the lube and a condom, which are on top of the nightstand, along with a towel.

As he holds up the condom packet, he says, "What would you think about us going bareback? After we both get tested for STDs, assuming we're both negative—and since we're exclusive—we could skip the condoms. What do you think?"

My eyes widen. "Oh my god, yes. I've never had sex without a condom." The thought of his bare-naked cock in my ass... the thought of him coming inside me. *Holy shit, yes.*

He leans close and kisses me. "We can get tested this week."

I grab his head and crush my mouth to his in a desperate,

hungry kiss. "Yes, please. I want you inside me—just you." The mere thought of it makes me so hard I ache.

I take the condom from him, rip open the packet, and roll it onto him, admiring every thick inch. He overwhelms me, both physically and emotionally, and it takes my breath away.

Tyler reaches out to stroke me, keeping me on edge. "How do you want me?"

I smile because he knows exactly how I want him. I roll onto my hands and knees, laying the towel beneath me, and he kneels behind me. His warm hands caress my ass cheeks, kneading them, spreading them. I feel his mouth on me as he peppers me with kisses, then soft bites. His breath is warm, his tongue teasing as he laps at me, lighting my nerves on fire. He gently tugs at my sac as he strokes my aching cock. The pleasure is overwhelming. I arch my back, moaning as he eats at me, driving me crazy.

My limbs are shaking. "Tyler, god," I groan, my head dipping down. I'm breathing hard, my lungs billowing.

Suddenly a lubed finger slips between my cheeks and teases my opening, making my already sensitive nerves sing. He slides it in deep, then withdraws, and does it again, over and over as he gets me ready for him. Then I hear him lubing himself.

One of his hands grips my hip, holding me still, while the other guides his cock to my opening. He presses gently against me, letting his weight do the work as he pushes forward. I gasp, my breaths long and shaky as he sinks inside.

Damn.

I moan loudly into my pillow as he fills me. Once he's fully seated, he grasps my hips, holding me firmly, pinning me in place as he starts to move. With each thrust, his cock drags against the sweet spot. My insides are tingling now with each graze, my breath catching in my throat.

His thrusts speed up, and soon he's riding me hard, his movements forceful. His hands steady me, his thighs slapping against mine. I reach between my legs and stroke myself, pulling hard on my cock. His hoarse cries and rough grunts fill my ears.

I can tell when he's about to come, because he reaches around me and jerks me off, his fist demanding. We come together. He shudders, his hips rocking into me with each spasm of his body.

My knees give out and I sink down onto the bed and onto my belly. He follows me down, still buried deep inside me, covering me with his body as he milks his orgasm.

One of his arms goes around my shoulders, holding me to him, and with his free hand, he turns my face to the side so we can kiss.

This is what I love—to be so wholly enveloped by him. To be surrounded by him and feel his strength and his power as he fucks me so perfectly.

I sigh when I feel his lips in my hair. One of his hands cradles my jaw, and we kiss. Our mingled breaths are rough, our lips hungry.

We roll to the side and lie still for a minute to catch our

breath. I wipe my abdomen with a corner of the towel. Tyler climbs out of bed, taking the towel with him, and goes to the bathroom to dispose of the condom.

Soon, he's back, climbing into bed and drawing me into his strong arms. He covers us both with a sheet and blanket.

When he presses his lips to my forehead, I cling to him and try not to cry as reality comes screaming back and the ache in my heart becomes unbearable.

His lips settle on mine, and we both taste the salt of tears. "It's going to be all right, I promise."

But we both are perfectly aware that he can't know that for sure.

ꙮ 21

Tyler Jamison

The next morning, I wake bright and early, as soon as the morning sun begins to light our room. Carefully, so as not to wake Ian, I climb out of bed and hit the bathroom.

As I stare at my toothbrush lying next to Ian's on the bathroom counter, I'm reminded of how important the little things are, and how much we take for granted. It's not just sex that's intimate, but cohabitating. Sharing a space, sharing our bodies, our lives. The thought of not being here with him, for any length of time, is gut-wrenching.

What if he needs me, and I'm not here for him?

What if he gets sick or lonely?

What if someone tries to take my place in his life?

I know he wouldn't just forget me the moment I was locked up, but Ian's a very attractive young man with so much to offer. It wouldn't surprise me if someone tried to worm his way into Ian's life.

I pull a change of clothes from our duffle bag and get dressed. When I return to the bedroom, Ian's awake, sitting up in bed. He looks a bit lost.

"Good morning, baby." I reach out to stroke his messy hair. "Did you sleep well?"

Still groggy, he nods.

"Why don't you get dressed, and then we'll go downstairs for a quick breakfast. We don't have a lot of time."

"I'd like to come back here sometime," he says as he swings his feet to the floor. "When we can stay longer."

"Beth and Shane are planning to stay here while she recovers from the birth of their new baby. Maybe we can come then. This place will be crawling with McIntyres."

"I would love that," Ian says as he heads to the bathroom.

After we're ready, I carry our bag downstairs and leave it by the front door. We wander into the kitchen.

Elly is at the stove. "Good morning, gentlemen. Are you ready for some breakfast?"

We sit at the kitchen table, and she brings us each a plate of eggs and sausage and toast.

She sets a basket of blueberry muffins on the table. "Help yourselves. They're still warm."

"Thank you, Elly," Ian says.

"Can I get you some coffee?" she asks.

"That would be great, thanks," I say. "Black for me. Ian likes his flavored—caramel, vanilla, anything sweet."

"I hope you two will come back soon," she says as she pats Ian's shoulder. "You're welcome here anytime."

We eat quickly, cognizant of the time. I need to be home by eight.

After saying our goodbyes to Elly and George, Ian and I get into my car and head back to the city. Ian's quiet on the drive home, but I don't press him.

We arrive back at the townhouse and walk in the door at seven-thirty.

Back to house arrest.

Without a word, Ian takes our overnight bag from me and heads upstairs. "I'll put our stuff away."

"Okay." I stare at his retreating back, at his tired steps as he climbs the stairs. "Do you want me to put on a pot of coffee?"

But I don't get a reply. It's possible he didn't hear me, but my gut instinct tells me otherwise.

A sense of unease crawls up my spine. I'm not afraid for myself, but I am afraid for Ian. I'd never forgive myself if our relationship did damage to his emotional state. Now I'm starting to realize just what his father meant when we first met, when he told me he and Ruth wouldn't let anyone undo all the good that's happened to Ian since they adopted him.

Shit. My relationship with Ian is everything to me, but maybe it's not always such a good thing for him.

I head into the kitchen to put on some coffee. While I'm waiting, I power up my laptop and sit at the kitchen table to check for e-mails that came in overnight. Last night at Kenilworth, we were both offline. Now it's time to touch base with reality.

I have an e-mail from Troy—he knew where we were last night, so I imagine he didn't worry when I didn't reply to him. He e-mailed to confirm that Lydia received his message and responded favorably. She agreed to the plea deal, thank god. Ian won't have to testify in court. That lifts a huge weight off me.

When the coffee is ready, I pour myself a cup. I get out the sugar and the caramel-vanilla creamer Ian likes, ready to make him a cup when he comes downstairs.

There's no sign of him, though, and I'm starting to worry. It shouldn't take him this long to unpack one bag.

I'm about to go check on him, but then I hear the water come on upstairs. He's fine. He's just taking a shower.

I remain seated at the table and finish wading through my e-mails. There are two from Jud, one from Andrea Davis in Internal Affairs, two from Bill Lesko.

No one has anything new or earth-shattering to share. They're all just checking in with me and reminding me of the terms of my suspension. Jud made it very clear the terms are non-negotiable and that I'd better follow the rules to the letter or risk serious repercussions.

As I have a second cup of coffee, I skim the news headlines.

I check the time when I realize the water's still running upstairs. Jesus, how long can he stay in there? He's going to turn into a prune. My scalp tingles when I estimate how long he's been up there. *Shit!*

Why the fuck wasn't I paying better attention?

I set my cup down hard on the table and bolt for the stairs, racing up to the second floor. I rush into our bedroom and head straight for the bathroom. The lights are out, and the room is filled with steam.

"Ian?" The glass walls are fogged over, so I have to open the door and see inside. I find Ian standing beneath the spray of water, leaning against the shower wall, his forehead resting on his arms. His shoulders shake as he sobs.

My heart breaks.

I did this to him.

I turn off what is now frigid water and step into the stall with him, wrapping my arms around his chilled body. "Shh, baby, it's okay." I press my lips to his hair, which is soaking wet and ice cold. He's shaking. "Damn it, Ian, you're freezing."

I step out and yank off my wet T-shirt before grabbing a towel to wrap around Ian's shoulders. I pull him out of the shower and into the bedroom, where I sit down and pull him onto my lap, cradling him in my arms. He's shivering violently, so I wrap us both in our comforter and hold him tight.

"It's okay." I press my lips to his temple. "You're okay."

"But for how long?" he asks, his voice little more than a croak.

I grab the discarded towel and use it to dry his hair. "Everything's going to be okay," I tell him. "We're going to be fine."

"You don't know that for sure."

"I do. Troy e-mailed to tell me the DA accepted our plea deal. I'm going to be charged with a misdemeanor now, which means I can plead guilty and only get a week or so in the county jail."

Ian pulls away and secures the towel around his waist. His nipples are puckered tightly from the cold. "I'm sorry," he mutters before he heads into the closet.

I follow him and stand in the open doorway, leaning against the doorjamb. "You don't need to apologize, Ian."

He rifles through the dresser and pulls out a pair of teal boxer-briefs and a pair of matching socks, which he hastily puts on. Then he pulls on jeans and a pink hoodie featuring a unicorn riding a sparkly rainbow. His choice of attire makes me smile.

The damp hair on top of his head sticks out in wild tufts, and he looks so damn young and so lost.

On his way out the door, he pauses in front of me, meeting my gaze head on. "I never needed anyone before, and now I need you too much." He says this with so much bitterness it scares me. He sounds like he's giving up.

As he starts to move past me, I grab his arm, stopping him in his tracks. Gripping his chin, I make him look me in the eye. "It's not too much. Do you think I don't need you just as much? I do." My voice breaks, and I swallow hard. "I can't lose you, Ian. I won't. Do you hear me?"

He tries to pull away, dismissing my words, but I hold him

fast, my grip on him hard enough to leave bruises. "I know this is hard and that you're scared. I am too. But I will *never* give up on you, or on us." I want to add *I hope you'll never give up on me*, but I don't. He's feeling enough pressure as it is without me adding more.

He relaxes his stance, no longer fighting me. "That may not be enough," he says. And this time, when he tries to walk away, I let him go.

I have the strength to hold on to him—I have enough strength for the both of us. But sometimes too much strength isn't a good thing if it leaves him bruised.

I watch him walk back into the bathroom. He runs water at the sink, and then I hear him brushing his teeth. I linger at the bathroom door just to make sure he's okay.

As he wipes his mouth, I tell him, "Coffee's ready. Come downstairs and I'll make you a cup."

Shrugging, he reaches for a comb and detangles his damp hair. After finishing, he drops his comb into the vanity drawer and walks past me out of the bathroom. "I'll make it."

* * *

While we sit at the kitchen table drinking our coffee, Ian avoids making eye contact with me. I think he's embarrassed by his earlier meltdown in the shower.

I realize that simply loving someone isn't always enough. There are forces outside our control that affect our lives. Things that can hurt him badly.

After we finish our coffee, Ian rinses out the cups and puts them in the dishwasher. I offer to help.

"It's okay," he says. "I'll do it."

Before I can insist, my phone rings, and I check the screen. "It's Jud." I leave the kitchen to take his call, not wanting Ian to hear anything that might further upset him. "Hi, Jud. What's up?"

"I just heard about the plea deal you made with the DA's office."

"Yes. It was accepted. It's a done deal."

"I see."

"You disapprove?" It's obvious by the tone of his voice.

"Son, I hate seeing you plead guilty when you didn't do anything wrong. It's not right. It was clearly an act of self-defense."

"Yes, but pleading otherwise would have resulted in Ian having to testify in court, and believe me, that's not an option." I realize that now even more than ever.

"How's he doing?"

"Not well."

"I'm sorry to hear that."

"He'll be okay. We just need to get past this."

After my call with Jud ends, I call Ian's father.

"Tyler, hello," he says, in his brusque voice. "How is everything?"

"As expected, I guess. I'm calling to let you know I made a plea deal with the DA's office. In exchange for pleading guilty, and thereby avoiding a trial, they've agreed to lower the charge to simple battery—a misdemeanor."

Martin exhales a relieved breath. "Tyler, I'm sorry you're in this position, but I'm grateful to you for sparing my son. How is he?"

I hesitate to tell him. He's already so sure my relationship with Ian will end up hurting him. But if I'm going to get off on the right foot with Martin, I have to be honest. "He's not doing so well right now."

"I guess that's not surprising, given the circumstances."

"He's afraid I'm going to jail."

"But the good news is, it won't be a long sentence. And you'll be kept separate from the general population, so it won't be too bad."

"I'll be fine. It's Ian I'm worried about."

"His mother and I will take care of him, don't worry about that. He can come home and stay with us for the duration. We'll keep a close watch on him."

"Martin?"

"Yeah?"

"Has Ian ever threatened to harm himself?" I can't bring myself to say the word *suicide*, but based on what I witnessed this morning, and the way he's acting, I can't rule it out.

He hesitates before answering. "He has, yes, not lately, but when he was a teenager. Why? Has it come up?"

"Let's just say I'm keeping a close eye on him."

"Understood. If you are incarcerated, his mother and I will

take care of him. I promise you that." He pauses. "One more thing, Tyler. I owe you an apology. I was wrong when I said you were bad for my son. I think you're exactly who he needs."

I'm stunned by his admission. "Thank you, sir. Your opinion means a lot to me. Your wife's and Layla's, too."

He chuckles. "I don't think you need to worry on the ladies' account. They're both smitten with you."

* * *

Later that afternoon, I manage to coax Ian into sitting down with me in the living room. We put on a movie and relax on the sofa.

Pretty soon we're snuggled together, neither one of us paying much attention to the film. He allows himself to relax in my arms.

Halfway through the movie, my phone chimes with an incoming call. I glance at the screen, hoping it's someone I can ignore, but it's not. It's Ian's father, which is odd as we'd just spoken earlier.

"I'm sorry, but I have to get this," I whisper to Ian, who's half asleep in my arms. I accept the call. "Jamison."

"Tyler." The urgency in Martin's tone puts me immediately on high alert. "I need your help. *We* need your help."

I straighten in my seat. "Of course. What do you need?"

"It's Layla. She never came home from school today, and we can't reach her or her bodyguard. They're not answering their phones. This goes completely against protocol, and Ruth and I are worried."

"I see." I don't dare say anything more with Ian right beside me.

"Ian's there, isn't he?" Martin says, picking up on my guarded response.

"That's right."

"Can you step away? We need to talk."

"Certainly. Just a moment." I kiss Ian's forehead as I gently extricate myself from his hold. "I'll be right back," I whisper.

I head down the hallway to the kitchen and step out onto the back porch, well out of earshot. "I can talk now," I tell Ian's father. Immediately, I switch to detective mode. "Tell me everything you know."

"Her last class today ended at two, and she should have come straight home after that. I've tried calling both Layla and Sean, but they're not answering their phones. Hers goes straight to voicemail, so it's either turned off or the battery's dead. For Sean not to answer his phone is inexcusable, and it violates protocol and his company's policies. I've contacted the security agency, but they can't reach him either."

"Have you called the police?"

"Yes. An officer already came to the house and searched her bedroom. He found a note in her dresser drawer, from Sean to Layla, suggesting that the two of them run off together. Now the cops are saying she's likely a runaway, but I don't believe that for a second. Layla would never agree to such a thing—

she doesn't even like Sean. Besides," he says, his voice shaking, "Layla wouldn't do that to us. She's in trouble, Tyler. I know she is."

"I'll call my captain and see what I can find out. With her medical issues, she'll be deemed an at-risk missing person, and they'll make her a top priority."

"Not if they think she's a runaway. Tyler, every hour she's missing puts her in greater danger. Without her medications—"

"Does she carry her meds with her?"

"No, they're kept here at home. And Ruth just checked. All of Layla's medications are here. Her insulin pump has enough insulin for roughly another twelve hours, but her antipsychotic medication has to be taken daily. Tyler, we need to find her fast. She might not be eating right—and stress makes her hallucinations worse. And she—" He chokes up. "She's a vulnerable young female, Tyler. I don't think I need to spell out what's at stake here."

Even though I doubt it myself, I have to ask. "And you're sure there's no possibility she ran off with Sean?"

"Absolutely. I'd bet my life on it."

When I hear a pained gasp behind me, I turn. Ian's standing in the doorway, a horrified expression on his face. "Ian—" Damn it. I didn't want him to find out this way. "I have to go, Martin. I'll call Jud Walker and report back to you." Then I end the call.

Ian pales. "What's going on?"

"That was your dad." I hate that I have to tell him this. "Layla didn't come home from school today, and no one can reach her or Sean."

I walk him back into the house and sit him down at the kitchen table.

"I need to call Jud," I say as I call up his number and begin pacing.

Jud answers almost immediately. "Walker."

"Jud, it's Tyler. Layla Alexander is missing—Ian's sister."

"Yes, I know. I've read the report. We have APBs out on her and her bodyguard. We've got people looking."

"Layla has serious health issues, Jud. She's dependent on medication."

"I know, Tyler. We're on it. I'll let you know as soon as we find anything."

"I can help—"

"No, you can't," Jud argues. "It would be a direct violation of the terms of your suspension. If you perform *any* law enforcement activities, you'll be putting your job on the line, and I won't be able to intercede on your behalf." His voice hardens. "Stay out of this, Tyler. I'm sorry, but you have to let us handle it."

"This is Ian's *sister*—"

"I'm aware of that, but my hands are tied, and so are yours. Sit tight. Hopefully we'll find her soon."

"Martin told me about the note that was found in Layla's bedroom. He's sure she didn't run off with her bodyguard. The note's a red herring, and that means Sean is—"

"Tyler, stay out of this," Jud warns. "That's an order."

I turn to Ian. "I have to ask, is there *any* chance your sister could have run off with Sean?"

"No!" he cries. "She can't stand him, Tyler. You heard her say so yourself."

I nod, feeling guilty for pressing Ian, but the questions I'm asking are standard procedure in a situation like this. "I know. I'm sorry, but I had to ask. Sean's missing, too. His agency can't locate him. Because of the note, the police are looking at the possibility that they ran away together."

Ian has a wild look in his eyes as he begins pacing. "What about her meds? Did she take them?"

"No. Your dad said all of her medications are at the house."

Ian checks the time. "She should have been home nearly two hours ago. My god, Tyler, what if he hurts her? What if he—" He grabs my arms. "Find her, Tyler. Please, I'm begging you." His eyes fill with tears. "Find her before something happens—before he hurts her."

Ian doesn't know what the consequences would be if I were to investigate Layla's disappearance—and I'm not about to tell him.

My job versus the life of his sister?

There's no question. There comes a time in every man's life when he has to weigh his options and make a choice. I'm making mine.

"I swear to you, Ian, I'll do everything in my power to find her." I refrain from adding the qualifier *alive*. He doesn't need to hear about crime statistics right now.

Ian's been through a lot lately, but losing his sister is something he would never recover from.

ᒷ 22

Ian Alexander

I follow Tyler as he retrieves his holster and straps it onto his chest. Then he slips on his jacket.

As he grabs extra ammo from the top shelf, I tell him, "I'm coming with you."

"No. You're staying here."

"There's no way in hell I'm staying home while you're out there looking for *my* sister. Either you let me come with you, or I follow you. Either way, I'm coming, and you can't stop me."

He studies me for a split second before he says, "Fine. Grab your jacket and let's go."

As we head south toward the university, Tyler starts rattling off instructions. "Call your parents and find out as much as you can about Layla's class schedule. I need to know which classes she was taking, room numbers, professors' names, any classmates she ever mentioned by name, friends, study partners—anything they can remember."

"Got it." I reach for my phone and call my mom.

Her voice breaks when she answers. "Ian?"

I can tell she's been crying. "Mom, it's okay. We'll find her. We need some information, though." I repeat everything Tyler said.

Tyler reaches into his jacket pocket and pulls out his little black notebook and a pen, which he hands to me. "Write down everything she can remember, no matter how small. And get Layla's license plate number."

While I'm talking to my mom, Tyler makes a call. "Shane, I gotta make this quick. Layla Alexander is missing—yes, Ian's sister. Ian and I are looking for her. I just wanted to give you a heads-up in case we need help with resources." He pauses a moment as he listens. And then, in a low voice, he says, "It doesn't matter, Shane. This is Ian's sister we're talking about." He listens again, then says, "Yes, I know what I'm doing. I'll keep you posted."

"What doesn't matter?" I ask Tyler when he sets down his phone.

He spares me quick glance. "It's nothing. What did you learn from your mom?"

Referring to my notes, I recite everything she told me. "Her last class of the day would have been philosophy at one o'clock, with a Professor Baker."

"Then that's where we start," Tyler says.

* * *

We arrive twenty minutes later at the University of Chicago and park in a visitor lot. Tyler grabs a map from an information kiosk, and we head across campus.

"Do you think her disappearance has anything to do with the school?" I ask as I follow him to a collection of ivy-covered brick buildings.

Tyler shakes his head. "I doubt it. But since this is where she would have been seen last, this is where we start. We retrace her steps."

We locate the building where her philosophy course is held and find the classroom on the second floor. It's after five o'clock now, three hours since her class ended. Currently, there's another class in session, but according to the sign posted outside the door, this class is taught by the same professor.

Tyler wastes no time knocking on the door, interrupting the professor mid-sentence.

The professor, a clean-cut guy in his mid-thirties, opens the door and sticks his head through the opening. "Do you mind? We're in the middle of class."

Out of habit, Tyler starts to reach into his jacket pocket for his badge, but then he stops himself. "I apologize for the interruption. You're Professor Baker?"

"Yes." The man looks from Tyler to me. "What's this about?"

Tyler can't rely on his affiliation with the police department to demand information, so I step in. "Professor, we're sorry for the interruption, but it's urgent. I'm Ian Alexander, Layla's brother. She's in your one o'clock class."

The man frowns. "Layla? Is everything okay? I was surprised when she missed class today. It's not like her to be absent. I hope she's not sick."

"She missed class?" I ask. *Shit.* She's been missing longer than we realized.

"Yes," the man says. Abruptly, he stops himself. "I'm sorry, but I really can't talk to you about this, not without Layla's permission. Student privacy laws, you know."

Tyler nods as he jots something down in his notebook. "Thanks for your time."

As the professor returns to his lecturing, Tyler consults my notes on the rest of Layla's class schedule.

We end up working our way backward through her schedule, locating each classroom and then trying to track down each of her professors—psychology, English, history, biology. Half of them are still on campus, and the other half have gone for the day. But the ones we speak to all give the same response.

Layla wasn't in class today.

I feel sick as the implication sinks in. She's been missing for *hours*, if not all day. I can't even bear to think about where she is, or what's happening to her. God, she must be terrified. "Tyler, what if she—"

"Ian, don't go there. You'll drive yourself crazy." Tyler pulls out his phone and makes a call. "Martin, I need the contact information for Layla's bodyguard. His home address, phone number, anything you can get from the agency."

We head back to the car, and by the time we're buckled in and ready to leave campus, my dad calls back with the information Tyler asked for. I write it all down in the notebook.

"Call Sean's number," Tyler tells me.

I try, but my call goes to voicemail. "Straight to voicemail."

"You have his address?"

"Yes." As I rattle it off, Tyler frowns. "Why the scowl?" I ask him.

"That's a rough neighborhood. I would expect Sean to be able to afford something better."

When we locate Sean's apartment, Tyler parks in front of a four-unit, beige concrete building, two apartments on the ground floor and two above. Two of the first-floor windows are boarded up with plywood decorated with graffiti. Trash cans on the side of the building are overflowing, and there's an abandoned sofa in the front yard.

Tyler points toward the spray-painted markings on the windows. "Those are gang symbols," he says as he withdraws his gun from his holster and checks the magazine. "Stay in the car and lock the doors. Honk if there's any trouble."

I reach for my door handle. "I'm coming with you."

Tyler gives me an exasperated look. "Ian, no."

"I'm not waiting in the car. We're doing this together." I open my door and step out.

Looking far from happy, Tyler gets out of the car and locks it with his key fob. "Then stay close behind me."

I follow him along the broken sidewalk to the front entrance, where the door hangs crookedly on broken hinges.

Tyler pushes me behind him as he pries the door open and peers inside the dimly lit building.

I follow right on his heels, immediately getting a strong whiff of urine. "This place reeks. I can't believe Sean lives here."

We head upstairs to Sean's apartment, 2B. The hallway is littered with old newspapers, fast food containers, and empty beer cans.

Tyler knocks on the door. "Chicago PD. Open up!" When there's no response, he pounds on the door. "Chicago PD! Open the door!"

Still no response.

Tyler reaches into his jacket and withdraws a black leather wallet, which he flips open. Inside are several slender picks that resemble tiny instruments of torture. He sticks one of the picks into the door lock, moves it around a bit, and then a moment later, the knob turns. He pushes the door open.

The apartment is a mess, with clothes and trash strewn across every surface. The coffee table's glass top is streaked with white residue.

"Somebody's doing drugs," I say, stating the obvious.

Tyler checks the kitchen and pantry, then nods down the apartment's only hallway. "It doesn't look like anyone's here, but let's do a quick sweep. Stay with me."

We search the first bedroom, then a tiny, outdated bathroom.

There's a closed door at the end of the hallway, and as we approach, Tyler raises a hand, signaling for me to be quiet and stand back against the wall. He reaches for the doorknob, turns it, and slowly pushes the door wide open.

The room is dark and dank, the curtains drawn to block out daylight. Light from the hallway shines into the room, illuminating a small sliver of the floor. As Tyler steps into the room, I follow right behind him. The bed is unmade. The burgundy carpet is littered with trash, and there's a mountain of clothes piled on the bed, next to an open suitcase. It looks like someone might have been packing.

When Tyler freezes, I notice there's something lying on the floor at the foot of the bed, mostly hidden from view. All we can see is a shoe.

"What is that?" I don't know why I'm whispering, because we're the only ones here.

Tyler flips on the room's single light. I follow him as he walks to the foot of the bed to get a better view.

Jesus, it's a body. A man. And he's clearly dead.

Sheer relief rushes through me, making me lightheaded. *It's not Layla.*

I take a closer look at the victim's blond hair. "My god, is that Sean? What the hell?"

"Don't touch anything," Tyler warns. He grabs a pair of latex gloves from his jacket pocket and pulls them on before he crouches beside the body and rolls it over.

We both stare down at Sean Dickerson's lifeless eyes. There's a hole in the center of his forehead. There's also a huge blood stain in the center of his chest, soaking his T-shirt.

That's when I notice the pool of blood beneath him, partially camouflaged by the dark burgundy carpet. "My god."

Tyler rises to his feet. "We have to go before the cops arrive. I'm surprised they didn't beat us here."

"Shouldn't we call 911 first? We can't just leave him here."

I see a flash of indecision cross Tyler's face before he shakes his head. "There's nothing we can do for Sean now. Let the cops do their jobs and find him themselves. Besides, if they know we're here, it will only complicate our efforts to find Layla."

"All right." He's right about Sean. And our first priority has to be finding Layla.

On our way out of the apartment, Tyler stops to rifle through a stack of unopened mail lying on the coffee table. He snags an envelope and tucks it into his jacket pocket.

"What'd you take?" I ask him.

"A pay stub for someone by the name of Chad Faulkner. I'm guessing it belongs to Sean's roommate as it's addressed to this apartment. It came from Tillerson Packaging—I know where that is. Let's go pay Chad a visit."

We drive across town to Tillerson Packaging, which turns out to be a manufacturer of food packaging supplies. Their building is located in an industrial park, and apparently second shift is in full force as the employee parking lot is filled with cars. Attached to the ugly gray manufacturing plant is a single-story white building.

Tyler checks his watch. "The administrative offices are closed by now, but the plant's open. Let's see what we can find out."

We park in a visitor lot and walk around to the back of the two-story factory. At a rear entrance, two middle-age men and an older woman congregate near a designated smoking shack.

Tyler approaches them without hesitation. "Do any of you know Chad Faulkner?"

They eye us warily.

The woman, a sixty-something with a short cap of white hair, nods. "What about him? I don't suppose you're here from the child support agency." She laughs.

The two men say nothing.

"No," Tyler says. "Chicago PD."

The woman narrows her eyes at Tyler. "Where's your badge?" She looks past Tyler to me. "And what do you want with Chad?" She sounds more curious than suspicious.

"Do you know if he's here now?" Tyler nods toward the open rear door that leads to the factory floor, which is bustling with activity.

She shakes her head. "No. He came in for first shift early this morning but left a couple hours later. Said he wasn't feeling well. What's it to you?"

"We're hoping he can help us find someone," Tyler says.

"Are you really a cop?" one of the men says. "You never showed us a badge."

Tyler grins. "Sorry, I left it in my other jacket." Then he turns to the woman. "I'll tell you what we want with Chad. His room-mate is dead. We thought he'd want to know."

The woman's pale blue eyes widen in surprise. "You mean Sean?"

Tyler nods.

"Holy shit," she says. "How'd he die?"

"He was murdered."

Tyler walks away without another word, and I follow. I have a new level of respect for my badass boyfriend. He's ballsy and clever. "If he is here," I say, "they'll run to tell Chad about Sean, and then he'll rush home."

Tyler nods. "It's a long shot, but yeah. That's the hope." Half-way across the parking lot, he stops dead in his tracks. "Ian, is that Layla's car?" He points to the next row over.

A bright red Fiat stands out like a sore thumb, sandwiched between a dark-blue Ford pickup truck and an older model silver Buick.

"Shit," I say as I race toward the car.

I don't even need to read the license plate number to know it's hers. There's a familiar pair of fuzzy pink dice hanging from the rearview mirror. I walk up to the driver's window and peer inside the car. There's nothing out of place in the front seat, but her backpack is lying on the backseat, open, the contents spilling out. When I spot her earbuds lying on the seat, my heart slams against my ribs.

Her earbuds.

She's never without them.

"Tyler—" My voice breaks. "Her earbuds."

As I reach for the door handle, Tyler stops me. "Don't touch anything," he says. "We don't want to leave any prints."

After pulling on a fresh pair of gloves, Tyler opens the car door, which is unlocked, and searches the car thoroughly—the glove box, under the front seats, above the visors. Then he moves to the backseat, checking every nook and cranny. He finds nothing out of the ordinary, except for her backpack.

"Her wallet is here," he says as he searches the contents of her backpack. "Along with cash and a credit card. She wasn't robbed." He hands me her wallet.

"Maybe he's holding her for a bigger sum," I say, thinking the obvious.

"You mean ransom?"

I nod. "We've always known it was a possibility. It's why we've always had bodyguards. Layla's has access to a small fortune."

Before Tyler can close the car door, I reach in and grab her earbuds. "These are coming with me. When we find her, she'll need them."

↝ 23

Ian Alexander

I want to scream. My sister is out there somewhere, and god knows what's happening to her. She must be terrified. And my god, what if someone has hurt her—I can't even contemplate the possibility.

We don't know where she is, or who has her. Or what they're doing to her. I try not to think about the possibilities, but it's hard not to.

My legs are shaking uncontrollably, my hands clenched on my lap. Tyler keeps glancing at me out of the corner of his eye, which tells me he's not just worried about Layla; he's also worried about me. He reaches over and clasps my hands.

As I stare out the front passenger window of Tyler's car, I listen to Tyler's phone conversation with my dad. They're on speaker.

He tells my dad about finding Sean's body, about Chad, and the fact that we found Layla's car at Chad's workplace. "Since Sean is dead, and Layla's car is here, we have to assume Chad either has her or knows who does."

In hindsight, I blame myself. Layla complained time and time again about Sean. She told me she didn't like him, how uncomfortable he made her feel. I chalked her concerns up to the fact that she's an independent young twenty-something who doesn't like being told what to do. But now I realize it was more than that. Her instincts were telling her something, and I didn't listen.

None of us did.

And now she's paying the price.

Tyler ends the call with my dad and pockets his phone. "Let's go," he says as he starts the engine.

Before he can back out of the parking spot, there's a knock on the driver's window. It's the woman we spoke to earlier. She looks... conflicted.

Tyler lowers his window. "Yes?"

"What do you really want with Chad?" the woman asks. "I'm Loretta, by the way."

Tyler glances at me, then back at the woman. "Loretta, a young woman is missing." He nods to me. "His sister. We're trying to find her, and we think Chad knows where she is."

She frowns as she bites her lip. "Like I said, he was here for first shift. He said he was going out for a smoke break, and when he came back in, he was agitated. Really antsy. A few minutes later, he said he was sick and had to go home."

"What time was that?" Tyler asks.

The woman thinks about it. "It was before lunch, maybe ten o'clock."

"Do you know if Chad is involved in any illegal activities? Is he using drugs? Selling them? Anything?"

"He does coke. And there are rumors that he deals out of this plant. I've never seen it myself, but I've heard others talk about it. But there's something else."

"What?" Tyler says.

"Today, I went out to my car on my lunch break. I usually eat in my car where it's quiet so I can read. While I was sitting in my car, I saw Chad pull into the parking lot. At first, I thought he must be feeling better and had returned to work. But when he got out of his car, he wasn't alone. He had a girl with him. They stopped to talk to one of the shift managers—Larry Johnson."

I lean across the center console, toward the open driver's window. "What did she look like?"

"Young, really pretty, with long black hair and dark eyes. She seemed out of it, like she was stoned or drunk. Chad and Mr. Johnson were arguing. I couldn't hear what they were saying, but it was definitely heated. Chad had his hand on the girl's arm, practically holding her upright. Then Mr. Johnson took her from him and put her in the backseat of his car. Chad got in the front passenger seat, and they drove off together."

"Do you know the make and model of the manager's car?" Tyler asks.

She shakes her head. "All I know is it's black and expensive."

"Thank you." Tyler pulls out his wallet and hands the woman a business card and some cash. "Here's my number, Loretta. If you think of anything else, or if you see Chad, please call me."

She nods as she glances at his card. "Detective," she says, and then she pockets the card. "You should have led with that, handsome. I'll call you if I hear anything."

After she leaves, Tyler raises his window and sits staring out through the front windshield. After a moment, he glances at me. "You okay?"

"No." My voice is tight, and I have a death grip on the door handle. "She's out there, Tyler, and who knows what's happening to her."

Tyler reaches over and grasps my hand. "You can't think like that, Ian. You have to stay focused on the here and now—on what we *can* do for her. Otherwise you'll fall apart, and you won't be able to help her." Tyler pulls out his wallet and counts his cash. "How much money do you have on you?"

"I usually carry a couple hundred bucks. Why?"

"I only have a hundred. We'll need more. Let's go find an ATM."

"What for?"

"We need cash so we can bribe someone in Tillerson's security office. We need to find out the make and model of Larry Johnson's car."

Tyler starts the engine and backs out of the parking space, and we go in search of a bank.

* * *

After we locate the closest automatic teller machine, we both withdraw the maximum amount of cash allowed. We return to Tillerson Packaging and park in the visitor lot next to the security building.

"It's amazing what you can learn from watching surveillance video," Tyler says, as we approach the company's security office, which is little more than a freestanding shack located in the parking lot.

Tyler raps on the door, and a uniformed security guard answers.

"Chicago PD," Tyler says. "I'd like to ask you some questions."

The guard opens the door to let us in. He stares at me curiously, probably wondering who the hell I am. I'm certainly not dressed like a cop.

"Where's your badge?" the guard asks Tyler.

Tyler ignores the question. "I need to see your parking lot surveillance video from earlier today, approximately eleven-thirty am to one pm."

The guard's brow furrows. "Do you have a warrant? You can't just barge in here—"

Tyler pulls out his wallet and counts out five crisp hundred-dollar bills. "Here's my warrant. Bring up the footage, then go take a bathroom break. We'll be gone before you get back."

The guy eyes Tyler with a great deal of suspicion, but then he grabs the cash and sticks the wad of money in his front trouser pocket. "Fine," he grumbles.

He sits down at the video console and scrubs back through the day's footage to the requested time mark. "You better not be here when I get back," he says as he rises. Without another word, he walks out, leaving us alone.

Tyler sits at the console and quickly scans the footage as I watch over his shoulder.

"There!" I say, pointing at the screen as Layla's Fiat enters the picture.

We follow the path of her car as it pulls into a parking spot next to a black sedan.

"That's a Mercedes," Tyler says as he retrieves his notebook and pen. Then he zooms in on the vehicle's license plate and jots down the number.

I stare in horror at the grainy footage as a man in his mid-thirties drags Layla out of the backseat of the Fiat. If it weren't for the guy holding her up, she would have collapsed on the pavement. "Jesus, look at her. Is she drugged?"

"Most likely," Tyler says.

We watch the rest of the interaction between the two men as they argue, both of them gesturing wildly. As Loretta said, after Johnson puts Layla in the backseat of his car, Chad gets in the front passenger seat and they drive off.

Just as Tyler had promised, we're gone from the security office before the guard returns.

"Now what?" I ask as we hurry back to Tyler's car.

"We need to find Larry Johnson. I suspect Chad's just a middleman. Johnson will lead us to Layla."

Tyler pulls out his phone and makes a call. "Jud, I need you to run a plate for me." He listens to the captain's reply. "I know that," Tyler replies tersely. "The plate, Jud. Please. I'm asking you to do this for me as a personal favor. I need the address." Another pause. "I understand that."

Tyler ends the call, and we sit.

"What was that about?" I ask. There was something in the tone of his voice that concerns me.

Tyler shakes his head dismissively. "It's nothing you need to worry about."

My stomach knots as I realize Tyler's hiding something from me.

His phone rings, and Tyler takes the call. "Yes?" He jots something down in his notebook. "Thanks, Jud." And then he ends the call and starts the engine.

"You got his address?" I ask.

"Yes."

We drive north to an affluent section of Lincoln Park. Tyler drives slowly down a residential street, past one gated residence after another. He slows to a crawl as we pass a stately, red-brick two-story. Through the open wrought-iron gate, we spot a black Mercedes parked in the open garage.

It's quite a domestic scene. Three teenage boys are shooting hoops in the driveway, while a woman waters flowerboxes on the front porch.

Tyler keeps driving and parks a couple of houses away. "Looks like Larry Johnson does all right for himself," he says as he shuts off the engine. "Now we wait."

I reach for my door handle. "I'm going over there. Layla might be—"

Tyler grabs my hand. "She's not here, Ian. Not at the guy's house. He must have taken her somewhere else. We just have to wait for him to show us where."

"I can't just sit here—"

"Yes, you can. The last thing we want to do is tip him off. We have to watch and wait. He'll take us to her."

That is, if she's still alive, I think. But I don't dare voice my fears.

ℰ 24

Tyler Jamison

Ian's a nervous wreck, about ready to jump out of his skin, and I can't say I blame him. His mind is working overtime imagining all the horrible things that could be happening to Layla. I don't let myself think about it. I can't. I have a sister, too. So I shut that part of my brain off and focus on what needs to be done.

As darkness falls, my pulse rate picks up. I'm counting on Johnson to lead us to Layla, but I could be wrong. It's possible she's dead and he's already disposed of her body. But I can't allow myself to think that way. He's going to take us to her.

If he doesn't, the chances of us finding her alive will dwindle quickly. And finding her any other way just isn't an option.

At nine-thirty, the Mercedes pulls out of the driveway and turns right.

"There!" Ian says, pointing. "He's leaving."

"I see him." As soon as the Mercedes is out of sight, I make a U-turn and follow. I just hope it's Johnson behind the wheel and not his wife or one of his kids. It's too dark for me to see who's driving.

The Mercedes hops onto Lake Shore Drive and heads south, back toward the south suburbs. I keep pace with the vehicle, careful not to lose him in Chicago's congested traffic.

"What if he realizes we're following him?" Ian asks.

"Black sedans are a dime a dozen in Chicago. He won't notice."

I follow when the Mercedes pulls off an exit. We're driving through a shit part of town now, rundown and depressed. If someone's conducting criminal operations, this is the place to do it.

I glance at Ian, who's gripping the door handle. Every inch of him radiates tension. I hate that he's here with me right now, because I have no idea what we might walk into, but leaving him at home would have been even riskier. At least by keeping him with me, I know where he is and what he's doing.

Johnson pulls through an open chain-link gate into the parking lot of what looks to be an abandoned warehouse covered in gang graffiti. I spot two unmarked white work vans parked inside the loading bay of a cavernous brick building. The Mercedes parks in front of a side door. It's dark out, and I can just barely make out Larry Johnson as he gets out of his car and walks inside the building.

I park across the street beneath a broken streetlight and shut off the engine.

"Now what do we do?" Ian whispers.

Despite the severity of the situation, I smile and reach for his hand. "Now we wait."

"For what?"

"For an idea of what's going on. I think there's more here than we realize."

A few minutes later, another car pulls into the lot and parks next to Johnson's Mercedes. Two men get out of the vehicle, and one of them pulls what looks like an unconscious woman out of the backseat, throws her over his shoulder, and disappears inside the building.

Shit. The enormity of what we're witnessing hits me. This isn't just a kidnapping. This is human trafficking. I reach for my phone and call Jud.

He answers immediately. "Tyler, what the hell's going on?"

"I think we found Layla at an abandoned warehouse on the south side. It appears we've uncovered a human trafficking ring. I just watched a man carry an unconscious woman into the building. I think there's a good chance Layla Alexander is here, too. Possibly more women." I give him the address.

"I'm sending units and a SWAT team," Jud says. "Tyler, you

need to get out of there. You can't be seen. Let us take it from here."

I end the call, not wanting to waste time arguing with Jud. There's no way in hell we're leaving—not without knowing if Layla is in there and what her condition is. Ian would never stand for it and, frankly, neither would I.

After I tuck my phone into my jacket pocket, I reach for Ian's hand. "SWAT is on their way. Now we sit tight."

Ian has a death grip on my hand as he stares at the building, his gaze pained. His chest rises and falls, hard and fast. I know this waiting is killing him.

"I should have taken her concerns about Sean more serious-ly," he says quietly, so much self-recrimination in his voice. "If only I'd listened to her."

I turn to face him, but he's hidden in the shadows. I doubt it's a coincidence that the streetlights on this block are all out. I'm sure the bulbs were intentionally destroyed.

"Whatever happens," I tell him, "it's not your fault. We all wish we'd done better for Layla. Right now, let's just focus on finding her."

"If it's a trafficking situation, then she's probably still alive, right?" he says, sounding hopeful.

"Right."

Moments later, headlights blind us as a half-dozen police cars arrive on scene and surround the warehouse. They come in silently, no blaring sirens to tip off the traffickers. A tactical van pulls in behind the squad cars, driving right through the open gate. The rear door of the van opens, and a unit dressed in night combat gear disperses and approaches the building in tight formation.

Almost immediately, we hear a volley of gunshots.

Ian lifts his door handle, but I reach over and capture his hand. "Not yet."

"What if she gets hurt in the raid? What if—"

I bring his hand to my mouth and kiss his knuckles. "Have faith, baby. These guys know what they're doing. They're trained for this, and they're her best chance for survival. If we walk into that melee, we're likely to get shot."

I notice someone in uniform walking across the street in our direction. "That's Jud," I say. I open my car door and meet him halfway. A moment later, Ian's right beside me.

"You shouldn't be here, Tyler," Jud says, scowling at me. He glances at Ian, then back at me.

I shake my head. "Forget it, Jud. I'm in this to the end."

"I won't be able to help you."

I take Ian's hand. "This is a family matter, Jud. I've made my choice."

Nodding, Jud sighs in resignation. "You're just like your father. He would have said the same thing—and to hell with the consequences." Jud reaches out and pats my arm. "At least stay back until we've cleared the building." He nods toward Ian. "We don't need both of the judge's kids in harm's way."

As Jud walks back toward the scene, Ian says, "What's he talking about? What consequences?"

I watch as Jud engages in a heated conversation with the leader of the SWAT team.

Ian grabs my arm. "What did he mean, Tyler?"

Shit. I really don't want to get into this with him right now, but I can't lie to him. "He means I shouldn't be here. It's a violation of my suspension."

Before I can say more, we hear a volley of gunfire coming from within the building. Ian flinches.

The shots go on for several moments until there's a sudden deafening silence. Just as Jud and a few other law enforcement leads head into the building, a caravan of ambulances arrives on scene, and the medical techs quickly exit their vehicles and begin unloading gurneys.

Ian breaks loose from me and sprints toward the warehouse.

"Ian, wait!" I chase after him, but he's got a decent head start on me.

I follow him into the building, which is nothing short of chaos. There are dead bodies lining the corridor—all apparently traffickers.

A member of the SWAT team blocks Ian's path.

"I'm looking for my sister," Ian yells as he tries to push past the officer.

"Sorry, buddy," the guy says. "No civilians."

"Is the building secured?" Jud asks as he comes up behind us.

The officer nods. "Yes, sir. All clear."

"Then let him through," Jud says. "Let them both through."

The officer steps back to let us pass. "At the end of the hall, turn right," he calls after us. "The girls are in the offices all up and down that hallway."

Ian and I stop at the first office we come to. The door is open and two SWAT team members are using bolt cutters to remove the handcuffs securing two naked African American teens to the bedframes of two single beds.

In the next room, another officer is freeing two more young women—a blonde and an Asian—similarly naked and cuffed to bedframes.

Ian moves to the next room and the next. "Layla!" he yells. "Layla!"

We stop at two more offices, each containing two girls. Two Latinas, an Asian, and an African American girl.

As Ian moves frantically to the next room, my skin starts to crawl.

It's possible she's not here. It's possible we're too late.

"Layla!" Ian yells as he moves to yet another room.

The long corridor is filled with teams of paramedics. Numerous gurneys appear. The young women are weak, tired, and scared. They're likely dehydrated and possibly drugged to keep them more manageable.

Ian races to the last office and charges inside. I'm right behind him, prepared to help him deal with whatever he finds.

But he comes up short. There's just one bed in this room, and it's empty. The blood-stained sheets have been yanked off the mattress and strewn on the floor, along with a filthy pillow. There are bloodstains on the soiled mattress. A metal chair lies toppled over beside the bed.

Ian turns to me, his eyes raw with pain. "She's not here. I was so sure she'd be here. Layla!" Ian screams so loud his voice cracks.

Suddenly, we hear a rattling... the sound of metal clanging against metal, followed by a muffled sob.

Ian drops to the floor and peers beneath the bed. "She's here, Tyler! She's here."

I rush to the other side of the bed and crouch down to find Layla huddled beneath it. She's naked and her hair is a tangled mess, hanging limply in her face. She stares at me, her dark eyes glassy and unfocused. She resembles a wild animal that's been cornered.

"Layla, it's okay," I say in a low voice. "It's me, Tyler." I reach for her, but she scuttles back. Her right wrist, rubbed raw and bleeding, is cuffed to the bed frame, preventing her escape. There's a ball gag in her mouth, and her lips are cracked and bloody, her chin stained with dry blood. Like a wild animal trying to escape a trap, she yanks on her cuffed wrist, trying in vain to pull free.

Ian lies on the floor and extends his hand to her. "Layla, sweetie, it's okay. We're here."

I'm shocked by the crazed look in her eyes. "Ian, she doesn't recognize us." *Jesus, how could anyone do this?*

Ian tries again, his voice gentle. "Layla? It's me, Ian. I'm here. Come out, sweetie. It's okay—you're safe."

She scuttles back, as far from us as she can go given that she's cuffed to the bed. Tears stream down her filthy cheeks, and she mumbles behind the gag.

"Did you find her?" Jud asks as he walks into the room.

"Yes," I say. "She's cuffed to the bed."

Jud turns around and walks toward the door. "I'll get the bolt cutters."

I pull out my phone and send a quick text to Martin.

Tyler: We found her. She's alive.

"Ian, keep distracting her," I say, as I move into position. She's trying so hard to get away from Ian that she's not paying me any attention. When she's within reach, I grab her. "I've got her."

As I carefully pull her out from beneath the bed, careful to protect her cuffed wrist attached to the metal bedframe, Ian crawls across the mattress to our side. Layla is fighting for her life, kicking and thrashing. She manages to land a few good blows against my chest and shoulder.

"Careful of her wrist," I tell Ian as I sit her down on the bed.

We can see now just how badly her wrist is damaged, the skin bloody and torn from struggling against the handcuffs.

She fights madly, clearly not aware of who we are.

Ian struggles to restrain her. "Remove the gag," he says.

I gingerly unfasten the leather strap and pry the ball from her mouth.

Immediately, she begins screaming, blood-curdling wails of terror that echo throughout the room. *That explains the ball gag.* They were using it to keep her quiet.

"Layla, it's me," Ian says, his voice breaking as he holds her to him. "It's Ian. I'm here."

She starts rocking mindlessly, her tangled hair hanging in her face, obscuring her vision. There are countless bruises covering her body, as well as smears of blood. I'm not entirely sure if the blood is hers or someone else's. There's blood on her chest and thighs and belly. She might have been raped, but it's impossible to know at this point.

Ian skims her battered body. "Her insulin pump and glucose monitor are gone." He struggles to shuck off his jacket, and I step in to help him.

I hand his jacket to him, and he drapes it over her. The screaming has stopped, and now she's whimpering like a wounded animal, clutching the jacket to her as she huddles beneath it.

Jud returns a moment later with the bolt cutters. As he cuts her free, she screams.

Layla covers her ears. "Stop it! Shut up! Shut up!" she screams, her voice raw.

Ian pulls her earbuds out of his pocket and sticks them in her ears. Then he connects them to his phone via Bluetooth. "This might help," he says, turning on a music app. "I've got a copy of her favorite playlist."

Immediately, she stills.

A paramedic enters the room, takes one look at Layla, and opens his med kit. "What do we know about this one?"

"She's a type one diabetic and paranoid schizophrenic," Ian says. "Her glucose monitor and insulin pump are missing."

As the paramedic reaches for her uninjured wrist to check her pulse, Layla jerks her arm free and struggles to get away.

Ian tightens his hold on her. "It's okay, Layla. He's trying to help you."

Out in the hallway, it's utter chaos. There are cops, detectives, SWAT team members, and paramedics rushing from room to room. Orders are shouted in gruff, brisk voices, and girls are crying.

Layla is still highly agitated. Ian is doing an admirable job of holding himself together as he tries to get through to her.

He looks directly into her eyes and brushes the hair back from her bruised and filthy face. "It's me, sis. You're safe now. We've got you."

I doubt she's making sense of anything he's saying.

My phone, which I put on silent, has been vibrating nonstop with repeated calls. I finally take a second to glance at the caller ID. It's Martin. I step out of the room to take his call.

"Tyler, please tell me my baby girl is okay."

"She's alive, Martin. An EMT is assessing her now. Her insulin pump is missing, and she's struggling emotionally. Ian's doing his best to try to calm her. She'll be taken to Cook County Hospital. You and Ruth should meet us there."

"Right. We're leaving now. Tyler—"

"Yeah?"

"I—*we*—" His voice breaks, and I hear a muffled cry as Ruth sobs in the background.

"It's okay, Martin," I tell him. My heart is hurting for both of them. "We'll meet you at the hospital."

"Thank you." And then he ends the call.

I step back into the room just as the paramedic administers an injection in Layla's thigh.

"He's giving her insulin," Ian says. "Her blood sugar levels are through the roof."

"I just spoke to your parents. They'll meet us at the hospital."

Ian nods as he rocks his sister in his arms. With one hand, he cradles the back of her head as she leans into his chest. His other arm is wrapped tightly around her.

I know he's not going to leave her side for a good long while. "You ride in the ambulance with your sister. I'll follow in the car."

Ian glances up at me, his emotions obvious in his eyes. His gaze locks onto mine, communicating far more than mere words ever could. *You saved her. You saved me.*

"Thank you," he whispers. "I knew you'd find her."

25

Ian Alexander

I about lose it when I see my parents walk hand-in-hand into the ER waiting room. I've never seen them looking so distraught. They're usually both so calm and collected. They stop and scan the room, and when they spot us, they rush over.

My mom pulls me into her arms, and then we're both crying.

"We found her, Mom," I say. "We found her."

As my dad hugs me tightly, Tyler stands nearby, keeping one eye on us as he talks quietly with his police captain.

"She's being examined now," I tell my parents. "They had to

sedate her because she was hysterical."

"When can we see her?" my mom asks, her voice shaking.

I shrug. "I don't know. They're trying to determine exactly what injuries she has—there was a lot of blood on her, so it was hard to tell. And they're having someone come in to do a psych evaluation."

My mother pales. "I need to see her." She turns her pained gaze to my dad, who's just as shaken, and clutches his arm. "Martin, please do something. I need to see her."

"I know, honey," he says as he pats my mom's hand. "I'll go talk to someone. But first—" He extends his hand to Tyler.

They shake, and then my dad pulls Tyler in for a hug. "We can never thank you enough, Tyler. There just aren't words."

"You don't have to thank me, sir."

My dad tears up. "I was wrong about you, Tyler. I'm sorry. I hope you can forgive me."

"Already have," Tyler says.

My heart swells with emotion at seeing my dad open up to Tyler this way. I knew he'd come around eventually, but I didn't realize how much it would mean to me until I saw it with my own eyes.

My mom hugs Tyler, too, as fresh tears stream down her cheeks. "Thank you for finding my baby," she says.

The automatic entry doors to the ER open, and Beth and Shane walk in, accompanied by Sam and Cooper. Tyler meets his sister halfway, and the two of them hug.

"That's Tyler's sister, Beth," I tell my parents. "And that's her husband, Shane McIntyre."

My dad nods. "McIntyre Security. I've heard of them."

After all the introductions are made, we continue our vigil, waiting for Layla's doctor to call my parents back. My father paces anxiously. Beth talks my mom into sitting down with her.

Tyler brings me a cup of something hot from a vending machine. "Here. Drink this before you fall down."

I take a sniff of something that smells really good, then a hesitant sip. "Mm." Peppermint hot chocolate. "Can you be any more perfect?"

He grins. "We missed lunch and dinner. I don't want you passing out."

I look at Tyler—really look at him. He's exhausted, too. He's worked tirelessly since we got the word that Layla was missing. He jumped into action and did what he does best—unravel a mystery and track down those responsible.

I reach out and touch his hair. "You saved my sister. In fact, you saved my whole family."

He catches my hand and holds it to his chest. "It was a joint effort. You were there with me every step of the way." He rubs the back of my hand with his thumb. "How are you holding up? Are you okay?"

I nod, but I don't trust myself to speak. I've done enough crying today. "She's going to be okay, right?"

He nods. "She'll be okay. We'll make sure of it."

I glance across the waiting room to see my father deep in conversation with Shane and Cooper. Sam is sitting with Beth and my mom. In spite of the traumatic circumstances, I'm glad to see our respective families are coming together.

A nurse opens the door leading to the examination area. "For Layla?"

My parents jump to attention, and Tyler and I join them as they're escorted back into the emergency ward.

We're met by Dr. Crawford, a petite brunette wearing a white lab coat and neon green running shoes. She stops us in the hallway outside one of the exam rooms. "Layla is still sedated," she tells us. "We've given her a new insulin pump, and her blood sugar levels are under control. Her blood alcohol level was quite high, but it's coming down. She's stabilized now, and we'll wake her soon. We'd like for you to be with her when we do, so she'll see some familiar faces. We're trying to keep her as calm and comfortable as possible."

My father's expression darkens. "Alcohol? She never drinks—what exactly did they do to her?"

"The good news is, there's no sign of sexual assault," Dr. Crawford says. "Neither vaginal nor anal."

"Jesus," my dad mutters as he pulls Mom close.

The doctor continues. "She has bruises and lacerations from being beaten and restrained. Her bloodwork shows the presence of alcohol and Rohypnol—the date rape drug. Also cocaine. She's going to be okay physically, but the emotional repercussions are likely to be significant. Right now, that's our main concern. We've already consulted with her psychiatrist, who's coming in to do an evaluation."

"Can I see her?" my mom asks.

Dr. Crawford nods to my parents. "Yes, both of you can come into the room. We'll wake her shortly." The doctor smiles apologetically at me and Tyler. "I think two visitors is enough for now, until we see how she's doing."

Mom turns to me. "Go home and rest, honey. Your dad and I will stay with Layla." Then she glances past me at Tyler. "Take him home, will you, Tyler? He looks like he's about to collapse."

"I will," Tyler says from behind me. He lays his hands on my shoulders and draws me back against his chest. "Let's go, sunshine."

I grin at the nickname, and my mom smiles at us.

$\backsim$ 26

Tyler Jamison

It's two in the morning by the time we get home from the hospital. We head straight upstairs and hit the bathroom to pee and brush our teeth. After showering, we climb into bed, both of us dead on our feet.

Ian turns to me, laying his head on my chest and hugging my waist. "I can't believe any of this," he murmurs. "It's unreal."

I lay my arm over his, my fingers clutching his forearm. "I saw your dad talking to Shane tonight. And just as we were leaving, I saw Jason Miller arrive at the hospital. He's one of Shane's guys—a former paramedic, now a bodyguard. I think your sister has a new protector."

"I don't know if she'll be able to trust anyone now."

"I'll call Jud in the morning and see if I can find out more about what happened and who was behind it. I hate being out of the loop like this."

"You're in trouble for what we did today, aren't you? How bad?"

I hesitate to tell him the truth because he's dealing with enough right now. He doesn't need to know I willfully flushed my twenty-plus-year career in law enforcement down the toilet today. "Don't worry, it's fine." Then I tip his face up to mine and kiss him.

"Tyler, I don't want you to get in trouble because of—"

"Ian, shut up and kiss me."

And he does.

* * *

The next morning, we shower and dress, then make breakfast together. While we're eating, my phone rings. "It's Jud."

"We apprehended Chad Faulkner and Larry Johnson last night," he says. "Faulkner confessed to killing Sean Dickerson. He also confessed to selling Layla to Johnson."

"Jesus."

"As it turns out," he continues, "Sean owed a lot of money to Chad, who was his dealer in addition to being his roommate. Chad was putting increasing pressure on Sean to pay up, so

Sean offered to trade Layla to Chad in lieu of payment. When Sean demanded cash from Chad to finance his getaway, Chad balked. The two fought, and Chad killed Sean. Chad then sold Layla up the chain to Johnson. We got to those girls just in time, Tyler. Johnson had planned to move all twelve of them out of the city last night." Jud pauses. "You did good work yesterday, Tyler."

"Thank you," I say, although I'm under no mistaken impression that my actions last night will change the outcome.

"You saved those girls—all of them. But I'm afraid that's not going to matter when it comes to the consequences of violating the terms of your suspension. Internal Affairs is already writing you up. There's nothing I can do, Tyler. The rules are clear, and my hands are tied. I'm sorry."

"I expected as much. Hey, I did what I had to do, and I'd do it all over again."

"Your dad would be so damn proud of you, son."

"Thanks. That means a lot, Jud."

"You'll always be family to me. So, ponder what you're going to do next. It sounds like it's time for a career change."

I smile at Ian, who's sitting across the table from me, listening to my half of the conversation and trying to figure out what's being said. I extend my arm across the table, and Ian smiles as he takes my hand. "Thanks, Jud. I appreciate everything."

"You're in trouble because of what we did, aren't you?" Ian asks when the call ends.

"Yes."

He squeezes my hand. "I'm so sorry."

"Don't be. I knew the choice I was making."

"Are you going to lose your job?"

I nod. "Yeah."

Ian looks shocked. "I—god, I don't know what to say. I—"

"You don't have to say anything, Ian. I don't regret any of it. You'll always come first. Jobs are replaceable, you aren't. Your sister isn't."

* * *

That evening, we return to the hospital to visit Layla, who has been moved into a private suite in the psych ward. As we approach her room, I'm not surprised to see Jason Miller standing guard outside her door.

I'm glad Martin took my advice and hired one of Shane's guys. Former military, former paramedic, now a bodyguard, Jason has all the skills needed to keep Layla safe and healthy. Plus, he's young enough—in his late twenties—that he'll fit in well with the college crowd. He looks the part, too, with his fit, tattooed body, short dark hair and trim beard.

"Good to see you, Jason," I say, offering him my hand.

"Hello, Tyler."

While Jason and I shake hands, Ian peeks inside Layla's room. The door is partly open, and I can see Martin and Ruth seated beside Layla's bed. Layla lies motionless beneath the covers as she stares at the ceiling. Even from here, I can see that her face

SOMEBODY TO HOLD 251

is covered in bruises. I hate to imagine what those bastards did to her.

After introducing Jason and Ian, I nod in Layla's direction. "So, it's official? You've been assigned to protect Layla?"

Jason nods. "As of oh-three-hundred." He smiles ruefully. "Unfortunately, my new client refuses to let me step foot inside her room."

Ian fights a grin. "Don't take it personally. She's been through an awful ordeal, and I don't think she trusts anyone outside of family right now." And then Ian leaves us to join his sister.

"She'll come around," I tell Jason. "Just give her time."

Jason nods. "Don't worry. I'm a very patient guy, and I have all the time in the world."

When I join the Alexanders, I find Ian sitting on his sister's bed, holding her hand. I notice the tray of untouched food on the dinner cart beside her bed. Ian tries to coax Layla into taking a bite of something, but she refuses.

I stand at the foot of her bed and take in a very bittersweet scene. I know her family is overjoyed to have her back, but they're clearly concerned about her state of mind.

Ian catches my gaze and shakes his head as if to say *she's not okay*.

"Hello, Layla," I say quietly.

She responds by closing her eyes, shutting out everyone in the room. This bruised and battered young woman is nothing like the bubbly Layla I've come to know.

Martin catches my gaze and nods toward the door. I follow

him out into the hallway, and he closes the door behind us.

"She's having a hard time processing what happened to her," he says in hushed tones. "She remembers going to Sean's apartment. She said he and Chad got into an argument, and when Sean demanded money from him, Chad shot him right in front of her. After that, her memories are hazy."

I nod. "When I saw her on video surveillance footage at Chad's workplace, she was clearly incapacitated. She must have been drugged. She couldn't even stand on her own."

Martin looks haunted. "Who knows what those bastards did to her. Even if she wasn't raped, they still hurt her. And those other girls... there's no telling what Layla might have seen or heard. She refuses to talk about what happened in the warehouse."

A moment later, the door to Layla's room opens and Ian joins us in the hall. "She wants to be alone," he says.

I pull him into my arms. "She's going to be okay, Ian. She just needs time."

Jason and I exchange a glance. "You're going to have your work cut out for you," I tell him.

ϐ 27

Ian Alexander

Tyler's court appearance is scheduled for tomorrow, at which time the judge is expected to approve the plea deal and announce the sentence. Tyler assures me he'll get no more than a week or two in the Cook County jail, but I'm not holding my breath. I won't be able to relax until we know for sure.

The two of us are seated on the sofa, our feet up on the coffee table as we binge-watch the new season of Disney's *Mandalorian.*

Tyler lays his arm across my shoulders and pulls me close.

"While I'm away, I want you to stay at the penthouse with Beth and Sam. Or you could stay with your family, if you prefer. I just don't want you staying here alone."

"Why?" I think I know why, but I want to hear it from him.

"Two reasons."

"I'm listening."

"Well, for starters, I'd feel better knowing you were with family, either yours or mine. You need a support system."

"What's the second reason?"

"Turner. It concerns me that you'd be here alone. Knowing what an ass he is, I wouldn't put it past him to come here and harass you. So, either you go stay with someone, or I'll have Miguel come stay here with you."

I run my hand along his thigh, squeezing the firm muscles beneath the denim. "Are you asking me, or telling me?"

He chuckles. "I guess that depends on your answer. I'm hoping you'll agree to my request—in which case I'm asking. But if you don't agree, then I'm *telling* you." His voice hardens. "I don't want you staying here alone, Ian. That's not an option."

I glance at him, studying his handsome profile. "What does it say about me that I get turned on when you get bossy?"

As he turns to face me, his hand comes up to cup my cheek. "It tells me we're well suited for each other, because yes, I can be bossy."

"*Can* be?" I laugh. "How about you *are*? Not that I'm complaining, mind you."

Tyler's hand slides to the back of my neck, gripping me firmly, and he kisses me. His mouth is demanding and insistent. *Swoon.* He sure knows how to get me going. All he has to do is pound his chest or growl at me and I melt.

"I'm a grown man, Tyler," I tell him as I try to keep a straight face. I don't really want to argue with him, but I want to see how he responds when I do. "I don't need you telling me what to do."

Of course, my growing erection is making me out to be a liar.

He notices, and his hand slides from my waist to palm my cock. He runs his hand down my length, and when I moan, he smiles. "Promise me you'll do as I ask and stay with friends or family."

I suck in a breath as I press myself against his palm. I want more. I *need* more. It's crazy what he does to me with just one touch.

His expression softens. "Honestly, Ian, I'd go batshit crazy stuck behind bars if I didn't know you were safe. Would you really do that to me?"

Shit. Now I feel like a total ass. "I'll stay with Beth."

He closes his eyes a moment, clearly relieved. "Thank you. I'll call her and make the arrangements."

I reach for his hand and put it back on my erection.

"You like this?" he says, pressing his palm against me.

I'm already hot and throbbing and needing a lot more than just a touch. It feels so damn good, I can't help moaning as I shamelessly grind against his hand.

He slides his fingers beneath the waistband of my sweats and pushes the fabric down, freeing me. Then his long fingers wrap around me.

"God, yes," I groan as I throw my head back onto the cushions.

* * *

We still haven't heard anything official about Tyler's job. He's expecting a letter any day. The whole thing infuriates me because Tyler saved my sister's life—not just Layla's but the lives of eleven other girls. He should get a freaking medal for that. But no, they're going to fire him. It's so unfair.

I know Tyler has to be heartbroken about losing his job. His career means everything to him. He was put in a difficult position, forced to choose between his job and my sister. "It's so unfair."

Tyler steps up behind me and lays his hands on my hips. "What's unfair?"

"You losing your job." My eyes sting, and I blink away tears. "What are you going to do next?"

"I've been giving it some thought. Finding Layla and those other girls made me realize how much I like helping people who are at risk. If we hadn't found those girls when we did, they would have been moved out of the city, and who knows if we would have found them. I think of those girls and their families... we impacted a lot of people's lives, Ian. We made a real difference, and not everyone can say that. I'd like to continue making a difference."

"How?"

"Well, I've been thinking about becoming a private investigator. For years now, I've been a homicide detective, investigating *murders.* What if I got involved earlier in the process? If I took on missing persons cases, I'd at least have a chance of finding them alive, before they become another murder statistic."

I pivot to face him. "You'd make a wonderful private eye, and I could help you. I could be your assistant—you know, like Robin to your Batman."

Tyler smiles. "Slow down, baby. I didn't say anything about you doing investigative work. It could get dangerous. You're not trained for that."

"But I could be. I loved helping you find Layla. I think I'd be pretty good at it—certainly I'd make a good assistant." I grab his hand and squeeze. "We could work *together*, Tyler. Just think about it."

He brushes my hair off my forehead. "I'll think about it."

Just the thought of us working on cases together is exhilarating. "This is something I really want to do. And you can teach me what you know. You could even teach me how to handle a gun."

"I would love for us to work together," he says. "I'm sure there are things you could do behind the scenes—research, for example. PI work requires a ton of research."

"You'd be my *boss*," I say, grinning. "You could tell me what to do. You know we both like that."

Laughing, Tyler pulls me into his arms. "All right, we'll figure something out."

* * *

That evening, Tyler and I go to my parents' house to see Layla, who was released from the hospital earlier in the day. When we arrive, we find my mom and dad in the living room, deep in conversation.

"Where's Layla?" I ask.

My mom points at the ceiling. "In her room."

I frown. "How's she doing?"

"She's very withdrawn," Mom says. "She's trying to pretend nothing happened. That can't be good for her."

"I'll try talking to her." I look to Tyler. "Do you want to come up with me?"

"I think you should talk to her alone," he says. "She'd probably feel more comfortable if it was just you. I'll wait here with your parents."

I head upstairs and find Jason seated in an armchair outside my sister's room, reading on a tablet.

"Is she still refusing to talk to you?" I ask him.

Jason nods. "Honestly, I don't blame her. I'm just hanging around hoping she'll change her mind."

I knock on her door. "Layla? It's me."

"Come in," she says.

I step inside her bedroom and close the door behind me.

Layla's sitting on her bed, leaning against a stack of pillows propped against the headboard. She's clutching a pillow, her chin resting on her arms, and her earbuds are in.

I take a seat on the bed. "Hey. How're you doing?"

She lifts her eyes to me, dark eyes that are filled with shadows. "Not so good." She takes out one earbud.

There are a multitude of bruises on her face. I try not to think about how those bruises got there. Or what those cretins might have done to her when she was drugged.

"How are the voices?" I ask.

"Bad. They've been bad since I woke up in the hospital. They say it's all my fault, that I brought this on myself."

"Layla, that's not true." I start to reach for her and stop. "Is it okay if I hug you?"

When she opens her arms, I scoot toward her and draw her close.

She tucks her head beneath my chin. "You saved me. You and Tyler."

"Well, Tyler did most of the saving. I helped, though. It was definitely a team effort."

"Is he here?"

"He's downstairs with Mom and Dad. He didn't want to intrude."

When I release Layla, she leans back against the pillows.

"Do you remember much of what happened?" I ask her.

She swallows hard. "I remember getting in the car with Sean to go to school. He asked me if we could make a stop—he said he needed to get something from his apartment. I didn't want to go because I was afraid I'd be late to class, but he said it would only take a few minutes. We drove to his apartment, and he said I had to come up with him, that he couldn't leave me alone in the car. So I went upstairs with him." Her voice breaks. "I didn't like Sean, but I never wished him harm. Seeing him killed like that—"

She shudders. "I can't believe his roommate shot him. And I can't believe Sean would sell me out like that. If I'd known he owed his roommate money, I could have paid it for him. Instead, he tried to *sell* me. How could he do that? He drugged me, although I can't figure out how."

"Did you drink anything on the way to his apartment?"

She thinks for a moment. "Just the only thing I ever drink— water from my own water bottle."

"He might have put something in your water. Do you remember any of what happened at the warehouse?"

She looks away. "I don't want to talk about that."

"How about Jason? Why won't you talk to him?"

"I don't want anything to do with any more bodyguards."

"You're going to have to, sis, if you want to return to school. You know Mom and Dad aren't going to let you go out alone, especially after what happened. And Jason's a good guy. Tyler wouldn't have recommended him if he wasn't a hundred percent trustworthy."

"He knows what happened to me, Ian. How could I ever face him?"

I reach for her hand and give it a squeeze. "I think you should give him a chance. Tyler trusts him, and that's good enough for me."

I sit with Layla until she gets tired and disappears into her bathroom to get ready for bed. I wait until she comes out dressed in her fleece pajamas, and I tuck her into bed.

"Did you take your meds?" I ask her, meaning her anti-psych medication.

"Yes."

I lie down with her for a while, and we check her sugar levels using the app on her phone. They're fine.

I stay until she dozes off.

When I leave her room, quietly shutting the door behind me, Jason is right where I left him.

"How's she doing?" he asks.

"The same. She's scared. She's afraid to face you because you know what happened to her."

Jason winces. "Poor kid."

"Just be patient with her."

"I will. I'll give her all the time she needs."

When I return to the living room, I find Tyler seated next to my mom. She's beaming at him, and my dad is hanging on his every word. I think it's safe to say he's won them over.

After all, he saved their daughter's life.

* * *

Later that night, as we lie in our bed, Tyler and I try not to dwell on what tomorrow will bring.

As I rest my head on his shoulder, I use my index fingers to draw shapes on his chest. "What time are you supposed to be in court tomorrow?"

"One o'clock." He turns to look me in the eye. "You're not planning to come to the courthouse, are you? I'd rather you didn't."

"Of course I'm coming. So are Beth and Sam and your mom."

Tyler sighs. "There's no reason for you to be there, Ian. They won't detain me immediately. I'll be able to come home afterward. They'll let me come to the jail on my own."

"There's every reason for us to be there," I say. "We love you, and we're coming to support you." I roll away from Tyler so he can't see the hurt on my face.

He turns with me and wraps his arm around my waist as he presses himself against me. "It's not that I don't want you there," he says. "I just don't want you to go through that."

I link my fingers with his. "I'll hate sleeping without you."

He presses his lips to my bare shoulder. "I know, baby. Me too. Sam and Beth will keep you so busy you won't even notice I'm gone."

"I don't believe that for a second." There's nothing on this earth that could distract me from the knowledge that Tyler is behind bars.

28

Ian Alexander

Tyler leaves early in the morning to meet with Troy, so they can strategize before their court appearance. Beth and Sam, along with Tyler's mom, Ingrid, are supposed to come by the townhouse to pick me up on their way to the courthouse. Nothing could keep us from being there for him.

There's a knock on the door at noon, and I answer it to find Sam standing there on the stoop, dressed in jeans and a white button-down shirt, along with a black leather jacket.

"Is there a rulebook that says all bodyguards have to wear black leather jackets?" I ask him. "You wear one. So do Miguel and Jason."

Sam laughs as he opens his jacket to reveal his holster. "They're essential for concealing handguns." He winks at me. "Plus, we look cool."

"Are you even allowed to bring that into the courthouse?"

"No. It'll have to stay in the Escalade with Joe. You ready? The ladies are waiting for us. Cooper and Shane will meet us there."

I lock up the townhouse and follow Sam out to the Escalade. He opens the rear passenger door, and I climb up into the back-seat to sit beside Ingrid, who's in the middle, with Beth on her other side. Sam takes the front passenger seat.

"Mr. Alexander," Joe Rucker says, in a deep, deep voice. He turns to me and nods. "Good to see you again."

"Ian, please," I tell him. "And thanks. It's good to see you too."

"Hello, ladies," I say, smiling at Ingrid and then leaning forward to address Beth.

Beth is wearing a light blue maternity dress beneath a white cotton sweater and flat sandals. Her long blonde hair is plaited in a single braid, and she looks stunning. Maternity glow must be a real thing because she has it in spades.

Ingrid is wearing a cream-colored pantsuit, her silver-blonde hair twisted up into a neat chignon. "Hello, sweetheart," she says as she takes my hand. "How are you holding up?"

I squeeze her hand, careful not to crush her slender fingers. "Shouldn't I be asking you that?"

She gives me a sad smile. "It's not every day a mother's son is convicted of a crime and sentenced to jail, but I know in my heart that Tyler did the right thing." She releases my hand so she can cup my cheek. "He was protecting *you,* dear boy, and I wouldn't expect any less of him. When Tyler loves, he gives his all."

My heart swells with emotion, and I find myself blinking back tears. I sniff. "We're not even there yet and already I'm on the verge of tears."

"It's all right," Ingrid says. "I know I'll cry." She opens her matching cream handbag and pulls out a pair of dark sunglasses. "I'm ready."

Sam turns to face the three of us in the backseat. "No doubt this is going to be rough." He reaches back and pats Ingrid's knee. "It's going to be all right, mama. Tyler's tough as nails."

Joe drives us to the Cook County Courthouse, a massive stone building with soaring pillars in front. As we pull up to the front entrance, Sam stows his handgun in a lockbox in the center console between the two front seats. Then he hops out and opens the rear passenger door for us.

I slide out, then I give Ingrid a hand, and lastly, Beth. Beth reaches into her purse and pulls out a pair of dark sunglasses, which she slips on. Sam's wearing shades as well.

"Great," I say. "I'll be the only one with red, teary eyes."

Sam puts his arm across my shoulders. "You can borrow mine if you need them."

Sam leads us inside the building, and we file through security, stepping through metal detectors manned by armed security guards. Then we head down a corridor until we reach the public entrance to the gallery.

As we're waiting in line to enter, I catch sight of Tyler and Troy standing farther down the hallway, preparing to enter the courtroom through a separate entrance.

Tyler has already spotted me, and his gaze locks onto mine. When he looks at me, everything else just fades away. It's like we're the only ones here, and we can speak without words. He looks so handsome in his suit and tie, standing tall and resolute, looking invincible. My throat tightens as I stare at his beautiful face. I'm so damn proud of him, of his courage and his principles. I'm so proud he's mine, and I'm his. It's killing me not to go to him, to stand by his side.

Tyler gives me a small, understanding smile before he nods to his mother and sister, and to Sam. Then he steps into the courtroom with Troy.

Sam gives me a nudge when it's our turn to enter the gallery. The four of us walk through the open double doors into the large public space, which is already more than half-filled. A group of people seated to our right wave at us, signaling they saved seats for us.

As we sit, I scan the row of chairs filled with a number of familiar faces, but I don't recall exactly who they all are except for Miguel. "Who are all these people?" I ask Sam, who is seated to my left.

He rattles off names faster than I can keep up. "Mack Donovan, Erin O'Connor, Dominic and Sophie Zaretti, Calum and Bridget McIntyre, Liam McIntyre, Lia McIntyre and Jonah Locke, Jamie McIntyre and Molly Ferguson, Jake and Annie McIntyre."

"That's a lot of McIntyres," I say.

Sam nods. "This family is tight. When one is in trouble, the rest come running, and they consider Tyler family."

Shane and Cooper arrive a moment later, taking the seats we saved for them, Cooper sitting next to Sam, and Shane beside Beth.

Ingrid is seated to my right. Her hands are folded in her lap, and she's clearly prepared as she clutches a tissue.

I lay my hand on hers. "All these people are here to show their support for Tyler."

Ingrid sniffs and nods. "I just wish there was something I could do for him," she says.

I can't see her eyes behind her dark sunglasses, but I have no doubt they're filled with pain and sorrow. "Just be brave. That's all he'd ask of any of us."

Then my father walks in, dressed in a suit, no indication that he's a judge himself. He sits in the empty chair directly behind me and squeezes my shoulder.

I turn back and whisper, "I didn't know you were coming."

Having my dad here, knowing he came to support Tyler, means the world to me. It means he's accepted wholeheartedly that Tyler is my partner.

"I'm here for the both of you," he says. He glances across the room at Tyler, who's seated with Troy. "Tyler's a good man."

There's a long docket of cases to be heard this afternoon. Tyler's case is just one of many, and we have to sit through a number of them before Tyler's name is called.

When the judge announces his case, Tyler stands, Troy at his side.

Immediately, Tyler catches my gaze. As we stare at each other, I swear he can see right into my soul. Even halfway across the room, the force of him touches me.

The judge presiding over today's cases is an older woman with black hair threaded with silver and pulled back into a bun. She slips on a pair of gold-rimmed glasses and skims the sheet of paper in her hands before glancing at Tyler. "Mr. Jamison?"

Tyler nods. "Yes, Your Honor."

"And that's your counsel there with you? Mr. Spencer?"

"Yes, ma'am," Troy says.

The judge continues speaking, but I zone out on her words as I focus on Tyler. He looks so dashing, so polished and professional. So heroic. He looks invincible, but above all, he looks at peace.

My nerves are fraying, and I'm aching to stand up and tell the judge what a farce this is, that Tyler was only protecting me. He's a hero, not a criminal. That it's Brad Turner who should be standing before the judge, not Tyler. It's all so unfair.

Ingrid turns her palm and links her fingers with mine, squeezing my hand tightly. "Everything's going to be all right, Ian. Have faith."

Have faith.

That's what Tyler has told me time and time again. But how can I have faith when the very person I need—like I need my next breath—is about to be convicted of a crime and sentenced to jail?

Tyler's gaze remains steadfast on the judge, his expression stoic. He appears calm and resigned, while I feel like I'm about to implode.

"Seven days in the Cook County Jail," the judge says as she raps her gavel on the bench.

At the sound of those words, my head fills with a deafening roar and I can't make out anything else.

My father leans forward and lays his hands on my shoulders, gripping them firmly. "It's okay, son. Just breathe."

My gaze bounces frantically around the room as I try to get myself under control, from my dad to the McIntyres to Tyler and his attorney, to the judge and the deputy on duty, to an audience full of complete strangers.

And then I see him—Brad Turner. He's here! He's here in the fucking courtroom watching the proceedings. He's here to gloat, no doubt.

Brad looks right at me, smiling as he winks at me.

As I shoot to my feet, my father and Sam both stand as well. The armed deputy presiding over the courtroom pivots in my direction, his hand automatically going to his sidearm. I struggle to catch my breath, and I can't hear anything over the roaring in my head.

Sam grabs my arm and leads me from my seat, down the aisle, and out the door into the corridor.

My father is right behind us. "Sit him down over here," my dad says as he steers me to a wooden bench.

Shaking, I drop down onto the bench and lean forward, hanging my head between my knees as I try to catch my breath. My head is spinning, my heart pounding. My vision narrows floor beneath me. "Tyler's going to jail, while that bastard sits in there and gloats."

Sam kneels in front of me, his hands on my knees. He's talking, but I can't make out what he's saying. My dad sits beside me and puts his arm across my shoulders. Then I notice Ingrid and Cooper and Beth are clustered around me.

I drop my gaze back to the floor. They're all talking at me, but I can't make sense of what they're saying. The only thing I can hear is the rushing pulse of blood in my ears.

Then Sam moves, and I notice a pair of polished black dress shoes right in front of me—shoes I'd recognize anywhere.

I glance up to see Tyler standing before me. He reaches down to grasp my arms and pull me to my feet. And then I'm in his arms, right there in front of everyone, held tight and secure, and the roar in my head begins to dissipate. I breathe in his familiar scent, his cologne, and it centers me.

"I'm sorry," I say, my words mumbled and barely coherent. "I'm sorry."

"Shh." His lips are near my ear, his warm breath on my skin. His hand grips the back of my neck, and he makes me look at him. "Just breathe, baby," he says, his voice low and rock steady. "Just breathe."

His steadiness is like a balm to my soul, and I close my eyes and melt into his embrace. As long as I have him, I can face anything.

29

Tyler Jamison

Shane puts his hand on my shoulder. "Do you guys need a ride home?"

"Thanks, but no. Troy offered us a ride."

I'm amazed at how circumstances can bring people together. Since he first came into my sister's life, Shane and I have mostly been at odds with each other. When he met Beth, he fell hard for her, but I wasn't ready to relinquish my role in her life. I had always been Beth's protector. I was her big brother. Hell, I helped my mom raise Beth after our dad died. It wasn't easy for me to back off and let Shane step in and assume the role of her protector. But he's more than proven himself worthy of my sister, and gradually he and I have become friends.

More than friends, really. We're family. I no longer have to shoulder all of the responsibility.

Shane squeezes my shoulder. "Let me know if you need anything tonight. Otherwise, we'll see you both in the morning."

Since I don't have to show up at the county jail for processing and intake until tomorrow morning at ten, I can spend the rest of the day and the night at home with Ian. In the morning, I'll drop him off at the penthouse on my way to jail.

As everyone heads home from the courthouse, I steer Ian to the main doors, and we wait for Troy to bring his car around. When I spot his black sedan, we exit the building and climb into the backseat.

"You doing okay?" Troy asks as he peers into the rearview mirror.

He's looking at Ian, not at me. He knows I'll be fine. It's Ian we're all worried about.

Ian nods but doesn't say anything.

I reach for his hand and place it on my thigh and link our fingers. He's still shaking, but his breathing has normalized. The panic attack has passed.

Before he left the courthouse, Martin made eye contact with me, and the message was clear. *Take care of my son.*

Once we're home, Ian heads for the kitchen, leaving me standing in the foyer. It's a familiar pattern—Ian running when he gets overwhelmed—but I don't mind. It's been a traumatic day, and I know he needs a few minutes to collect himself.

I hang up my jacket in the front hall closet, then follow after him. I stand in the kitchen doorway and watch as he opens the fridge door and peers inside, then closes it. He opens the cupboard door, then closes it. Then he goes back to the fridge.

I'm not sure what he's searching for. I don't think he knows either. He just needs to keep busy.

Finally, I address the elephant in the room. "Are we going to talk about it?"

He stills for a moment, then grabs the coffee pot, heads to the sink, and turns on the water. "I don't want to talk about it," he snaps. "I don't even want to think about it. If we just ignore it, maybe it will go away."

"Ian." I cross the room to stand behind him, my hands going to his hips. "Come on."

He pulls away from me and pours the water into the coffeemaker.

When he slams the glass pot into the maker, nearly hard enough to break it, I have to put my foot down. "Ian, stop." I turn him so he's facing me.

Ian looks out the window that overlooks the back patio, effectively shutting me out.

I lift him and set him on the kitchen counter in front of me.

"Hey!" he says, his gaze shoots back to me. He's pissed.

I wrap my arms around his hips and step between his legs. "We need to talk about this."

"I'm not like you, Tyler, and I never will be," he snaps. "I wear my heart on my sleeve, while you're so freaking strong. Nothing scares you. Nothing ever gets to you."

"I don't expect you to be like me. When have I ever—"

"How can you possibly not be disappointed in me? *You're* the one going to prison, and yet I'm the one falling apart."

I slide my hands up to cup his face. "First of all, I'm going to *jail*, not prison. There's a big difference between the two. And it's only for a few days. You don't have to worry about me because I'll be housed separately from the general population. I'll essentially be in solitary confinement—I won't come into contact with any other inmates. The truth is, I'll be bored, Ian. I'll be locked up with nothing to do but sit around and worry about *you*. And if I don't cause any trouble, they'll let me out a few days early."

My phone rings, but I ignore it. A moment later, it rings again.

"You should at least see who it is," Ian says. "It could be important."

I pull my phone out of my pocket and check the call history. Jud called twice. "Shit."

"Who was it?" Ian asks.

"Jud."

I hit redial, and a moment later, Jud answers. "Tyler."

"Hello, Jud."

"I regret having to tell you this, but Chicago PD has officially terminated your employment, effective immediately. You'll be receiving a letter in the mail." He chokes up a moment and then clears his throat. "You're a fine officer, Tyler, and a good man. I can't think of anyone more dedicated. Losing you is a huge loss to the department, and to Chicago. I'm sorry."

Even though I knew this was coming, it's still a shock. Everything I've worked for has evaporated. My professional career, my identity—it has all been wiped away by a single phone call. "I understand, sir. And, Jud, it's not your fault. I knew exactly what I was doing."

As I end the call with Jud, my heart pounds in my chest. All I ever wanted was to follow in my father's footsteps. To help people. To serve my city. And now that's been taken away from me.

Ian runs his fingers through my hair. "Was that—"

"Yes. It's official. I'm out of a job."

Ian's fingers tighten on my scalp. He leans forward to press his forehead to mine. "I'm sorry."

When I realize I'm holding my breath, I suck in air. I've known this was coming. I need to put it behind me and move on. Ian needs me to be strong. "I was expecting it."

"I know, but still—it has to be devastating."

I gaze up into his eyes and am held captive by the fierce love I see in them. "Choosing to find Layla was the easiest decision I've ever made, Ian. There was never any doubt."

Ian lowers his mouth to mine, his lips soft and gentle as he kisses me.

* * *

The next morning, I carry Ian's luggage out to my car. I'll drive him to the penthouse, then leave my car in the parking garage. Shane will give me a ride to the jail. The only thing I'll be bringing with me is my identification and the clothes on my back. And those things will be taken away from me during intake, while I'm processed as I join the ranks of Chicago's convicted criminals.

Ian exits the townhouse, locks the door behind him, and jogs down the steps to the driveway. I glance up at him as I'm putting his luggage in the trunk and marvel at how young he looks. Sometimes I forget he's still in his twenties.

"Ready?" I ask him.

He nods as he opens the front passenger door. "Will I be able to talk to you while you're in the slammer?" he asks. "Can you make phone calls?"

I'm glad to hear him in a better frame of mind this morning. "Yes, I'll have phone privileges. I'll call you as soon as I can."

After we arrive at Shane's apartment building, I escort Ian up to the penthouse. When the elevator doors slide open, Beth is waiting for us in the foyer, along with Luke, who's standing beside her, holding his mama's hand.

As soon as we step out of the elevator, Luke walks straight over to Ian and asks to be picked up. Beth wraps her arms around me and holds me for a long while, saying nothing but communicating everything.

I pull back and gaze down into her blue-green eyes, which are so like mine. "I'll be fine," I tell her. "I'm long overdue for a vacation." Then I tip my head to Ian, who's tickling a squealing Luke, and lower my voice. "Take good care of him."

She nods. "We will."

Shane, Sam, and Cooper join us in the foyer, all of them stoic.

"Are you ready?" Shane asks me.

I nod. Then I pull Ian into my arms and hold him tight. I swear I can feel his heart beating against my chest, and mine against his. A knot forms in my throat, and I swallow hard. I'm not bothered by the thought of spending a few nights in jail. I just hate leaving him.

"I'll see you soon," I murmur against his temple. Then I kiss him, taking a moment to savor his scent and take comfort from it. The memory is going to have to last me for a while.

Ian's arms tighten around my waist. "Be good so they'll let you out early."

"Yeah," Cooper says. "Don't start any food fights and no brawling."

"I'll do my best," I say, grinning because I know Ian will be fine here. They'll keep him occupied.

Sam laughs as he picks up Ian's luggage. "And whatever you do, don't join a prison gang or get a tattoo."

"Don't you dare get a tattoo without me," Ian says, looking truly affronted.

Laughing, I kiss Ian. "I promise I won't. Now behave yourself."

And then, after saying our goodbyes, Shane and I step into the elevator. My gaze remains locked on Ian until the doors close.

* * *

It's weird being on this side of the prisoner intake process. As soon as I report to the jail, I'm quickly ushered into a private room. A guard takes my driver's license and hands me a uniform—khaki slacks and a matching short-sleeved shirt. I change out of my street clothes, put on the uniform, and wait.

I've lost count of how many people I've put behind bars over the years. Now it's my turn.

I go through the motions of intake, paying very little attention to what's happening. Part of my brain has shut down, and the other part is focused on Ian. I know he'll be fine. Beth will mother him, and Sam will keep him busy. Luke will entertain him, and Cooper will make sure he's well fed. And Shane will watch over all of them.

Before long I'm taken to what will be my accommodations for the next few days at least. I have a single cell, with one twin bunk affixed to the wall, a sink, a toilet, and a small table and chair, both bolted to the floor. There's a small, glass-block window high up on the exterior wall that lets in natural light. The opposite wall is nothing but steel bars with a pass-through for food trays. It looks like I'll be eating in my room.

Hearing the metal clang as the guard closes my cell door and locks it is surreal. I've stood on the outside of these bars many times while I interviewed inmates, but never in my life did I dream I'd find myself on the inside of one of these cells.

But I also never dreamed I'd have someone in my life whom

I loved so much that I'd give up my career for him without a second thought.

For the next hour, I pace the length of my cell, stalking back and forth like a caged animal, all the time wondering if Ian's all right.

ℰ 30

Ian Alexander

S o, what do you want to do?" Sam asks as he watches me unpack.

"Nothing."

After he and Beth showed me to my suite—a spacious room with a king-size bed and a private bath—Sam has been my constant shadow. He sits at the foot of my bed and watches me put away my stuff.

I put my toiletries in the bathroom and hang up my clothes. I put socks and underwear in a dresser drawer. My phone charger goes on the nightstand.

"You don't have to babysit me," I tell him. "I'm not going to fall apart."

Sam shrugs. "I have my instructions."

I stop to look at him. "From whom?"

He rolls his eyes at me. "Who do you think?"

Smiling, I sit down next to Sam. "I appreciate the support. But I'm fine, really."

"There's a basketball court on the roof," he says. "We could shoot hoops."

"I'm not much into sports."

"There's a full-service fitness center in the building that we can use, and we've got a home theater here in the apartment. Do you want to watch a movie?"

"Maybe later." I check my phone for a message from Tyler, but there's nothing. I do have a text from my mom, checking up on me.

I look at the time. I've been here barely an hour. "Do you think he's locked up yet?"

Sam bumps his shoulder against mine. "All right, that's enough of that. No brooding. I've got an Xbox in my room. Do you want to play *Call of Duty?*"

"Isn't that really violent? Thanks, but I'll pass. I'm stressed out enough as it is."

Sam frowns. "You're not making this easy."

That makes me smile. "I can't believe Tyler gave you *instructions.*"

"He called last night. He said, 'Keep Ian occupied. Keep him busy. Don't let him dwell on the fact that I'm locked up.'"

The knowledge that Tyler is taking care of me, even remotely, warms my heart. "That sounds like him."

"Eeen!" Luke squeals as he runs into my room. Beth follows behind him. Cooper brings up the rear and stands in the open doorway with his arms crossed over his chest as he watches our little gathering.

Luke hands me his beloved toy camera. Then he attempts to pull himself up onto the bed. I lift help him up and sit him between me and Sam. As he says something I can't possibly understand, he hands me the camera.

"He wants you to take his picture," Beth says, translating.

I pretend to take his picture, which thrills him. Then he takes the camera from me and climbs right onto my lap.

Cooper pushes away from the doorjamb. "Tyler seems to be taking it pretty well, all things considered."

Beth shakes her head. "I can't believe they fired him."

"Has he said what he's going to do next?" Cooper asks.

I nod. "He's thinking about going into private investigation. Saving my sister and those other girls really had an impact on him. He said it was nice to be able to prevent deaths instead of solving murder cases after the fact."

Cooper nods. "I can see him doing that."

Beth sits next to me. "I think he'd make a wonderful PI—ooophf!" Flinching, she presses a hand to her abdomen.

"Are you okay?" I ask her.

She seems a little pale to me, although it's hard to tell since she's so fair.

She nods. "I'm fine. I've been having Braxton-Hicks contractions on and off all day."

"All right, who's hungry?" Cooper asks. "It's about time for lunch. What sounds good?"

Luke scrambles off the bed and runs to Cooper, throwing his arms around the man's legs and jabbering something incomprehensible.

Cooper scoops the toddler up into his arms. "I know you're hungry, little man. Lunch is coming right up."

* * *

The first day of Tyler's incarceration goes by slowly. My parents call to check up on me, and we talk for a while. I ask to talk to Layla, to check on her, but they tell me she's napping.

"Has she spoken to Jason yet?" I ask my mom.

"No. I can hardly get her to talk to me."

After we eat lunch, the four of us plus Luke go up onto the roof. Shane had a playground built up here so that Beth and Luke could spend time outside in the fresh air and sunshine. A reinforced plexiglass barrier surrounds the space so there's no danger of anyone—i.e., Luke—getting anywhere near the edge of the building. There are potted trees up here and planters filled with ferns and flowers. It's a beautiful, park-like setting.

"How about we cook out tonight?" Cooper says. "Burgers and steaks?"

"Sounds good to me," Sam says, as he hugs Cooper from behind.

While Luke chases a soccer ball around, Cooper cleans the gas grill. Beth and I sit on some padded benches around a fire-pit—sans fire.

I watch her frown and shift position, her hand pressed against her back. "Are you okay?"

She gives me a weak smile. "My back hurts."

A moment later, we hear the sound of a basketball bouncing. Sam's dribbling the ball as Luke tries to steal it from him.

"Is there anything I can do to help?" I ask her. She's Tyler's sister, and that makes her my family, too.

"No, but thanks," she says as she arches her back.

When my phone rings, I frantically fish it out of my pocket. I check the caller ID and see that's an unregistered Chicago number. "This might be Tyler!" I accept the call. "Hello?"

"Ian, hi."

"Tyler!" Then to Beth, I whisper, "It's Tyler."

She smiles. "I figured that."

"How are you?" I ask him. "Are you okay?"

"I'm fine. I haven't come into contact with anyone other than my guards. I was outside a little while ago, by myself, to get some exercise. Right now, I'm taking advantage of my phone privileges to call you. How are you doing?"

"I'm fine." I shoot to my feet and walk to the far side of the recreational area so we can talk in private. "I miss you."

"I miss you, too." He laughs. "It's been four hours, but who's counting?"

"I am."

"What are you doing?"

"We're up on the roof so Luke can play outside. He's chasing a basketball with Sam right now. Cooper's cleaning the grill so we can cook out this evening. Are you sure you're all right?"

"Yes. Everyone here's been great. I think they feel sorry for me."

"They should. You shouldn't be there."

"Ian, don't worry about me. Just think of this as a forced timeout. I'll be out before you know it."

"I just want you home."

"I know. Me too."

* * *

We have an impromptu picnic up on the roof shortly after Shane gets home from work.

After dinner, I go looking for Sam. When I come across the suite he shares with Cooper, the door is wide open, and I can hear their voices coming from within.

I step into their room. "Hey guys."

"In here," Cooper calls out from the bathroom.

I follow the sounds of their voices into the bathroom, where I find Sam seated on a tall stool, shirtless, with a towel draped over his shoulders. Cooper is trimming Sam's undercut with a pair of clippers.

"You are multi-talented," I tell Cooper as I hop up onto the counter to watch.

Cooper brushes the short red strands of hair off Sam's shoulders. "How does that look?" he asks.

Sam peers at his reflection in the bathroom mirror as he runs his fingers through his undercut. Then he reaches up and releases his manbun from its hair tie. "Cut it off."

"Are you serious?" Cooper asks, sounding more than a little skeptical.

"Yeah. Cut it off. Leave about an inch on top so I can spike it."

Cooper meets Sam's gaze in the bathroom mirror. "Are you sure?"

"It's just hair. I can always grow it back if I want to."

"All right," Cooper says. He brushes the long strands of red hair on top of Sam's head, then grabs a pair of scissors off the bathroom counter and starts cutting.

Cooper reaches for a bottle of hair gel and applies it to the shorter strands, finger combing them to stick up. "How's that?"

"Perfect," Sam says.

Luke runs into the bathroom, followed by an exhausted-looking Beth.

"He wants to say goodnight," she says. "It's time for his bath."

When Luke sees Cooper playing with Sam's newly-gelled hair, he raises his arms to be picked up.

"You want some hair gel, too?" Cooper asks.

Luke squeals excitedly as he tries to grab the tube.

"Is it okay with mama?" Cooper asks Beth.

She laughs. "Sure, go for it. I'm about to wash his hair anyway."

Cooper sits Luke on Sam's lap and applies gel to the hair on top of the baby's head, spiking the strands.

As Sam steps off the stool, holding Luke in his arms, Cooper turns his gaze to me. "You're next." He motions toward the stool. "Want a haircut? I can trim your undercut."

I laugh. "No, thanks. I'm good."

Shane walks into the bathroom. "Sounds like I'm missing out on all the fun."

"Dada," Luke squeals as he reaches for his father.

As Shane takes the baby in his arms, Luke shows off his spiked hair.

"I see that," Shane says. "You look amazing."

"All right, young man. It's time for your bath," Beth says.

"I'll take care of it," Shane says to Beth. "You go put your feet up and rest, sweetheart."

After the haircuts are over, and we kiss Luke goodnight, Sam and I end up in the home theater, where we watch *Terminator*.

"I don't blame Sarah Connor," I say when she finally hooks up with Kyle Reese. "Growing up, I had such a crush on him. What about you? Who was your teenage crush?"

Sam ponders my question for a moment before he says, "You know the movie *Avatar*? Remember the soldier who was in charge?" Sam says with a grin.

"You mean the gray-haired guy with a scar? The bad guy?"

"Yeah, he's the one." Sam laughs. "I guess I have a thing for silver foxes."

"I should think so since you have one of your own."

Sam grins. "Damn right I do."

We call it quits after the first Terminator movie. It's getting late, and I'm tired. My lack of sleep last night is catching up with me.

After taking a long shower, I put on my flannel PJ bottoms and a T-shirt of Tyler's that I brought with me, and head to the kitchen for something to drink.

The apartment is pretty quiet now, with most of the lights off. The only light I see is coming from the kitchen. As I approach, I hear quiet voices.

"Are you sure, sweetheart?" That sounds like Shane. "I really think we should go to the hospital, just to be sure."

"I'm fine, Shane," Beth says. "They're just Braxton-Hicks contractions."

"I'd feel better if we got you checked out."

"It's late, and we have company. I really don't want to go to the hospital."

"Cooper and Sam can manage things here."

"Honey." She falls quiet a moment, and then she laughs softly. Actually, it's more like a giggle.

A moment later, Shane walks out of the kitchen carrying Beth. She's dressed in a nightgown and a silk robe, her feet bare. Her head rests against his shoulder.

When Shane spots me, he nods to me and keeps moving as

he carries his wife to bed.

Okay, that was pretty hot.

I help myself to a bottle of cold water and an apple, then I head back to my room. After I crawl into bed, I send a late-night text to Layla, just to check in with her.

She replies immediately, so I call her. "I didn't know if you'd be up this late."

"I can't sleep."

"How are you feeling?"

"Not great. Everything hurts. Every muscle in my body is bruised. My sugars are fine, but the mean girls are being particularly bitchy tonight. The voices have been worse ever since... you know."

"Stress always makes your hallucinations worse."

"They say it's all my fault."

"That's not true, Layla, and you know it." My heart hurts for her. Life is hard enough without having voices in your head constantly trying to drag you down.

She sighs. "I know. I'm trying to block them out. I have an appointment with my therapist tomorrow."

"What about Jason?"

"What about him?" she asks, sounding a bit wary.

"Have you talked to him yet?"

She hesitates. "No."

"Layla, don't blame Jason for what Sean did."

"How can I trust another bodyguard? Sean was supposed to protect me, and he *sold me*, Ian. He fucking *sold me* to his drug dealer. What kind of asshat does that? What kind of miserable, low-life, scum-sucking—" She cuts off and then I hear a muffled sob. "I keep reliving it over and over in my head, like a movie stuck on repeat. I can't stop thinking about it."

"I'm so sorry, sis. Do you want me to come over? I can come right now."

"No. Honestly, I just want to be alone."

"You can always talk to Mom," I tell her. "Or even to Jason. He'd understand."

She sighs. "I can't do that. He's probably disgusted with me."

"Who, Jason?"

"Yes."

"Layla, no. He just wants to *help* you."

"I hate that he knows what happened to me." She sounds so dejected.

After Layla and I end our call, I watch a little YouTube until I can't keep my eyes open any longer and I'm in danger of dropping my phone on my face.

This big bed feels so empty without Tyler. It amazes me how much I've come to depend on him in such a short time. I wrap my arms around the spare pillow, wishing it were him, and wait for exhaustion to take me under.

* * *

Somehow, I end up back home in the apartment I shared with my birth mom. Back in the beginning, before I became Ian

Alexander. When I was just Ian.

I'm upstairs in the little bedroom, and the door is locked from the outside. It's getting dark out. I know because there's no sunlight coming through the partially boarded-up window.

I'm hungry.

And cold.

And scared.

I hear voices downstairs... several of them, all men. They're laughing loudly. I hear my mommy sometimes, talking, laughing. Sometimes I hear her cry out like she's in pain. And the more she cries out, the more they laugh.

I grab my blanket and my pillow and my stuffed dog and I hide in the closet. Sometimes I talk to myself so I can't hear them downstairs.

Just as I'm falling asleep, I hear the bedroom door open. I listen to quiet footsteps approaching the closet. And then the closet door opens, and a man crouches down to look at me with a sad expression on his face.

"It's okay, buddy," he says. "You're safe."

I stare at the dark-haired man. "Tyler?"

I shoot up in bed as my heart thunders. I'm covered in sweat, and it takes me a minute to realize where I am.

I'm at the penthouse.

It was just a dream.

I lie back down and stare up into the darkness while my pulse races.

For the millionth time, I wonder if my birth mom is even

still alive. And I wonder if she ever thinks about me.

31

Tyler Jamison

I have no idea what time it is—I just know that it's pitch black outside my solitary window. I sit on my bunk and listen to the night sounds of this remote section of the jail. Nights are eerily quiet. Occasionally, I hear footsteps as the guards make their rounds. Once in a while, I detect the jangle of keys, the snick of a lock turning, or the clang of a metal door closing.

Mostly, I pace my cell and hope Ian's doing all right.

I'm allowed to go outside twice a day, for thirty minutes at a time. I usually pace the enclosed courtyard, maybe shoot a few hoops or do some calisthenics. It's nice to get outside—it certainly makes me appreciate the outdoors in a way I never have. I've always taken my freedom for granted, but incarceration gives me a whole new viewpoint. After I get out of here, I think a road trip is definitely in order. I know Ian would be up for it.

I've been able to call Ian twice, my mother once, and my sister once. Beth has been having those fake contractions off and on for a few days now, and I'm sure that's bringing back some unpleasant memories. I imagine Shane is a wreck. After what happened the last time, with Luke's premature birth, I don't blame him. Hopefully, everything will go smoothly this time and she'll give birth in a hospital at full term.

I've had a lot of time to think over the past couple of days... endless hours, in fact. I have to admit, losing my job—my entire life's career—hurts. Badly.

When I was a kid, I'd watch my dad come home from work every evening, stow his firearm in a lock box, and change out of his uniform into street clothes. Like any young child, I thought my father was invincible. But of course, he wasn't. A whacked out drug addict took my dad's life, destroying my family in the process.

Beth was just an infant at the time. She never even got to know him. But I knew him. I idolized him and I still miss him every day of my life.

He was my hero.

My throat tightens, and my chest feels like it's being squeezed in a vise. "I'm sorry, Dad," I say, the words catching in my throat. "I'm so sorry."

My eyes burn as hot tears blur my vision.

Pressing my hands to my face, I try desperately to hold back the tears. I'm supposed to be the strong one. There are people who need me to be strong—Ian, my sister, my mom. But lately it feels like it's been one emotional event after another—coming out, Valdez going after Ian, the fight with Turner, Turner pressuring Ian for sex, Layla, losing my job, and now I'm locked in a cage like a common criminal.

Blindly, I reach for my pillow and press it to my face to muffle the agonizing sobs that take me by surprise.

* * *

During my waking hours, I plan what I'm going to do with my life. First thing I need to do is sell my condo in Lincoln Park. Since I have very few bills, the proceeds from the sale will tide me over for more than a few years. Ian's townhouse is paid off so there's no mortgage. My car is paid off. Really, our only bills are groceries, utilities, and random sundries. There's also my grandparents' townhouse in Hyde Park, which I still own. Beth lived there before she moved in with Shane. I rent it out, and it's a great source of extra income.

I can use the proceeds from selling my condo to fund my new PI business. The more I think about it, the more I like the idea. I meant what I said to Ian about taking great satisfaction in finding Layla before it was too late—not to mention rescuing eleven other young women who were destined for a life of sexual abuse.

Finally, just after lunch on the fourth day of my incarceration, a guard comes to my cell.

"Ready to go home, detective?" he says as he unlocks my cell door.

"I'm no longer a detective," I tell him as I step out into the corridor.

He frowns. "Yeah, I heard about that. Sorry, man. That blows."

After I make a quick call to let Ian know I'm being released, a guard walks me to an office where I'm given my own clothes and my ID. I change, and then I have some papers to sign as my release is processed. Finally, I'm escorted through a side exit and a series of secure gates that lead to a visitor parking lot where Ian waits for me, along with Cooper and Sam.

The minute I step through the final gate, Ian runs up and throws his arms around me. We stand there for a good long time, holding each other and ignoring our amused audience—Sam and Cooper, the two armed guards stationed at the gate, and a few random strangers hanging out in the parking lot.

Ian kisses me soundly, in front of everyone.

I kiss him back, relieved to have him in my arms once again. He feels like *home*.

By the time Sam and Cooper drop us off at the apartment building, we load Ian's suitcase into the trunk of my car and head home. It's raining this afternoon, so Ian and I dash up the front steps and into the townhouse. I've never been so glad to walk through that front door.

Inside, Ian drops his luggage and wraps his arms around me. I back him into the wall and kiss him until we're both breathless.

For the first time in a long while, there aren't any clouds hanging over our heads—well, except for Brad Turner. I haven't forgotten about him. But after serving my sentence, I'm free to come and go as I please. Free to follow my own path, wherever that leads.

Ian grabs my hand and pulls me toward the stairs. "Come upstairs with me right now. I need you."

* * *

As Ian pulls me into our bedroom, I put on the brakes. "Ian, wait. I need a shower first." I feel like I'm covered in grime and the stink of incarceration. I was only behind bars for a handful of days, but simply being there has left an indelible mark on me. I doubt one hot shower will be enough to remove the stench.

"Sure, babe," he says, nodding with an abundance of sympathy. "Whatever you need."

I walk into the bathroom, strip off my clothes, and step into a hot spray of water. I stand there for a good while, letting the water beat down on me, letting it saturate my hair and scorch my skin. I just want to feel clean again.

I feel numb.

I thought I could serve my sentence and come out of jail unscathed—that it wouldn't affect me or change me—but I was wrong. It's only now just creeping up on me. I feel disconnected from my own life. From my own identity. If I'm not a cop, who am I?

I scrub my skin with soap, then wash my hair and rinse off. After drying off, I walk back into the bedroom with just a towel wrapped around my waist.

Ian's sitting on the bed, watching me warily. "Feel better?"

"Marginally." *Not really, but it's a start.*

Ian walks up to me and fingercombs my damp hair. "You're home now," he says. "That's all that matters."

* * *

"So, what was it like in jail?" Ian asks me when we're lying together in bed, wrapped in each other's arms. His head rests against my shoulder; his arm is around my waist.

I stroke his hair. "Pretty uneventful, actually. I was alone nearly all the time. Sleeping was difficult because I had trouble relaxing. Every little noise, every footstep put me on high alert. And on top of all that, I missed you like crazy. What about you? How did it go at Beth's?"

"She and Sam did their best to keep me busy. I didn't sleep well either. I kept having crazy dreams, actually they were more like nightmares. I dreamed I was back in that god-awful closet, only this time it was you who came to let me out."

I kiss his forehead. "I'll always come for you."

Ian draws a lazy pattern on my chest with his finger. His

touch is soothing, but it's also arousing, making my skin heat up and my dick stir. I roll him to his back, moving with him so that I'm on top, my hips cradled between his thighs. He gazes up at me, his expression a mix of desire and anticipation.

"I missed you, Ian." I kiss my way down his throat, past the crook of his neck, to his sternum. I gently tongue one of his nipple piercings, and with a cry he arches beneath me. I continue trailing kisses down his abs, past his navel, to the base of his erection, breathing in his scent.

Ian groans when I wrap my fingers around the base of his cock. And then I draw him into my mouth, taking him as far back as I can. He lets out a heated breath, followed by a moan.

I suck and lick him until he's shaking. His hands grip my biceps as he holds onto me for dear life. Hearing his desperate cries makes me even harder. His heated flesh throbs against my tongue and lips, and I know he's on the verge of coming.

"Tyler, wait," he gasps as his hands latch onto my head to still my movements. "I want to come with you."

I release him and reach for a condom. After sheathing myself and lubing up, I slide a finger inside him, stroking him until he's squirming with impatience. And when he's ready for me, I slowly sink my length inside him, one sweet inch at a time, while he fists himself.

I pace myself, trying to draw out as much pleasure as I can for both of us. Our gazes lock, and we're both breathing hard. We come together in a gasping rush of pleasure, perfectly in tune with each other.

* * *

At midnight that night, after Ian has fallen asleep, I get out of bed and dress in jeans and a plain black T-shirt. Civilian clothes, because that's what I am now—a civilian.

I leave a note for Ian, in case he wakes up before I get back, and I quietly leave the townhouse. There's something I need to do before I can move forward. I have some unfinished business.

After a drive across town, I stand at the door to Brad Turner's apartment, feeling a sense of calm. I'm not here as a cop. I don't have a badge or a warrant, although I am armed.

No, this time I'm here as Ian's boyfriend—Ian's very pissed off boyfriend.

I knock on Turner's door and wait, biting my tongue against the impulse to yell *Police! Open the door!* That's going to be a hard habit to break.

Finally, I hear the rattling of the chain, followed by the deadbolt turning. The door opens, and Brad Turner stands looking a bit disheveled, dressed in sweatpants and a soiled, white muscle shirt.

His eyes narrow on me. "What the fuck do you want?"

I push my way inside and close the door behind me. We're standing in his small, cluttered living room. When my eye catches sight of a studded leather collar and leash lying on the coffee table, I see red. "I hope I'm not interrupting anything."

Before he can utter a word, I grab Turner by the front of his shirt and slam him against the wall.

"You can't do this," he says. He sounds belligerent, but the stark terror I see in his eyes says something different. "I'll have you fired for this."

Too late for that, pal.

"Listen carefully, asshole," I say through gritted teeth. "If I *ever* catch you within a mile of Ian—if you ever call him or text him again—I swear to god I will end you. Am I making myself clear? You stay the hell away from Ian, or I will kill you. And I promise, if I do, no one will ever find the body."

Turner's mouth falls open, but no words come out.

"Say it, Brad. I want to hear you say the words."

"I'll stay away from him, I swear!"

I wrap my fingers around his throat and squeeze, cutting off his air, just like he did to Ian and god knows how many other men. Only I'm not playing a sex game with him. This is for real.

I watch his face darken as he chokes. "You're not such a tough guy now, are you, Brad?" I nail him with a glare. "This is your one and only warning."

I release him and step back, prepared for him to lunge at me. Hell, I'm prepared for anything. But he doesn't retaliate. Gasping for air, he wilts before my eyes, his knees giving out on him.

Without a second look, I walk out the door and exit the building. Despite having ended my career in law enforcement, I feel more empowered than I ever have in my life.

Ian's mine, and I won't let this motherfucker, or any other, hurt him.

✌ 32

Ian Alexander

Tyler? Where are you, babe?"

"I'm in the living room."

I find Tyler seated on the sofa, tablet in hand and his black reading glasses perched on his nose. He's in a much better frame of mind than he was yesterday when we got home. "You look hot, like in a sexy professor kind of way."

Lifting his blue-green eyes to me, he gives me a look that I've come to recognize. His *bossy* look.

I sit on the coffee table in front of him and peer down at his tablet. "What are you reading?"

He glances at me over the top of his glasses. "I'm studying for the Illinois private investigator's license exam."

"Oh, my god, I want to take it too. What do you have to do to qualify?"

He removes his glasses and hooks them on the neckline of his T-shirt. "Are you at least twenty-one years of age?"

Now it's my turn to give him a look. "Duh."

He cocks a dark eyebrow. "Just answer the questions, please."

Oooh, he's using his cop voice. Swoon. "I am."

"Have you ever been convicted of a felony?"

"No."

"Are you of good moral character?"

"I hope so. Yes."

"Well, there's more to it, but basically yes, I believe you're eligible to be a licensed PI in our fair state."

I take his tablet from him and set it aside so I can straddle his lap. "I want to get licensed. I want to learn how to shoot a gun, and I want to take self-defense classes."

He studies me. "You're serious about this, aren't you?"

"I'm absolutely serious. I think I'd be good at it. I don't have all the experience you do, but I can learn. I knew I'd never be good at an office job, where I'd have to sit behind a desk all day and stare at the same four walls. But this is different. We'd be out and about, constantly on the move, unless we're stuck in the car on a stake-out—but then, I'd be with *you*, and there's no one I'd rather spend my time with. I'm serious, Tyler. I think this is something I'd be good at. Let me do this with you. Let me help you save people."

Tyler smiles. "All right. If you really think this is what you want to do... then yes. You need to pass the exam, take a gun training course so you can obtain a concealed carry permit, and take some self-defense classes. I could use a little more training, too, in that regard."

I'm so excited I could explode. Not just because he's agreeing, but because he's taking me seriously. I grab his shirt and lean in to kiss him. "Thank you."

His hand curls around the back of my neck. "I would love for us to work together, but you have to listen to me, all right? I won't let you put yourself in danger. You have to promise you'll do as I say."

"Whatever you say, boss." At this point, I'd agree to just about anything.

He laughs. "I'd be your partner, not your boss."

"Jamison Investigations," I say, trying out the sound of it. "That has a nice ring to it."

He cocks his head. "How about Jamison and Alexander? That's more equitable, don't you think?"

I laugh. "That sounds like a wedding invitation." And then, when I realize what I just said, my face heats. *I can't believe I said that out loud.*

But Tyler's not laughing. "It does sound like a wedding invitation." He pulls me closer for a kiss. When he draws back, he gazes into my eyes as if searching for something.

"That sounds good to me," I say, my voice suddenly breathy.

"I always feel like I'm rushing things. I practically invited myself to move in with you when we'd only known each other a few weeks. I told you I loved you—"

My heart starts pounding. "Yeah, but I said it first."

"And now, I know it's *way* too soon, but I—"

"It's not. Ask me."

"I can't imagine a life without you, Ian. Whenever I think of the future, you're always in it. I picture us together. And after seeing you holding Luke, I can't stop imagining you with a baby in your arms—our baby. You're my family, Ian. You're everything I've ever wanted."

I swallow hard against the knot in my throat as my chest constricts. But it's not anxiety this time that's making it hard for me to breathe. It's anticipation. My heart feels like it might explode. "You still haven't asked me, Tyler."

"It's not too soon? Because if it is, I'll wait. I'm not going anywhere. I'll wait as long as you—"

I crush my mouth to his, partially to stop him from talking himself out of it, and partially because I want to breathe him in. "Shut up and ask me."

He smiles. "Ian Alexander, would you do me the honor of allowing me to be your husband?"

"Oh, my god, that's the most beautiful proposal I've ever heard." I wipe my teary eyes. "Look what you've made me do. I'm a wreck now."

"You didn't actually answer me," he says with a smile.

"Yes! The answer is yes."

"So, we're doing it? We're getting married?"

"You'd better believe we are." I smile as Tyler pulls me onto the sofa and rolls me to my back.

He lifts my shirt and kisses his way up my abdomen, to my nipples, which he teases with the tip of his tongue. Lighting streaks down my spine, and my cock stirs.

Tyler whips my T-shirt off me and tosses it aside. I reach up and unbutton his shirt, revealing a broad, masculine chest that never fails to arouse me.

The notion that we'll spend the rest of our lives together, as husbands, fills me with unimaginable joy. "Ian Jamison," I say aloud, wanting to hear how it sounds.

Tyler smiles. "You'd take my name?"

I run my hands over his chest to his arms and wrap my fingers around his biceps. "Are you kidding? Hell, yes. I want the whole world to know I belong to you."

Tyler's phone chimes with an incoming text. He glances at the screen. "It's the doctor's office. My results are in."

"What are you waiting for? Look and see."

Tyler taps the link in the text message, and it takes him to the online patient portal. "All negative," he says.

I dig my phone out of my back pocket and find a similar message. I check my results. "Negative," I tell him. "You know what this means, don't you?"

He grins. "I do. It means no more condoms, baby. Just me and you."

Epilogue

Tyler Jamison
two months later

Construction is well underway on the carriage house addition that will contain the offices of Jamison Investigations, Inc. I suggested to Ian that we call ourselves Jamison-Alexander Investigations, to be fair, but he thought that was too much of a mouthful, and that Jamison was enough.

Besides, as he loves to point out, when we're married and he takes my name—which he *insists* on doing—then Jamison Investigations will cover the both of us.

The remodeling plans call for a waiting room, a private office for us to share, and a conference room, all on the ground floor. We're putting in a small apartment above the office, and we're expanding the garage to make room for our recently-purchased work vehicles: two late-model gray Honda Accords. They'll blend in well in any environment and allow us to do covert surveillance without drawing attention to ourselves.

Both of us passed the licensing exam required to be a private investigator in the state of Illinois. I have obtained my concealed carry permit, and Ian is working on getting his. We're both signing up to take Liam McIntyre's self-defense class at McIntyre Security.

We've officially formed the business and have started advertising. Now we await our first client.

I sold my condo a week ago, so there's plenty of money in the bank to tide me over until the business starts earning a profit. Not that money is a problem. Ian has told me repeatedly that I'll never have to worry about money. And I've told him, repeatedly, that I prefer to pay my own way. I have my pride.

I'm in the kitchen making coffee while Ian's outside supervising the delivery of our office furniture. I add vanilla and caramel flavoring to Ian's cup of coffee, and enough sweetener to fell a horse, and give it a stir. I add a dollop of whipped cream to the top and some cinnamon sprinkles just because he likes it. The other cup is plain black coffee.

As I walk out the kitchen door to the back patio, two cups of coffee in hand, I spot Ian standing on the driveway. He's conferring with our new office manager, Jerry Harshman, who is a god send.

Jerry is a formerly homeless US veteran who Ian befriended a couple of years ago. Ian offered Jerry a job, he accepted, and now he's supervising the renovations to the carriage house.

Fortunately for us, Jerry was a depot manager when he was in the Army, and he has excellent organizational skills. Ian's just glad to know the man is finally off the street and has a secure roof over his head and hot food in his belly. Free use of the apartment is part of his compensation package, in addition to receiving a salary and medical benefits.

"Coffee?" I say as I join them. They're busy watching the crew unload the truck and carry in our new office furniture.

I hand Ian his caramel-vanilla-whipped cream concoction—it might as well be a milkshake as far as I'm concerned. I offer the cup of black coffee to Jerry.

"Thanks, Tyler," Jerry says in his deep, baritone voice.

Jerry's a tall, sturdy guy with broad shoulders. I guess him to be in his early seventies. His iron gray hair is buzzed short, regulation Army. He's almost always dressed in fatigues, a dark green T-shirt, and a worn pair of combat boots. His weathered skin is burnished by the sun, and his palms are calloused from years of hard physical work. His blue eyes reflect a great deal of wisdom born of experience, combined with a dry sense of humor.

With a clipboard in hand, Jerry ticks off the desks, office chairs, tables, and other assorted office furniture as it's unloaded from the truck. "The computers, phones, fax machine, and the rest of the tech equipment is scheduled to arrive tomorrow," he says. "The new phone lines and Internet access will be installed the following day. By Friday, we'll be fully functional."

"Great job," I tell him. "Thank you."

As Jerry wanders inside the office to direct the delivery team as to where everything should go, Ian gives me a pleased smile. "He is doing a great job."

I nod. "Hiring him was a great decision."

"Jerry refused to take any handouts, but when I offered him a *job*—a way to earn what he needed—he jumped at the chance."

My phone chimes with an incoming message. I glance down and see that it's from my sister. She's replying to my earlier text to see how she's feeling. She's due any day now.

"Who is it?" Ian asks.

"It's from Beth." I show him my phone screen.

Beth: I'm hanging in there. Won't be long now. Poor Shane is a wreck. LOL

Ian laughs. "Poor guy. I hope he survives the delivery."

I take in the newly remodeled carriage house and the bustling activity as the new furniture is unloaded. My life has taken so many unexpected turns—meeting Ian, coming out, finding the other half of my soul, and now embarking on a new career that will allow us to work together and really make a difference in people's lives.

When Ian takes my hand and links our fingers, I turn to face him. I see so much optimism and excitement in his eyes.

My phone rings. It's a local Chicago number, but I don't recognize it. I accept the call. "Tyler Jamison."

"Mr. Jamison, hello. My name is Randy Pearce. I, uh, I want to hire you to find my missing wife. The cops keep interviewing me—I think they suspect I had something to do with her disappearance, but I swear to you I didn't. I need you to find her. I'm afraid she might be in trouble. Can you help me, please?"

Our first case.

"Mr. Pearce, can you meet with me this afternoon? I'll need to get some information from you."

"Of course. Anything you need. I love my wife, Mr. Jamison. I want her back safe and sound."

"We'll do everything in our power to find her."

After getting the man's address, I tell him Ian and I will be at his place within the hour.

"Looks like we have our first case," I tell Ian. "A missing woman. That was her husband on the phone."

Ian's eyes widen. "Oh, my god. This is really happening."

"It is. Let's get to work."

* * *

Thank you so much for reading *Somebody to Hold!* I hope you enjoyed book two of Tyler and Ian's series. Stay tuned for news of their next release.

If you're interested in reading more about Shane and Beth, Sam and Cooper, and the rest of the McIntyre clan, check out

Vulnerable, the first book in the McIntyre Security Bodyguard Series.

If you're interested in reading my other gay romance novel, Sam and Cooper's first novel, check out *Ruined*. It's part of the McIntyre Security Bodyguard series, but it can be read as a standalone.

If you'd like to sign up for my newsletter, visit my website: www.aprilwilsonauthor.com

For links to my audiobooks, visit my website: www.aprilwilsonauthor.com/audiobooks

For updates of future releases, follow me on Facebook or subscribe to my newsletter. I interact daily with readers in my Facebook reader group where I post frequent updates and share weekly teasers. Come join me!

* * *

Books by April Wilson

McIntyre Security Bodyguard Series:

Vulnerable

Fearless

Shane -- a novella

Broken

Shattered

Imperfect

Ruined

Hostage

Redeemed

Marry Me -- a novella

Snowbound -- a novella

Regret

With This Ring -- a novella

Regret

Collateral Damage

(more coming...)

Tyler Jamison Novels:

Somebody to Love

Somebody to Hold

(more coming...)

British Billionaires Romance Series:

Charmed

(more coming...)

Audiobooks by April Wilson

For links to my audiobooks, please visit my website:
www.aprilwilsonauthor.com/audiobooks

Made in the USA
Coppell, TX
09 July 2021

58738175R00187